Red Dog, Red Dog

Patrick Lane is the author of *There Is a Season* (2004), his highly acclaimed memoir, which won the Lieutenant Governor's Award for Literary Excellence and the inaugural British Columbia Award for Canadian Non-fiction. One of the country's most celebrated poets, he has received numerous awards, including the Governor General's Award and two National Magazine Awards. Lane lives near Victoria, B.C., with his wife, the poet Lorna Crozier. *Red Dog, Red Dog* is his debut novel and was longlisted for the Giller Prize.

ALSO BY PATRICK LANE

There is a Season: A Memoir

Praise for Red Dog, Red Dog

'Lane is undeniably an accomplished writer . . . and his achievement here is his evocation of a forbidding landscape as the element in which these embittered characters have their being . . . It is fitting that Lane's oracular first novel ends not conclusively but with a hint of the continuation of the kind of story it has told so well.'

Times Literary Supplement

'Occasionally a novel comes out of nowhere and blows you away. This is one of those . . . The writing is reminiscent of Cormac McCarthy at times, spare and beautifully crafted; at other points it recalls William Faulkner. This is an impressive debut from a name to watch.'

Waterstone's Books Quarterly

'Not since reading John McGahern's That They May Face The Rising Sun have I come across a novel which so surely places the lives of its characters in the context of their landscape; but whereas with McGahern that landscape was local, intimate, and rewarding to those who worked it well, Patrick Lane's land is wild and barren, unforgiving, and populated by a scarred and hunted people.

Red Dog, Red Dog is a shock of a novel; immaculately crafted, deeply thoughtful, and with a broken-hearted wisdom about the ways in which damage can fall through the generations. There is little to celebrate in the world these characters inhabit, but much to admire about the way Lane has revealed it to his readers. A work of great and unconsoled love.'

Jon McGregor, author of If Nobody Speaks of Remarkable Things

Red Dog, Red Dog

PATRICK LANE

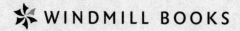

Published by Windmill Books 2010

2 4 6 8 10 9 7 5 3 1

First published in Great Britain in 2009 by William Heinemann

Windmill Books
The Random House Group Limited
20 Vauxhall Bridge Road, London SW1V 2SA

Addresses for companies within The Random House Group Limited can be
found at: www.randomhouse.co.uk/offices.htm

The Random House Group Limited Reg. No. 954009

www.rbooks.co.uk

A CIP catalogue record for this book
is available from the British Library

ISBN 9780099537434

The Random House Group Limited supports The Forest Stewardship
Council (FSC), the leading international forest certification organisation. All
our titles that are printed on Greenpeace approved FSC certified paper carry the
FSC logo. Our paper procurement policy can be found at:
www.rbooks.co.uk/environment

Printed and bound in Great Britain by
CPI Bookmarque Ltd, Croydon, CR0 4TD

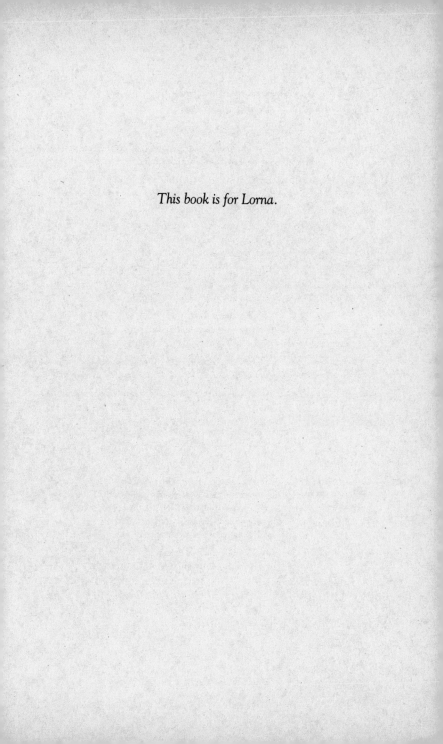

This book is for Lorna.

Red Dog
Red Dog

1

It didn't take him long to bury me. He scrabbled at the thin till, gravel and chunk clay sprawling out from his cracked shovel and dull pick. The sweatband on his straw hat got darker and darker as he bent to his task, the air heavy with the silt of stars. Heat hung from his neck like a yoke on an ox. The hair on his fingers was matted wool, grains of earth glinting there in the fur, the sky fraught with moon. Two trees leaned their gnarled branches down on him, bitter apples withering, their skin flayed with scab and the froth dust of wormholes, shimmering with bleached light.

He lifted me from the crib where I'd whispered my breath for six long months and rolled me in the sheet Mother had left me lying on when I was born. My baby sweat had marked the cloth a yellowed grey. I loved him holding me. He bound me tight in thin cotton and lifted me onto a leftover square of tent canvas, folding me up. My body moved light as a bird carcass among his fingers.

Fold upon fold.

I watched from a branch of the apple tree in the neg-
lected orchard, his little Alice, and knew the tears were
flowing down the inside of his skull, his dark eyes dry as
glass. What he worked to bury he'd thought was his to hold.
I knew he was imprinting my body onto the skin of his
hands and whatever he was to bear in the days and nights
he had left, be it axe or gun, hammer, wheel, or wonder, it
would be me he was holding, the dead daughter who had
followed hard on the heels of Rose, the first girl-child to go
to earth, and me to follow, his second to last.

We were the between children, Rose and me. Before us
was the one she wanted, Eddy, and two years later Tom, the
afterthought boy no one planned. My mother loved Eddy,
her first son, and for her, her only one. The baby who came
after all of us was of another mother, a daughter born
without a name.

Father said Mother killed both Rose and me from malice
and deliberate neglect, but the truth was different. Mother
had only emptiness in her for her kind. That she said she
was in a dark place after our births doesn't change what
she did and didn't do. Her heart beat for her first son, Eddy,
and when he came, she was at last at least happy. He would
become for her the lover she was sure of, a boy, an almost
man. Little Rose lived only a week, and me for nine days shy
of half a year. Every day and night of those long months was
a journey toward my grave. It was a long road I travelled in
that crib, no help from Mother, who said she sickened at
our births. There was only care from Tom and it not enough

to keep either of us whole. I suckled on cow's milk he'd soaked a rag in, a tag-end of cotton the nipple I knew. Little Rose had refused what he tried to give. Born for death, she went willingly to it. Tom tried to touch us clean, the only one who did.

Poor Mother. What milk she had came out white as water run through alkaline clay. I tasted her for a day or two, no more, her milk strained into a cup she, grudging, gave to Eddy, who gave it to Tom. That she denied me had to do with her dreams, where and who she came from. The past makes us what we are. We fail daily in our desire to be whole. Mother and Father's lives were always less.

It's the mirror of things torments us in the night. We imagine ourselves when we cry out at the coming darkness. In the day we see ourselves in what and who is closest to our grief. Night and day Mother saw herself in me, saw the little girl she once was looking back at her, and though she was wrong in what she imagined, it didn't change her. It was the same with Rose. Mother wouldn't go near her. She said it was impossible for her to see such a thing come out of her, sticks for legs and a swollen belly, eyes clamped down and a skin rope around her neck. She looked at who Rose was and would be, and couldn't bear it. It was the same with me. I can't bear it, Mother would say to Rose when she came into the crib room, Eddy small beside her. Why are you alive? Father picked up Rose when she was three days old and laid my sister's tiny body upon Mother's belly in the hope she might put it to her breast. Take her away, Mother said to Father, and he did, Little Rose's lungs whistling, gone

3

poorly from the cord that had strangled her coming out. Her breathing was a slow and laboured song. She lasted seven days, Tom slipping into the crib room to stroke her red skin, her green-stick bones, wetting her lips with the milk she never licked down. Rose stared past him at the walls, her tiny fists clenched tight.

While Rose lay dying, Father stormed. Both Eddy and Tom walked careful as he did, hiding where they could when he fell into a rage. There were stuttering fires going off inside him. They'd both seen them, outcries only Father knew, flaring in him like bad stars. They watched their father from afar, spying out his moves, his silences, his drunken wildness when the anger came up, the solitude he seemed to treasure. The night he finished burying Little Rose the boys peered through the cracked boards in the root cellar roof and watched him piss on the tattered corn. His heavy cock frightened them, the thick whorl of his water bubbling in the dirt. Staring, they couldn't see themselves the same, something unimaginable in their childish eyes.

Father had come in to see Rose every day while she still breathed. He didn't touch her but for the one time he gave her to Mother, only gazed through the bars as she sank deeper away. His stillness there seemed to the boys what care might be, never having known it for themselves.

A Wednesday to a Wednesday, and as Mother said to Father when Rose breathed her last: *Wednesday's child is full of woe*. Father cried out at those words and held them over Mother from that day forth.

I followed close on Rose, Father pinning Mother's body

and laying inside her the seed that would give him the daughter he wanted. Mother trying to hold him off was to no avail. He parted her legs with his rough knees and rode until his need took hold. Her revenge was sweet. The egg she gave him was as weak as the one before.

It was different earlier when she'd wanted a son. She'd waited through three years of wandering the West. He brought her to the valley then. A week after moving into the house on Ranch Road her egg was ready and she trapped Elmer when he was falling-down drunk, pushed him down in the empty living room onto the red fir floor, and pulled him into her. He'd shouted out but there's no stopping a man's body though the man might want it otherwise. Who knows who he yelled for? Father cursed his lust, but drunk as he was he couldn't stop her.

So she said.

Who was she trying for but a boy? She climbed off him with a terrible smile after he spilled and lay there on his back, his hardness fled from him, her thighs wet with his leavings.

That was Eddy and the story of his making.

Mother said she was delirious with fever the year after Eddy was born when Father had his way with her, and Father said he was passed out drunk the night Tom was conceived. They both lied as they always had. After Eddy, there was a need for Tom though they didn't know it. They didn't know what he would be or what he'd do in the years, but there was something in him that made them wonder. To them he was unlike, but unlike who or what? Tom had in him a weighted wish they might have called a heart had they known how to speak of it. But how was Tom to know anything of that? He was simply there, a baby, then a boy. What child knows to ask who he is? Eddy saw their confusion at this second son. He loved Tom for his burden. There are some who must do the world's work. Tom had in him the spirit of a crow and the heart of a wren. He was born to blood and hiding.

When Father carried me out among the last few apple trees, he didn't know Eddy and Tom were watching. Deep in the orchard he placed me on a fleece he'd cut that spring from a lamb. Then he took three bluebird feathers from his hatband and stuck them into the canvas shroud that covered me. Father dug my grave as he did Little Rose's, each scrape with his hands, each shovelful measured against Mother's failings. He said she wanted me dead, but he was wrong. She just didn't want me in the world she wept in. He said Mother wasn't worthy of a girl, and no matter his protestations of love for the daughters he never seemed destined to raise, he believed Mother killed with her outright neglect any daughter he might've had grow into a woman to look after him in the years to come. His dying days were around him, just not known. Cluttered gravel and hard clay surround my bier just as they do the body of my sister.

This is a desert land and good earth is hard to find. Withered apples hung above Father's head as he placed me in the hole he'd dug and whispered what words he had. I lay on the lambskin and watched him place his face in his rough palms. It was a wonder to him to taste salt water for the first time since he was a boy.

Father had set at Rose's tiny head a river stone. Rose quartz, it blistered with bruised light. Mine would be an alien stone dropped by a glacier in the days when the earth was ice, blue as the sky in the hour before the dawn. He said his sister loved blue stones. He named me for her: Alice. He'd found the stone in the hills above Sugar Lake and brought it to the field, the weight of it hanging from his hard arms. It lay above me solitary as a coyote that's missed its prey.

Oh, my sisters, the stories swirl. They are wrong water trapped by rocks. The words I was told turn on themselves. There were nights Father sat by the humped blue stone at the head of my grave with his whiskey bottle in his fist and told me tales. He talked to me, but sometimes I think it was as easily the night. When the moon was full, he'd stagger out from the root cellar and come to the orchard singing some country song from the years, "Cowboy Jubilee." "Tumbling Tumbleweed." When he was settled on the ground, he'd drink and mumble about the days when he was a boy. He felt safe out there with me. I was the daughter he thought he'd known. The past he gave me was the only gift he had beyond the blue feathers he stuck into my shroud, the stone he laid for me.

His oldest stories were told to him by his mother. I had only been in the earth a week when he remembered for me the time of his grandmother. She was a little girl coming up out of the Montana Territory back in the last century. There were three wagons and three families. His grandmother was seven years old when she saved the pup from her father, who wanted to eat it.

Father turned silent when he said that. It was like he expected me to question him, but who was I to speak? I lay in my grave and waited until he began again. It was a long story told through a bottle. Most of his stories were. Sometimes he'd stop and rage at those days, angry at a world he thought had done him wrong. And sometimes he'd stop in the telling and stare into the dirt as if an answer was there if only he could find it. He'd poke his finger among pebbles and rearrange them into squares and circles or push them into tracks of dust. He'd look long at what he'd made and then scatter the gravel with his boot. Who knows what he saw there, what he was thinking in the night.

He told me each family dug a hole in the earth at the southern lip of the Great Sandhills, winter coming before summer was full over, the blizzards seething without respite. They were trapped two hundred miles from where they were headed. Three wagons and the snow piled up in drifts, the ground beneath their feet stiffened sand that froze in grotesque crystals, chunks of meteors they thought were buried angels, the way they sparkled in the sun. They'd eaten what they could of the animals, the rest stolen by cats and wolves. The women and children lay in their holes in the ground and heard the howling from above while the men climbed ladders made from alder trunks and leather thongs, wasting bullets on wraiths come out of the dunes, grey wolves whose hunger became the sound of snow falling.

Three families and early winter in the Territories. Fort Macleod lay far ahead of them, a place made impossible by snow. Each night of the journey they'd sat around their fires and spoken of the dream, the land they'd break, the wilderness turned into something they could own, a farm, a ranch, a barn, a home. It was 1886, my father said, just thirteen years after American wolvers massacred the Assiniboine in the Cypress Hills. They'd risen in the night to kill the men who'd stolen their horses, but that was likely a lie, Father said. I think they just wanted to shoot some Indians, he told me.

Sometimes I think the only truth he knew was the past, the stories like the mazes he made with pebbles in the sand. He said the families had come up out of the Territories across the old Medicine Line and crossed over to the dry lands north of the Cypress Hills against all common sense, the Frenchman River south the safer, surer way, ready water and wood, the hills to protect them from storms. He never told me why they left so late, August no time to start such a journey. It seems there are no stories but those where a hand touches a rein and a horse turns its head, the animal knowing what the man does not, asking with its glance why they are leaving grass and water for a desert. The first storm came down from the north like a millwheel into their lives. It caught them when the moon turned August into September. They'd travelled a bare nine miles in the snow before they stopped, two of the horses dead under the whip, broken in the hip-high drifts.

Father would mutter, then lift his bottle of whiskey. He'd hold it up to the moon. He liked to look through it to the false light as he listened to the wind in the bunch grass. He said the men tied the wagons together, the last horses kept alive into December, when what feed they had was gone,

9

only melted snow for water, and they began to shoot the animals, one by one, trying to live off the meat. Each night they left a man in the snow to guard the dwindling stock against the predations of the wolves. What they didn't bring down into their holes was left for the wild ones, offal and bones, bits of tattered hide. Their hunting was next to nothing, a rare antelope, jack rabbits, until even they were gone. A skinny deer or two, no more, and all the while digging their holes deeper to keep alive, canvas and blankets stretched across alder sticks their roof. Father said the blizzard wind is a ghost that eats you, fallen snow lifted from the drifts to fly again.

When his mother told him the story, she used to smile when she got to the part about that little girl hiding from her father night after night and him never finding her or the pup. He said his mother chuckled to tell it, his great-grandfather dreaming of that dog, nothing to scavenge but bones strewn from the wolves foraging above the hole he'd dug.

Father would go quiet then. He always did when he talked about his mother. His voice would lull away and then he'd mumble into his hands. For god's sake, he'd say, it was cold and the months dragged on, the meat gone and the families living on hope, dry wood nowhere to find, their fires mean, the earthen rooms clogged with rancid smoke. Mealy flour, dried beans and peas, and not much more. I can smell it, he'd say, and then he'd lay his hand on the stone he'd placed for me and say: But I bet you want to know what happened to the little girl who was my grandmother?

He'd wait then, his ear cocked to the moon. When there was no answer, he'd go on.

Well, he'd say, she'd been allowed to choose one thing to take with her on the trek to Fort Macleod. One thing only, there being little room on the wagon for incidentals, and of all things possible she chose a pup. Then in late February, she woke up one night to find her father trying to steal it up the alder ladder so he could kill the dog away from her, they were that hungry. The puppy's squeal, its whine or whimper, woke her and, sullen, he gave it back. She knew the pup would die if ever she let it out of her sight.

She carried that puppy from ladder to hole, family to family, night after night, three and sometimes two steps ahead of her father. She kept it alive a month and more till the end of March when their smudge was spotted by a band of passing Cree who dropped an antelope carcass down their smoke hole. Three times the Indians came by with meat, but nothing was said, the families huddled in their caves, listening to the soft sound of the hooves of the unshod horses in the snow.

What happened, how they made it through to Fort Macleod after that winter of '87 in the Great Sandhills, was never told. Their trek on foot that spring through the drylands where the bones of dinosaurs grew like nightmares from the sand, their wandering west through nameless grasses that rose above their waists, the cats and wolves and rattlesnakes, weren't the stories that tormented him. It was that little girl, her pup, and the father who hunted in the dark. This story always made him smile when he told it.

There were nights he couldn't sleep when he'd come out to us and nights he never tried to sleep, him and his shotgun. He'd stand under the apple trees and try to shoot the stars. He'd aim at the moon and try to kill it. He'd shout about his sister, his leaving her behind so many years ago when he ran away from his father, his mother slipping him out the door before the dawn while his father slept.

Father and his stories of the past.

I remember the night I was buried, remember the stones and pebbles falling upon me. There was no moon when I left my flesh behind and travelled over the dry grass of the orchard graveyard. I crossed with Father over the gravel he'd strewn to keep the weeds down in spring, the yellow poppies in the yard parting before his boots. I went from my grave to the house where Mother was sleeping. Seeing her there, I thought a mother's love is strong and sometimes death is love enough.

Mother's father had hanged himself in their barn, the crops dead in the fields three years and the last steers sick with Wooden Tongue from eating thistles he'd foraged from the fields. She'd watched her father's body swing above the rats come out to feed on the handful of grain he'd scattered in bitterness, as if to say what they had was worthless, only good for vermin.

But Mother always told the boys her life went bad the day she first saw Elmer Stark striding tall down the correction line to the farm where she and her mother, Nettie, had waited for a man in the years after her father died. It took a long time for him to come. Elmer Stark. Lillian was already seventeen.

There was that last daughter I spoke of, the one who was not Mother's. That baby was our half-sister, born from a woman Father brought out of the night to deliver in Mother's bed. Another daughter, this one born to Mother's curses. Father burned that baby in the orchard, a girl like Rose and me. She died unknown to all.

I named her Starry Night.

What happened to the mother in the years to come I do not know.

2

It was stone country where a bone cage could last a thousand years under the moon, its ribs a perch for Vesper sparrows, its skull a home for Harvest mice. The hills rose parched from the still lakes, the mountains beyond them faded to a mauve so pale they seemed stones under ice. Sagebrush and bitterroot weathered the September night. In the desiccated grass of a vacant lot, a rattlesnake followed in the tracks of a Kangaroo mouse, a Fiery Searcher beetle clambered over the dried body of a dead Wood rat in the dust, and a magpie slept inside its wings on a branch of dying chokecherry, the berries hard as dog knots. Stars shone like sparks thrown from shattered quartz, Orion reeling in the southern sky and Mars sullen and red in the west.

In the heart of it was a valley leading nowhere out but north or south. North was going toward narrower cuts of rock, deeper winters, darker forests, and even more desolate towns that turned into villages, villages into clusters of trailers and isolated shacks in the trees, nothing beyond but bush that ran clear to the tundra. South was going toward the desert states where there was no place a man could get work unless he was Indian or wetback, someone willing to take cash wages half what anyone else might ask. The only way you could stay alive down in Washington or Idaho was to break your back in the onion fields and orchards, set chokers on a gypo logging show, or steal. East were mountains piled upon mountains, the Monashee giving over to the Selkirks and Purcells, and finally the Rockies and the Great Plains. To the west was a rolling plateau where nothing lived but moose, bear, and screaming, black-headed jays. At the edge of the plateau, the rolling forest rose up the Coast Range until it dwindled against the scree, and on the other side of the peaks and glaciers was the sea, something most people in the valley had only heard of, never seen, the Pacific with its waves rolling over the dead bodies of seals and salmon, eagles and gulls shrieking.

The town squatted in a bowl beneath desert hills, its scattered lights odd fires stared at from up on the Commonage where a rattlesnake could be seen lifting its wedge head from the heat-trail of a white-footed mouse and staring down at the three lakes, Swan in the north, Kalamalka to the south, and Okanagan in the west, the Bluebush hills and mountains hanging above them in a pall. Against the sky were rocky outcrops with their swales of rotted snow where nothing grew but lichens, pale explosions that held fast to the rough knuckles of granite as the long winds came steady out of the north. In the valley confluence where the lakes met were the dusty streets and avenues of the town shrouded by tired elms and maples. What the snake saw only it could know.

It was the hour after moonset, dawn close by. The darkness held hard on the Monashee Mountains. Eddy walked thin down a back alley halfway up the east hillside, his eyes blinkered, their blue faded to a mottled white, the colour of the junk in his veins. Ankle-deep yellow clay lifted and swam around his boots. Silica whirlwinds, they shivered behind his heels as they settled back into soft pools. He moved slowly between broken fences and sagging, fretful sheds. The open windows of houses gazed blind into backyards, sleepers heavy in narrow beds, sheets damp and crumpled at their feet. In the alley, wheat grass and cheat grass draped their seed heads over the shallow ruts. A single stem of spear grass brushed against Eddy's pant leg and left two seeds caught in the wisps of cotton on his worn cuff. He waded on through dust, the seeds waiting for their moment to fall in what might be some giving dirt, some spot where life might find a place to hide in winter. The alley held the illusion of water, thin waves of powdered clay shot through with the dead leaves of grass and chicory.

A slender ghost, lean as a willow wand, Eddy flowed in the languid glow of the heroin he'd shot up a half-hour before. Sergeant Stanley's German shepherd slept uneasy on its paws in the run next to the ashes of a burned-out shed. Eddy had set the shed on fire the week before. He'd watched the flames from his car on the hill above and imagined Stanley in the dark staring at the wild fire, raging.

Sergeant Stanley was nowhere around. Eddy knew he was likely taking his usual time with some frightened girl he'd picked up and squired out to the west side of the lake on some false, misleading threat or charge. Eddy had seen Stanley's women. The cop took his due with all of them, each one owing him her body in unfair exchange for the cell she didn't want to see, the father, friend, or husband she'd never tell. When he was a boy, he'd crouched behind a chokecherry bush up on the Commonage and seen Stanley with his pants open, a scared girl on her knees beside the police car, working for her life as she bruised her knees on rock shards in the clay.

The shed had been the first thing.

The dog would be the second.

The German shepherd, Prince, was Stanley's joy. When the Sergeant came home from rutting with some wretched girl in a deserted shack or cul-de-sac up the Commonage Road or out in the Coldstream Valley, he always walked down to visit his dog before going into the house. Eddy had been watching and imagined Stanley's wife hearing her husband's car pull up with its red bud pulsing. She'd be waiting for him in their bed, quiet and still in a cotton nightgown tight around her ankles, eyes open in the dark. Stanley would go to the caged kennel-run first and kneel to the surge of his dog's devotion, its tireless love. His wife knew each step he took, counted him down the side of the house and across the yard to the alley. She waited breathless until it was time to count him back, staring under her lids at the closed door.

Eddy knew Stanley wouldn't expect anyone to come again. And if he did conjure someone who burned things, how could he imagine him coming back to kill his dog? Stanley was still trying to figure out the fire. He might have thought it had been set by children playing with matches, but why would a child take the chance to play with fire in a policeman's shed? Eddy knew Stanley would come round to it sooner or later, but between knowing and doing were twists and turns the man hadn't negotiated yet.

If Stanley thought of Eddy at all, it was as a feral boy, the kind he looked toward when something went wrong in town. Eight years earlier, Eddy and his friend Harry had broken into the Royal Canadian Legion bar late one night, stealing liquor and taking all the money in the cash box, which was kept under the till. They were fourteen years old. The next night, the two of them got drunk in the park on a bottle of the whiskey they'd stolen and they ended up on Main Street throwing handfuls of quarters, nickels, and dimes to a packed crowd of drunks outside the hotel. Sergeant Stanley arrested Eddy, Harry having slipped away into the crowd. Richard Smythe, the town's judge, sent him down to Boyco, the boys' correctional school in Vancouver, despite Eddy being a year too young. Stanley wanted to teach Eddy a lesson. So did Father. Eddy never forgot Sergeant Stanley arresting him or the year that followed in that prison. There was something dead in Eddy's head when he came back from the coast. The boy he'd been was no longer there, and in his place was someone gone past feeling, who thought nothing of pain, his own or anyone else's. Even Father stepped sideways when Eddy walked behind him.

He's a throwback, Father had said to Mother a month after Eddy returned home. My own father's come out in him, he said.

You shut up, said Mother, her hands ripe with peach skins, jars boiling on the wood stove. You could've saved him from Boyco. You could've talked to the judge and got him probation, but no, not you. He went to that place because of what you told them to do and no matter how many times you deny it, I know the truth. It was you did to Eddy.

You don't know nothing, Father said.

Don't fight, Tom would cry into their anger. What about Eddy? he'd say. What about him?

You shut up too, Mother would say, rounding on him from the sink, her paring knife a blur in a peach's flesh. Why wasn't it you sent away?

You're crazy, said Father. You've always been so ever since the girls.

Shutup, shutup!

Eddy remembered Tom's pleading for him, the slammed doors, Father's truck heading up the driveway ruts, Mother cutting peaches into halves, the blunt of her thumb as she firked another peach pit out into the sink.

Eddy knew what had happened to him. That they didn't care or didn't know didn't seem to matter any more. What mattered now was that Stanley hadn't connected the fire to him. Shoulders hunched, thumbs hooked to his worn pockets, Eddy shambled down the alley. In front of him a shrew struggled across the clay, its naked paws swimming in the dust. He shifted his foot. The shrew was under his boot, something alive, something dead. What was in his head was the ball of ground meat laced with rat poison. As he walked on, his right hand slipped into his pocket and he moulded the wet pork ball in his fingers.

Eddy had been coming quietly at night for a week, talking to the dog, scratching behind its black ears, its tongue lapping at his fingers. The dog trusted him and wouldn't bark. The night he set the shed on fire he'd offered the shepherd a bit of fresh ground pork as the flames began to lick the cedar walls. The dog had only sniffed at the meat and growled, but after a few more visits it waited at the pig-wire fence for him to come, swallowing the gift each time.

So what if he'd been throwing money and laughing at the drunks scrambling in the gutter for coins? But it wasn't just being sent to the coast, it was the three days before he was put on the train, his two nights in the cells. Stanley was worse than the guards and older boys in Boyco. Twenty-two years old now and he had never stopped living what happened.

The iron clothesline pole at the corner of the dog run shot up into the night, a twist of rusted wire choked in its weathered ring. He stopped past the ashes of the shed, singed grass from the shed fire dibbling his boots. He grinned at the dog's black nose shoved through the pig-wire.

The shepherd whimpered. Eddy thought he could smell the remnant heat of the sun withering out from the pole, dust-cake thick in his nose. He pulled his fist from his pocket and held the meat out.

He whispered through dry lips: Hey, pretty dog. How's it going?

The German shepherd wagged its tail and whined.

3

the party was deep into its third night when Billy Holdman and Norman Christensen started to fight. The people had flowed out of the kitchen after them and formed a circle in the gravel turnaround at the back of the house. Under their feet were the dried fronds of summer's dead poppies, frayed remnants of flowers grown from seed Mother had scattered there when Tom and Eddy were boys, along with the wreckage of years, rock crush and weeds, scraps of bark and hay, old blood from slaughtered animals, cigarette butts, lost nuts and bolts, oil, plantain, sawdust, chicken feathers, broken glass and scrabbled dirt, all that grew or was dropped or discarded, things of little use. The men and women surrounding Billy and Norman were like children on a playground who'd found something suffering and wanted to watch its struggle, a squirrel part-crushed by a passing car, a hawk with a broken wing, a crippled child going violently nowhere in a wagon without wheels, the handle stubbed into the dirt.

Tom knew there was no question of who was going to win. He'd seen Billy fight before. His thick body and heavy arms were enough to warn most away, but not Norman. He didn't have a hope as he danced around drunk, half Billy's size and some years younger, his useless fists flailing. Norman wasn't a fighter. He spent his days and nights living in books, his belief that there was a truth to be found there. Norman had said once to Tom that what he imagined mattered to him. It was like the world map he'd torn from a *National Geographic* magazine and nailed to the wall in his basement room, a black X marking the place where the town should have been, no name there but for his enigmatic sign.

Girls had followed their men outside. They hung off strong arms and shoulders in their poodle cuts and pageboys, white blouses under pastel sweaters, circle skirts flounced out by crinolines, or narrow skirts tight to the hips, high heels, some worn, some new, the gravel crackling under them. The men stood beside their girls unaware, their bodies leaning forward, intent on the fight.

Billy, finally tired of Norman's useless blows, picked up a hoe he'd seen in the trampled grass at the edge of the gravel and swung it, catching Norman high by the ear where his sideburn was and peeling back his cheek. The flap hung off the line of his jaw like a rubber rag. Norman's teeth bright there in the yard light, quick stars in his red mouth.

His tongue poked out for what seemed a long time, though it was only a moment, probing to see what the edges were to his face, and finding none, it retreated behind the molars, one silver tooth shining far back in the cave of his head. Then the fists Norman had were hands again, fingers trying to put his face back together, the air whistling as he breathed wet from his new mouth.

It was strange how the blood took a moment before it bloomed. When it did it was like sudden roses. Billy had the hoe up behind him and was going to swing again for Norman's head when Tom grabbed it just below the blade, gripping the neck tight. Billy balked at the impediment, his hands clenched around what he thought was his to do with what he wanted. Tom held on where the steel blade was bound to the shaft and looked into Billy's eyes. There were limits somewhere. They rested out there beyond the edges of the land. Tom had searched for them since he'd been a child. He'd walked into the high hills and deep into the gullies and arroyos, but he'd never found them.

Suddenly, Billy let go of the handle and turned in a tight circle. Tom, alone with the hoe, stumbled over someone's boot. Two men, laughing, shoved Tom back into the ring. Tom steadied himself and flung the hoe, sending it deep into the sprawl of the tattered vegetable garden beyond the cars and pickup trucks parked slant in the first rows of ragged pea vines and dried-out corn. The hoe carved the air in awkward flight till it landed shaft down, vertical somehow like a starved skeleton among the hanging pods of runner beans.

Billy, you fuck, said Tom.

Nothing and no one ever tried to stop Billy. He came from a stump farm to the east of town in the foothills of the Monashee. Thin dirt and boulders had been his inheritance, the land as much him as anything he knew. He was the oldest child of a father who'd died under a load of logs sprung from the rusted-out cables of a truck on a hairpin turn south of Spuzzi Lake. Billy was given the weight of his father's brood when he was fourteen. His mother had pulled him from school, the oldest of the kids, and sent him to work setting chokers behind a tractor on a logging show. Billy had grown up hard, the years he'd laboured to feed and clothe his tribe only making him tougher. He had many ways, few of them clean, none of them legitimate.

Billy raged away through the crowd and back to the house. Fucking Starks, he said to his fists as if the clenched hands had a hearing all their own. Norman, that little shit. Who the fuck does he think he is!

Norman staggered a couple of steps and sank down slow onto the shards of rock, the circle of drunks leaning in, their breathing stopped. Norman lay there on his side, curled up like a cat in sleep. His ripped face rested on one hand, the other hand caught in his crotch. There was no moan in him, not yet, the blow of the blade still a shock in his stunned flesh.

The flare of flames from the burning barrel beside the shed spilled comet tails into the sky. Wayne Reid had been feeding it with the last posts and boards from the east yard fence someone had torn down and kicked to pieces. The fire blazed as he ululated, his voice tremolo, his fat cheeks juddering. He stood beyond the crowd, spread-legged under the willow tree, his face white as lard. Wayne turned twice around and let go both cylinders into the night sky from the shotgun that had been up till then hanging from its nails above the kitchen door. The party, the fight, and too much liquor had got him going. He came from town money, his father running the Chevy dealership off Main Street. He'd spent his young life looking for an outlaw hero and found both Billy and Eddy, Billy not caring about him one way or another, and Eddy hating him for the money he came from, for his weakness, his spoiled life. Tom glanced quickly over the crowd and saw Wayne waving the shotgun, a fat boy who liked to be close to destruction, knowing nothing of its cost.

Norman began to grunt through the blood and tears blotted on his skin. Tom got down beside him on one knee. Take it easy. It'll be all right, he said, the people around him leering at Norman, who was holding the flap of his cheek in his hand as if he could somehow stick it back onto the cartilage and bone it had been chopped from.

Please, said Norman. It's my face.

Vera Spikula came out of the crowd, pushed Tom aside, and knelt by Norman, her hand stroking his forehead, her brown ponytail swaying to her soothing cries. Tom remembered other victims he'd seen Vera with. She seemed to move from man to boy to man, each time ending up the worse for her caring. She had run away from a dead-end bush farm five years ago in yellow shoes she'd stolen from her mother. She was a girl with a heart full of misguided love. She mothered every man she met and forgave each one their sometimes casual use of her. There on her knees, she was like someone in a picture praying. Then, like a strange bird blown in from some other planet, a child-sized girl was standing in front of Tom. She stared at him, one eye partly closed, her face shadowed by the barrel fire behind her. Looking at her, he thought of the ring-necked pheasants his father had loved, birds that had been brought to the valley years ago from China and were still not quite believed by anyone, so alien were they to those who saw and hunted them. The strange girl stepped by him, her shoulder brushing against his ribs.

Tom had seen women look at blood before, but this girl was different. She seemed drawn to what she saw, as if to her Norman's ripped face was a way of climbing through his flesh inside him. She wasn't afraid and because she wasn't he knew she was rare. Small as she was and given her awe, he knew she'd need protecting. As for the other girls in the crowd, they stood in the glow of the drum fire, their voices whispering the ways of men, already making up a story about the fight to tell and so to be repeated for days in town. The girl with Vera wasn't excited the way the rest of them were. She looked like she was thinking deep about what runs through a man's heart.

After a few moments, the crowd began to break up, the excitement over, most of them heading back into the house for a drink. A few couples drifted toward their cars or trucks to do whatever it was they needed quiet for. When Tom stood up, he saw Joe Urbanowski with Billy's dealer friend from the coast, Lester Coombs, Joe propped against the back wall of the house by the water barrel in polished cowboy boots, narrow jeans tucked into them. Lester leaned there beside Joe, laughing, his bald head gleaming under the moon. Joe, insolent, stared hard at Tom. He was Billy's creature, and Tom knew he'd do whatever was necessary to keep Billy happy. Had it looked like Billy might have been in trouble during the fight, Joe would have tried to step in.

You guys seen enough yet? Tom called out.

Joe lifted away from the wall and swivelled on his boots, his heels harsh in the gravel. He walked slowly into the house, Lester following. They didn't look back, the screen door slamming behind them.

Vera was still on her knees beside Norman, the other girl standing above them with her arms crossed under her breasts. She didn't look more than five feet tall in her scuffed blue shoes. Vera pulled up Norman's shirt and held it across his cheek as she got him to his knees. Help me, Marilyn, she said. I can't do this on my own.

The girl ignored Vera, turning instead to Tom and smiling. Tom stared at her, thinking it odd how he'd been looking up at the Milky Way and now was seeing the same soft stars in her left eye socket drifting. He stepped around her and heaved Norman to his feet, taking one arm over his shoulder and leaving the other to dangle upon Vera's chest. Marilyn stood a moment in front of the three of them, reached out with her finger, and touched it to the blood on Norman's face, as if curious at what had come out of him.

Vera made a noise like something squeezed.

Marilyn looked up from her wet finger at Tom and said: This's some party.

Yeah, Tom replied as he began to slow-walk Norman toward his rusted Ford. Tom asked Vera if she could drive Norman home. Yes, she said, Norman stuttering that he wanted to go to the hospital but didn't want any stitches, his voice plaintive as a child's.

It's okay, Vera said to Norman. I'll look after you. Marilyn trailed behind them as she plucked at bits of grass and leaf on the hem of her skirt.

When they got to Norman's truck, Tom opened the door and helped him up onto the seat, Vera scrambling around to the driver's side. His keys are likely in his pocket, Tom said. She slid across the seat and fumbled them from his pants, Norman holding his face together, groaning. Hey, Tom, his words coming in soft blurts. Whut'd he do that for?

Your guess is as good as mine, said Tom. You know what Billy's like.

Marilyn had climbed up on the running board and was looking in at Norman. Get down, Tom said as Vera started the truck, a cloud of exhaust rising from under the tailgate. He put his hands on Marilyn's waist and lifted her off.

Then the shotgun again.

God *damn* you, Wayne!

Wayne stood under the willow, shouting Jesus! Jesus! Jesus! He raised the shotgun and let go yet another couple of rounds into the branches above him, broken leaves falling around his shoes as Tom came up.

What the hell, Wayne! Tom said, wondering for a moment where he'd got the shells from and then remembering the box he kept on top of the fridge. He took the shotgun from him, blue smoke wisping from the barrels. Wayne staggered back and fell over a black-haired girl Tom hadn't seen in the shadows. She was on her hands and knees under the verge of the tree near where it met the broken fence, her belly heaving.

The twelve-gauge shot Wayne had let loose rained down on the squash leaves in the garden, leaden seeds falling from the sky. Some of the last went *pling plink pling* on the scarecrow hat of the hoe. Tom figured he was the only one to hear the pellets fall, the others there too crazed to know the wonder of the sound.

He glanced into the darkness at the side of the shed. A woman he'd seen a few times at the bar downtown was bent over the hood of a pickup, her skirt up around her waist, her panties around an ankle, the man behind her flashing the white moons of his ass. Tom heard the woman saying, Hurry, honey, hurry, someone'll see, the man going faster, buttocks and belly, the white flesh going *slap slap slap*. Tom looked away, and for a brief moment caught the silhouettes of his brother and Harry as they stared down from Eddy's high window. They were there and then they were gone, the window an empty vault of light. Eddy had been up there in his room ever since Billy and Lester Coombs had arrived, Eddy making his drug buy from Billy as soon as the two of them had come into the house.

The bullet nose of his pale green Studebaker was parked

under the fir tree, the car pointed straight at Ranch Road, no one daring to touch it or, worse, block it off. Eddy always wanted a clear route out. The car had been Father's pride. It was only a year old when he won it off Harvey Jellison in a crooked poker game three months after Eddy was sent to the coast with Father's blessing. Eddy got the car after Father was buried and fair enough. Tom got the shotgun. He still had the leather vest his father used to wear when he went into the hills, side pocket loops that held shotgun shells, the back of it a quilted black satin stitched across the shoulders with the name his father said he earned riding saddle bronc on the rodeo circuit back in the Twenties. Written in curlicues with crimson thread, Elmer's moniker: *The Chocteau Kid.* Tom always carried the clasp knife he'd found in Father's pocket the night he buried him.

The strange girl looked over at Tom, her curled brown hair shining with bits of light thrown off by the dying barrel fire beside her.

Like fire, he said, thinking of touching her waist with his hands.

What did you say? asked Wayne.

Nothing, said Tom, the shotgun in the crook of his arm. He broke the gun open, the spent shells falling into the uncut grass to get lost until the following spring.

4

father grieved his life, he grieved the sister he left behind on the farm in Saskatchewan, and he grieved his daughters. Because he didn't have us long, he missed us more. He carried in his heavy hands the wrongs he'd done in this life. He sat and tried to wring himself away, but there was no ridding himself of what he wore under his skin. He raged at his sons for no other reason than that they'd been born boys. He'd perch on his heels beside Little Rose's stone and sing his songs. "Roll Along Moonlight" and "The Drunkard's Son" warbled from his lips, desert tunes from the forgotten times. He'd sing "Blue Okanagan" as he drank from a bottle of Crown Royal, little Buddy Reynolds lilting on his tongue.

When Tom hid down by the well, he'd watch his father's lips move, Father singing of boots and saddles, dogs and cattle, the lonesome blue of sage, or telling of the days he roamed the prairie, and of darker times, earlier, when he was a boy. Tom's eyes marked every move Father made, blunt fingers lifted to a cheek, a boot shifted in the dirt, a shoulder hunched. He thought if he learned each gesture, grunt, and shrug, he'd learn the man.

Sometimes Tom would go to see the graves in the old orchard, the few trees left there gaunt with thin suckers appearing among their branches every spring, branches that would blossom but rarely produce fruit. He'd go out and stand on that glacial drift, clumps of grass, rocks, and pebbles, hardened clay, the dust of years under his feet. Father had buried his fair share of animals there. What was it about those men that they liked to put things in the ground? Father, his father, the father before him. They went back forever, those men. It must have been the wars, though Father said no one in his family ever fought in one. Why would they fight for something not their own? Maybe it was too much peace drove them to blood and burying.

Father almost never told stories to the boys in the early years. He'd drive Tom away when he bothered him. Father was mostly not there, off somewhere on what Mother called a toot, or he'd be covered in grease under his truck fixing something. He had little time for tales then, it seemed, except on those nights he'd sit with us in the orchard.

There was the one night I saw Tom come up on Father when he was sitting on the step at the back porch. Who knows why Tom's begging that day got a story out of him? Anyway, he told Tom about the one time he and his sister, Alice, had been taken down to Minot, North Dakota, to visit family. When he was there, he met his grandfather. The man told him that when his own father was young he'd run off to

Illinois from Kentucky, having got himself disowned fighting over a slave girl he didn't know he'd been sharing with his father. He lost the argument they had, his father finally shooting him, the bullet in his side left there to nag him for the rest of his life. Father's great-grandfather left Kentucky and never returned. He married a girl from the Bulliner clan in southern Illinois. Tom sat quietly and listened as the tale unwound about a feud that started between the Bulliner and Henderson clans in Bloody Williamson County back in 1869 during a card game. Elmer's great-grandfather had been there that day when one of his wife's family was called a lying son of a bitch over a bad poker hand. He had stood with the Bulliners, the long feud that started that day with the Hendersons a fight he could call his own. He ended up killing three men and helping bury sixteen others, women and children among them. He was shot twice, finally leaving ten years later, heading west with his wife to the Dakotas. Father told Tom that family mattered back then, that the only war the Starks had time for was a vendetta. When he told the story, he grabbed Tom and shook him. Nothing's changed, he said. You remember that.

When Tom was a child, no matter his father's loudness or violence, it was always clear what he stood for. His mother frightened him too, with her changes and her unquenchable needs. It was different with Eddy. He always said he knew who she was, no matter what she did. But Tom thought Mother touched Eddy too many times when he was small. Her kissing him all over sometimes went too far, that mouth of hers searching out the bits of him, her red lips leaving signs on his fair skin, Eddy looking up at her from his clear blue eyes.

Eddy was in Mother's clutch when he was younger, but things changed. After his year away, he'd still go to her, but Tom didn't know if it was simply to satisfy her demands or to play with her need for him. Sometimes Eddy would make her wait for him as he listened to her pleading for attention. Tom would sit alone in the kitchen, Father already gone to work and his mother and brother in her bedroom, and he would worry his life. He came to feel his birth was a mistake, the need he had for them all, leaving him bewildered. He always felt he was searching, but for what he didn't know.

Tom tried to talk to Eddy about their father's hate or love, but Eddy didn't seem to care. He told Tom once that hate and love were just words in movies. Tom had read those words in books and even though he could find nothing in his own life that resembled the stories he read, he still believed in them. Father used to say that the country they lived in was too big for any tale to hold it. He said a story gets lost each time you try to fit it into the land.

Remorse was what rode Father down in those years. He never reconciled himself to his life. It's strange how men try to appease the misery they feel, but regret is wasted on them. Father said he was only true to his daughters, but in the end there was no one to believe him, least of all us. We loved him, no matter the past and his many lies. He never had us long enough to hurt. But where was he when I wizened in my crib? What bar, back alley, cul-de-sac, or turnaround?

Eddy rarely came out to the graves. Tom would ask him to come and listen with him, but Eddy never wanted to. He could see everything he needed from his window at the back of the house. Many a night he saw Father bemoaning out there as he prayed to Rose and me, but Eddy never wondered how far back it went, father to son forever. Eddy had no need of squatting in the night, no need to beg a story. The grieving for a sister or a daughter was Father's lament, not his.

When Eddy came back from Vancouver, he drew a hood over his skull. There were no words anyone could say that could lift it. It was the caul Eddy saw through. Before he went down to the coast, Mother was greedy for his love. When he was little, he'd earned his place at her breast. It was as if when he was born he took in devotion with her milk. God knows, it poured for him. She breast-fed him till he was four. He'd walk in from the yard and pull aside her apron, drink from a breast as if from a skin sack while Tom sat in his high chair staring at what wasn't his.

Mother stroked Eddy even as she held on to her dream of a dancehall in San Francisco, taking off her dress in some fancy hotel room in Spokane for any man but Father. She kept her losses intact, this wrong or that, the emptiness of everyone but herself. She denied Tom to give to Eddy, who took as his due what he wanted from her, giving back his absence. Tom's childhood wishes were field stones gathered from desert ground. Eddy saw them in his brother's wretched stare and did for him what he could, giving him the care Tom got from no one else.

When Mother wasn't around, Eddy would drag Tom in the wagon he'd built out of an apple box, the baby buggy wheels ones he'd found in a ditch down some road. He cotter-pinned them to the axles with bent nails and whittled a handle from a broken rake. On wash days, Mother would tie Tom in a harness and rope him to the clothesline with a ring clip. Tom would run back and forth from pole to porch, the ring screaming down the clothesline wire as he called for Eddy, but Eddy wouldn't come. He'd be in the garden with Mother, that wagon of his between the rows piled high with weeds, her patting Eddy's head as he dragged it through the clay-thick mud, hauling the weeds to the refuse pile by the poplar trees. There was an innocence in Eddy when he was small, no matter the trouble and grief that surrounded them. Like Tom, Eddy knew no other life. The misery others saw as they passed by the house was not what Eddy knew. He was a child and what child thinks his life less?

Mother's need for Eddy was endless, and she was never far from his mind. It was as if he could smell her lament far off. When he caught the scent of her woe, he'd head home in his patched pants and dirty canvas runners. When he was bigger, he had the rusty bike he'd painted yellow from a can taken from some pillaged garage. He could be chasing some girl down an alley in town or struggling with one on a porch, breaking some basement window or using a stolen skeleton-key to unlock a house left empty too long. In the middle of things there would come a moment when he'd stop and turn away from a girl's wet mouth, a wallet on a chest of drawers, or a purse hanging from a kitchen chair.

The day Eddy was sent away, Mother had stood on the platform at the train station along with the others. In the coach-car window a young Mountie fresh from Regina stood behind her boy, the policeman smiling down at her as she wept. Eddy stared straight ahead in the desperate hope that somehow someone would appear at the end of the railway car, some father other than his own who would tell him it was all a mistake, that Eddy would be all right, safe from Stanley, protected from what was to come. But his mother's tears changed nothing. Eddy's two nights in the cell below the Courthouse, his body breaking under the Sergeant's hands as he was held down on the steel cot, all that and more had pushed him into a canyon there was no bottom to. From then on, all he ever did was brag that he'd die young.

Tom and Eddy never talked about what had happened when he was gone. What story Eddy might have had was just another part of the family's silence, Eddy pretending he was the same as he was before and Tom knowing he wasn't. There were stories enough about what happened to boys sent down to Boyco. Some never returned, choosing to drift on the streets of Vancouver or Seattle, and others who came back for a week or a month and then were never seen again. Some stayed on in town, sullen or boasting, some turned violent, and there were others so lonely their presence became unbearable, their families driving them away. They lived in the villages strung along the valley, boys no one dared go near for fear of the pain and anger in them.

What Eddy had hidden away drew Tom to his brother,

Eddy's emptiness sometimes so loud it made Tom afraid. Father had wanted Eddy broken and he was, though who Eddy had built out of the pieces he was left with was not the boy his father thought he'd get back. Mother never wanted to wake up Eddy's silence, the words Eddy had buried too dangerous to be said aloud. Silence ruled the house, no one speaking of what they'd done.

When Mother was young, she'd imagined a wild life and it was not on a desolate farm in a forgotten valley. Years ago Father had given her the taste of who she could be when he bought her a Jitney dance for a dime, whirling her on the horsehair floor in the dancehall at Watrous. The bands came up from Minneapolis and Spokane, out from Winnipeg and Calgary, to play their magical tunes on Manitou Beach, the salt lake crusted around them. Before Father ever came she'd listened to dance music on the crystal radio in the farm kitchen. She'd heard Guy Watkins call the tunes on the radio from Danceland. The crystal radio whispered to her the syncopated beats from the far cities. She'd be perched on a chair with her ear to the fragile coils of copper wire listening to "My Heart Stood Still," and "The Desert Song." She practised the imagined steps of the slow fox trot, a pretend permanent wave in her hair. Her heels and toes went mad with a Charleston she invented from looking at pictures in a magazine of Joan Crawford in a movie, her father laughing aloud as she pranced around, her mother, Nettie, shaking her head.

Mother's needs became Eddy's to serve, for him to hold her when she was drunk and hallucinating over some injury imagined or real, caused by Father or not, or when she was crying over some memory from the past, the farm and the early years, her mother's breast cancer, her father's suicide. It could simply have been the loneliness of the land, no one her age near enough to know, the places she might have been just pictures in a borrowed magazine. It was up to Eddy to sidetrack Father and keep him away from her, find a lost or hidden bottle to put in her hands, fill a bowl with crisp radish roses from the water jar, lay out on a plate tag-ends of Farmer's sausage, and slices of store-bought bread slavered with margarine and strawberry jam. Eddy climbed up on her bed when he was a child and when he was grown. Only his soothing touch could quiet her when she was drunk and crying. Eddy would lie on the covers and let her hold him as she stroked his cheeks. She said his hands were heavy angels. She said they brought her peace.

She blamed Father for all her losses. Her room was locked each night and Father, drunk as he might have been, never dared to enter it. He might splutter his rage at the door but he never tried to break it down. Her looks could wither, her sharp words cut. Tom would hover in the kitchen and listen to them shouting. Then the back door would slam and Father would head to the Legion or to whatever widow's door would open for him. That's when Mother called Eddy. Tom would creep down the hall after his brother and sit on the floor with his back to her door, his arms around his scant knees, his thin face buried like a blunt blade in his chest, echoes of hymns he'd learned when he was small spinning in his head. These were holy songs Mother had drawn from her own childhood, tales from the other west, the prairie flatlands she spoke of when she told of her youth to him and Eddy in their early years. Nettie had taught her daughter prayer, keeping her on her knees when she was small, thanking God for the little they had. Mother would sing "Tell Me the Old, Old Story," her boys intoning the words as they waited for her story to come.

Each fragment would begin with, *I remember*, Mother staring over their heads at the moon in the night window, talking to them as if she could explain what living used to be. Tom was hungry for the past. He wanted to know each day and night of Mother's life. In that way he thought he'd know himself, the *why* of what he was. He'd ask for the stories again and again, listening close in hopes that the new telling would reveal something hidden, some clue, some key as to a puzzle he didn't know the nature of. Her words were the catechism he memorized, every detail burned into his mind.

Tell me again, he'd say. Tell me the night of the Indians, and Mother would, so long as Eddy was near. She'd only tell it in the winter when the snow was on the ground. It had happened the year she was thirteen and the Indians came to the farm out of a two-day blizzard, her father and Nettie gone to Nokomis and stuck there in town, the wind and snow having buried the roads. She was only a girl when she opened the night door to Indians, thinking it was her parents come home somehow through the snow, drifts deep across the road. Five Cree, Mother would say, dressed as strange as anyone could imagine, one with a crushed top hat and a cape made from a black-bear hide so he looked like an animal alive split open by a knife, his flannel shirt underneath a bright red as if made of meat so that she thought she could see his lungs breathing there. Icicles hung down from the brim of his hat, his hair. They made a tinkling noise as he stood in the door, his mouth moving them as they melted with his breath. The others were as strange in deer hide capes or wool coats with brass buttons, beads on their pants and shirts. Mother always said how dirty they were, smelling of rancid fat smeared on their skin, and not washed since god-knows-when. Savages come in out of the storm, she said, and she certain she'd be raped and murdered where she stood.

What's rape, Tom once asked, and Mother told him not to interrupt. Eddy snickered at the question. Mother had given food to the Indians from what there was, thin meat left on a deer haunch hanging in the shed. As the man with the bear hide cut off gristle strips with his knife, she boiled shrunken potatoes and cabbage from the bins, and broke for them the bread Nettie had made before they left, dried prunes and crabapples put up in jars, whatever there was, the brown coal fire in the stove smouldering. They ate all there was and then they slept on the floor curled around the stove like animals, clouds of steam coming off them like the dawn mist off a sour slough.

Mother waited for hours as she peered around the edge of the curtain that hung in the doorway between her bedroom and the kitchen. She said she must have slept a little, for the Indians were gone in the morning when she awoke, nothing left but their smell. Her father was angry when he and her mother finally got back two days later, the storm abated, the roads still mostly blocked, the wagon and horses finding their way among the drifts, the sky as clear as it always was in winter, brighter than the sun itself. Her father swore he'd hunt the Indians down for breaking into the house as they did, and he made sure his daughter wasn't touched, Nettie laying Mother down on the bed and probing her with a finger to prove her purity. She'd go on to tell that every few weeks for a year they'd find the gift of a haunch of venison, moose, or bear, a brace of geese or grouse, even gophers strung on a rawhide loop hanging from the gatepost, all left there by the Cree. Twice, Nettie saw them through the window on their horses. Mother's father hated what he saw as charity, not thanks. He couldn't abide being beholden to them for anything, a bunch of savages who'd smelled up his house. Afterward, some of the older girls at school wouldn't speak to her. The few that did said they'd heard their mothers talking about how her father had raged about it at the bar in Nokomis, telling people that Indians had come to his house and raped his daughter.

The men in town looked at her in a different way after her father's telling. They thought me easy prey, she would say. In their minds one rape was as another. What did *they* know, she'd say, her breathing quick. Once, two friends of her father's wiled her into an alley behind the feed store with promises of chocolate, but her father stopped their play, their hands slipping out from under her dress. He cursed her for being what she was, he didn't curse them.

My father lay in wait many a night but could never catch the Indians leaving meat, Mother said. He ate it grudgingly when my mother cooked it, saying over and over that he could feed his own family without the damned Cree paying for fouling his daughter, my mother looking at him through narrow eyes, her tight hands hidden in her apron.

Mother told that story more than once, decorating it or stripping it down to nothing, a few words: *The Indians came. They left us food. Father hated them being there with me when he was gone.* Each time, Tom yearned to know more. He knew there was something that wasn't being told. He could tell by the darkness in her eyes, the way she'd look into the corners of the room as if her father might appear, as if the Indians were still there, huddled around the stove. As if the gifts they left were for more than food and shelter, but if not for those, then for what?

Tom would ask her what each man was like, the colour of their beads, what kind of buttons, bone or brass or iron. Were they like the Indians who lived on the reserve up at the head of the lake or like the Indians in the movies? He thought if he could see it all, could touch the things they wore, their guns and knives, their gloves and leggings, he'd understand what happened.

Eventually the stories about the old days dropped away and there was little telling of them again. Yet Mother would still read to them, drunk or sober. The Bible, always, when they were little, one of the few books she had in the house. She frightened Tom with the curses of Jeremiah, the suffering of Job. It was as if she enjoyed watching him flinch from her.

Eddy would smile when she made Tom hold the black book. She'd place the Bible in his hands when he was small and when he first looked down at the words he thought they were crushed insects. He came to believe there was a seeing in those words. The Bible was his first reading, the book he kept close as he grew. He'd trace the verses with his finger and place the prophecies in his head where he could recall them. To him the Bible's words were a passionate army. Isaiah raged in his young mind, Jeremiah doomed his hours. Verses chilled him. *And thorns shall come up in her palaces, nettles and brambles in the fortress thereof; and it shall be a habitation of dragons, and a court for owls.* He'd track words across pages in the same way he tracked a Spruce grouse up a draw. Elusive and wily though the holy book might be, Tom believed whoever wrote it left a track. There were times he would sit in front of the Bible and stare at a single sentence and get no further. Words sometimes hung in his head for days as he tried to shape them into meanings he could understand. One day he was sitting in the bathroom, the door locked, counting the red fishes on the shower curtain again, and he heard Mother as she passed by in the hall. Her voice scared him as the words slipped under the door. *O daughter of my people*, she said. *Gird thee with sackcloth, and wallow thyself in ashes.*

It was Tom's name Little Rose called out to me when I lay in my last breathing. *Tom*, she said, *Tom.* He was the brother she turned me to, the hands I knew alive when he fed me stolen milk, a boy I watch over dead. I saw him then for what he was, his solemn face beyond the bars of my crib. He was a boy gone early to old. He was born in the wrong season, wind in a rocky country, desert snow. He carried a sack of grief in his heart, in his eyes the story of us all.

I listened to the howls of the coyotes in the hills, the seething grasses, and the clatter of the far trees. Even the stones cried out. I lie among them now, a shroud around my bones, and try to think of what love might be and I remember Tom, just nine, and the dog he saved that would be with him five years more.

It was early summer. The pup was the only one alive in a litter he'd found at the town dump in a tied gunny sack tucked under a rusted bedspring. He'd been foraging for batteries, anything of copper, the chance of silver, some fork or knife, a cup. The potato sack had moved in the clutter beside a broken baby-carriage and Tom, seeing something hidden that might be alive in such a place, pulled the sack out into the sun. He took his jackknife and cut the cord that bound the bag, the pups and dam rolling out, all of them dead except for the one Eddy would name Docker, then barely alive, matted and wet from shit and urine. The auburn dam was a spaniel with a stump for a tail. The bitch had tumbled from the sack, this single pup attached to a cold hind teat, sucking, blind. Tom had to push his finger between the gums to free it from its mother.

He carried the pup home inside his shirt and hid it in the root cellar in an empty apple box with an old blanket he took from the house for it to lie on. He knew what Father would say if he found out he'd brought an animal home. Father didn't want chickens or geese, a steer or a sow, any more than he wanted a budgie bird, a cat or a dog. If he did ever talk of having a dog around the place it would be a Rottweiler or mastiff. Mostly, he didn't want anything around that would add to the bother he thought he already had with a wife and two sons. But when Tom brought the pup home, Father was away, down in Washington with some woman he'd found with money to spend and a body to share. He carried pork chop bones for the pup to gnaw on with its needle teeth, and bits of stewed chicken or marmot Tom had scavenged from the kitchen's leavings. Each day Tom snuck a cup of milk to the cellar, dipped a corner of his shirt into the milk, and let the pup suck just as I had suckled in my crib when Tom brought milk for me.

Two weeks later, Father came home and staggered through the moonlight to his root hole in the ground. He had worn out his welcome in Wenatchee and had scuttled home, some enraged husband roaming the desert roads in search of him. It was summer and the cellar was cool. There was no point in him going into the house, for Mother would have woken at his step and the usual fight begun. Instead, he'd stumbled down to the root cellar and passed out on the cot. He woke to the pup's mewling cries as Tom stood by the apple box with the pup in his hands, trying to stuff the dog inside his shirt. Wild-eyed, thin white hair damp on his forehead, the red pup squirming in his hands, Tom stared at Father, caught by him in an act of love.

Father roared: What the hell is wrong with you?

He reared up off the cot as Tom ran out the door and up the sandstone steps, Tom fleeing through the rough grass into the orchard, then down the bank of the failing creek and around the cracked clay margin of the summer slough. He didn't come back for days. It was Eddy brought him home finally. Tom had hidden the puppy in a cubbyhole cave near a windowless shack in a cul-de-sac arroyo off Cheater Creek, keeping it safe in a cage he'd made with old boards he'd found behind a deserted barn in a nearby field. Father took Tom down to the shed above the root cellar and beat him with his belt for what he called disobedience. He swore to Mother he'd beat the lies, the rebellion out of him, and he tried, but Tom said nothing to his father about where he'd been or where the pup was hidden. After the beatings, he'd walk back to the house behind his father, his bare feet in the boot prints his father left, each step he took hardening him. Fear his father as he did, he was willing to die in order to save his pup's life.

It was the summer of the beatings. Father demanded that Tom obey him. He forbade him from leaving the gravel reach of the yard. Tom was not to go near the road or out past the well. When Father was driving a logging truck in the watershed west of Sugar Lake, Mother was to watch Tom, but no matter how close she kept her eye on him, he would slip out of the yard, bits of food in his pockets, a jam jar of milk inside his belt. He would stay away the day and sometimes a day and a night, but Father would not give in to his son. Such rebellion was impossible for him to accept. He swore to Mother he'd teach the boy to obey, but after two months of Tom escaping and Father beating him, Mother said that unless Father was going to tie his son up in the root cellar or chain him to the clothesline pole, he might as well let him bring the dog home.

She had always denied Tom, and most days she might wish him far from home, but seeing Father dragging him down the path to the root cellar week after week began to plague her. Eddy had pleaded with her to make Father let Tom keep the dog, and in the end, worn down from seeing Tom limp back up the path with Father in front of him threading his heavy belt through the loops in his pants, she finally stood up to him. After hours of fighting and longer days of heavy, bitter silence, Father reluctantly agreed, promising Mother he'd do nothing to hurt the dog, and Tom brought his pup back from the arroyo. Father and Mother watched him cross the orchard, Eddy close behind, the puppy tumbling alongside Tom, tied to his wrist with a twist of binder twine.

Two days later, Father took the pup into the shed and chopped its tail off with the kindling hatchet. When Tom cried out, Father said: It's a spaniel, for Christ's sake! That's what they do to spaniels, they cut their tails off. If we're going to have one around here then it might as well look the way the dog is supposed to look.

Tom tied off the stump and bound it with a rag dipped in iodine he'd taken from the medicine box in the bathroom. Tom never said a word more about it to Father. He carried the pup up to his room in the attic and kept it there till the stump healed. Father said he didn't know what the damned fuss was all about.

Tom loved that dog more than he loved anything in the world, even Eddy. They roamed together in the fields and hills. Docker would sit at his feet when Tom shot a Willow grouse or a Blue. The dog would quiver, waiting for the sign, the long ears decorated by now with burrs and grass seeds. When Tom told the dog to fetch, Docker would run in a red blur and bring the bird back to his whistle.

A boy and his dog.

I'd see them when they set off for the hills, the rifle slung from Tom's hand, that dog at his heels. I followed him when he ranged the fields and hills. He'd take the Cooey .22 out across the farms and up into the dry coulees and arroyos. He'd hunt rabbits and squirrels, chipmunks and marmots. He got so he could shoot the head off a Spruce grouse from thirty feet, leaving the breast meat clean for eating. He'd come home with a sling of grouse, the birds tied one to one by baling twine knotted round the scales of their feet. From a distance, coming across the last fields home, he looked like some feathered creature, his shoulders and arms draped in the bodies of birds, a golden boy with white hair, Docker barking at his heels, delirious with joy.

His quietness when he saw a pheasant break from bunch grass and ride a complaint down the wind was a beauty all its own. He knew the creatures of the sloughs and swamps, the dry clay hills and the Ponderosa meadows. He would lie on a rocky outcrop of shale high above Grey Ditch and stare across the valley to Ranch Road and Cheater Creek. There were the times he'd circle round and come upon the house from behind. He'd cross the old orchard from Pottery Road and at our graves he'd kneel, in his hands the white skull of a mink he'd found or an eagle's feather he'd watched fall from the clouds, and he'd set the treasure on the stones that marked our place.

5

he fight had begun when Norman had been trying to impress anyone drunk or sober that he was smarter than they were. His latest obsession was Nietzsche. He'd been standing with his back to the counter where the liquor was, going on about someone called Übermensch who'd walked a tightrope above a crowd of fools. Billy, who would've thought anyone walking a tightrope stupid, had gone over to grab a couple of Lucky Lager from the cold water in the sink and heard Norman explaining to some girl about Superman. Billy thought he was talking about the comic book and said to no one in particular that he liked reading Superman. Norman, who had saved every issue of Captain Marvel and Batman comics that had ever come out, prized Superman most of all, but that wasn't who he was talking about.

What the hell do *you* know about Superman?

Norman's question had been an insult, for he had no love

for Billy Holdman, but he was drunk and had forgotten where Billy came from, the pride that rides wild out of worthlessness. Norman was deep into a bottle of scotch. His question didn't invite an answer, for all he wanted to do was show off. Billy was only interested in the two beers he was holding in one hand, both bottles for himself, and the double gin he held in the other. The drink wasn't for Vera, the girl he'd come with, but for Crystal, who was at the kitchen table, and who Billy knew would follow him out to his pickup truck or upstairs to the spare bedroom regardless of what Vera thought.

Crystal had the calculating half-dreams of the poor. She'd grown up in a shotgun trailer with old towels for curtains. If anyone looked close at her they'd find a hole in a stocking, a seam stitched by a bad needle, a hem come down, or a twist in a sweater woven wrong. She had the curse of coming from nothing, all her plans a map leading her someday into a beat-up trailer worse than the one she came from, pregnant, with two bawling kids and bruises on her cheeks. To her a skirt and sweater in the end were just things a boy took off, blonde hair something they could grab. Tom figured the day Crystal was born she'd opened her eyes to a wrong world. Eddy said Crystal Wright was the kind of girl men fed upon, Billy, Joe, Harry, and the rest. Both brothers were right.

Eddy and Tom had looked up to Billy when they were boys. He was older, but like them and most of their friends, he came from raw milk, wild meat, and stolen eggs. When Billy went to work in the bush, the money he earned went to his mother to feed the family. What he got to spend on himself came from riffling the pockets of some passed-out Indian in an alley back of the bar who still had treaty money on him, a logger three sheets to the wind, or a white-trash girl on her worn heels. He also sold things that could be sold to someone else, copper wire stripped from a house going up or coming down, stolen batteries melted down for lead, a car radio or a record player lifted from a house, or the soiled and oil-streaked hard-earned dollars and cents some garage or corner store man had the foolishness to leave in a tin box or till over a Sunday night.

When he got a little older, Billy discovered gambling. He was razor-sharp at reading a car or horse, a dog or a fighting cock, and his betting on racing or fighting either man or beast or bird usually resulted in him having more money than when he arrived. He had one sure source of cash and that was the dog fights. His last pit of the season was coming up on Saturday out at Carl Janek's farm.

When Tom was a boy, he'd seen Billy sell his slow-witted sister, Nancy, out of a coal shed down by the tracks for nickels and dimes to older boys. Later, the story went, he sold her to men who could get no other woman, men from the bars or back streets who'd tried and never got a last dance, men who didn't know how to get anyone except in their wretched hand-held dreams. Nancy was at the party in tow of Lester Coombs, who was in town again. Billy had brought him out to the party to show off his big connection from Vancouver. Before letting him in that afternoon, Eddy had made Lester turn over the pistol he carried, Lester taking the Smith & Wesson .22 out of his belt from under his leather jacket, and Eddy putting it away in the tub of the wringer washing machine. Lester said the pistol had better still be there for him to get when he left. Eddy and Tom had just looked at him, this guy from the coast who probably thought they were all a bunch of rednecks, good only for buying what he'd brought for Billy to sell.

———

The party had begun two nights before, the word having gone down into the town and out into the country that there was a wild time to be had Saturday night at Eddy Stark's house. Saturday afternoon Mother locked herself in her bedroom at the corner of the house, the snap of the deadbolt loud as it slipped into its slot. The iron bars lag-bolted into her one window completed what Mother called her privacy. She told Eddy and Tom she had a knife and was prepared should some drunk try to break into her room. Eddy had told her that she'd be all right. It's just a party, he'd said. Mother didn't try to answer that and neither did Tom.

Mother had been down her own roads and couldn't bear Eddy's parties, the drinking, cards, and dancing, cars and trucks coming and going in flares of dust and grit at all hours of the night and day, people dragging themselves around the house trying to sleep off their carouse. Such chaos was too much for her who thought she'd lived through enough in her life. Over the years she'd become solitary, reclusive, alien to all but family, though Tom reckoned her being a stranger to family too. She had no friends. What women she might have known when she and Father moved to the valley had drifted away after Rose disappeared. Their questions about her vanishing were left unanswered but for Mother looking at some nosy woman in the door through half-closed eyes and shaking her head. She told whoever asked that there had been no birth, only a death, and though neighbour women could add up the months and figure she'd carried to term, they said nothing to anyone, certain they knew all that went on in the Stark house out on Ranch Road. The women stopped coming to the house. Sometimes they could be seen sitting in cars driving by, their heads turned, mouths grim as they stared, their men keeping their eyes on the ruts and ditches.

In his last years, Father began wandering around drunk with the shotgun at night. Deadbolt or not, it made Mother nervous. Father knew where he was to sleep and it wasn't with her. Tom was careful around him and would run into the orchard when Father started muttering, gun in hand. Tom would lie near the graves and watch the house until everything was still. The bats told him Father was passed out and sleeping. Only when the yard was quiet did the bats return through the cracks in the fascia to their attic roosts. Eddy wasn't afraid, but after a while he had respect enough for Father's ways to disappear into the night and not return till dawn. The cot in the root cellar was Father's place when he was drunk and otherwise the couch in the living room, but he never lasted a whole night in either place.

Mother had asked Eddy to put the bolt in her door the night of her small revenge. She had left a kitchen chair out where Father was wont to walk. He tripped over it, accidentally springing both barrels of the shotgun in the dark. When Tom heard Father yell about it the next day, he knew she'd left the chair out deliberately, but she swore she hadn't and that Father ought to have known better than to be walking around the house at night with a loaded gun. She'd asked Tom and Eddy: Who does he think he's hunting, if not me?

There was no clear answer to that. It could well have been Mother, though both boys thought it was the sworn phantom enemies Father complained about from week to week, men who'd caused him harm at some time or another. His losing the tractor to the bank in 1949 was one such misery. The Reo dump truck being seized seven years ago had been his last chance to own his life. After that, he drove Cat or logging truck for outfits that hadn't gone under, losing jobs because of his anger, his sneering at others, him telling them they didn't know their ass from a hole in the ground when it came to making a dollar in the bush.

What Father earned he kept for himself, giving Mother a handful of change a night or two after pay day, a few crumpled, leftover dollar bills from his shirt pocket. The rest he'd spent in the bars gambling and drinking. The food he brought home he'd traded for: carrots, onions, and potatoes given to him by some farmer in exchange for a hind-quarter from a moose or a deer he'd shot out of season. Flour and sugar, salt, lard, and rice he'd get from Winning Chow down at the New Dawn Café. He'd dicker with the Chinaman in exchange for a side of pork he'd lifted from someone's smokehouse, chickens he'd stolen from a coop down Oyama way, the birds stuffed into potato sacks, their beaks poking through the coarse weave. What other the family ate, Mother grew or the boys hunted for, stole, or bought on credit at the grocery store, Mr. Olafson phoning every few weeks, reminding them of the money they owed, taking the occasional dollar the boys brought and marking it down in his book, a balance never reached.

There were two holes in the wall by the china cabinet that Tom could put his foot inside. One shotgun blast had gone right through to the other side so Tom could peer from the hall into the dining room. Father would be far gone when he began to wander the house for lack of sleep. He'd search the rooms for bottles he'd hidden and forgotten. The blowing apart of the dining-room wall was enough to make Mother fear his bursting in and holding her to account with the shotgun while he demanded what he thought was his right. Mother said to whichever of her sons was near enough to hear: God knows what right he thinks he was entitled to. God knows.

They'd hear him shout at her from the yard about how it was no wonder he went looking for other women. I'm still a man!

Go to hell, she'd hiss.

Tom came into the house, put the shotgun back up on its nails, and stared down the hall at Mother's door. He'd seen her two days ago, squirrelling away her bottles of Seagram's 83, a galvanized pail for her needs, cigarettes, and various foods. She said she was not about to emerge into what she called Eddy's craziness, saying to Tom, Father's come out in him again, and that was true enough for both of them, though Tom felt what blood he had was different than what pumped in his brother's skull.

Tom imagined Mother in her bed, honing her paring knife on a fingernail file as she muttered imprecations at the man who'd ruined her life. All those years of moving from farm to ranch to town, to the poor land they lived on now, what she called their half-assed bit of nothing. He'd promised her more and she'd got less, each day and month and year eating into that dream until there was nothing left but bits of threadbare rag, something to line the nests of field mice, the burrows of rats. Tom could hear her through the bedroom door ask Eddy as he was kneading her back, her muscles thin ropes in his Vaseline hands: Just who does he think he is? Tom knew Eddy gave little thought to what she said, having heard it all too many times before.

In the afternoons when Father was off working in the bush, Eddy would go down the hall to see Mother, and one morning Tom thought of a way to climb inside their secrecy. Mother always went to the garden early in the afternoon, where she argued with the young corn that seemed slow to grow and worried the peas, driving in stakes and tying them up with string so they wouldn't sag and rot. One day he waited in his attic bedroom until he heard her leave the house, then he went downstairs to her room where he made a hurried nest in the shadows under her bed, pushing the empty bottles against the wall into the drift of torn magazines and crinkled candy wrappers. He was eight years old.

His bare foot was braced against the wall and the other hooked to a spring. It seemed to him he was crawling upside down on the bottom of her mattress. One hand gripped the hind leg of the bed, the other the mattress rim. The quilt hung from the side of the bed like a curtain. He rested his cheek on the floor and peered out from behind the cotton squares and waited for Mother to return, terrified of what she would do if she caught him hiding there.

He waited a long time before he heard her come back in the house. She went to the record player in the living room and put on "Stormy Weather," turning it up so she could hear it all the way into her room. As Tom watched from under the bed, she seemed to him to be a girl again, light on her feet as she turned on the floor. It was like she was dancing by her salt lake, a place she'd told him about one time.

Just as the song ended, Eddy opened the door, his face empty. Mother smiled and told him to play the record again. He went to put it on again and when he came back, she held out her arms. Tom hadn't known his brother could dance. Eddy glided with her by the bed. Tom watched him from under the quilt, his brother's face appearing and disappearing as he turned in slow circles. Mother's eyes were closed, but Eddy's were open, staring into the room, and there was a look on his face Tom had never seen before. It was as if his brother had lost something, but what it was Tom didn't know, this thing he was doing, holding Mother and moving as if she was nothing in his arms, and then the rasp of the needle in its grooves on the turntable, the *wish-tic, wish-tic, wish-tic* and the click of the record arm rising, the turntable spinning to a halt. She went to the bed then, Eddy lying down beside her, the two of them above and Tom below. Looking up, Tom could see the shapes of their bodies in the grey mattress. Tom lay still, listening as Mother's breathing became laboured in sleep, lulled by Eddy's sing-song, *husha husha hush!* It was a sound Tom had heard over the years through the door. Tom remembered the feeling that was in the room, and though he couldn't have put a name to it back then he knew what it was now. Loneliness. That's what had been in there, not just his mother's and his brother's, but his too, him lying there under the bed, utterly alone, and waiting.

Tom went down the hall and knocked on Mother's door the secret code of three sharp raps and two lighter taps. He could hear her on the other side of the door, like a trapped fox. Are you all right? he asked.

Who's been shooting that gun?

Don't worry, he said. It was just someone fooling around. Do you need anything? He knew she had a cache of kubasaw, process cheese, and salted crackers stored in shoeboxes in the closet, more than enough, given her lack of appetite. All she seemed to want to eat were her radishes. Eddy cut them with his knife into roses and put them in sealed water jars in the refrigerator. She'd said often enough they were all that kept her blood running.

Where's Eddy?

Up in his room where he always is, said Tom.

Mother was quiet for a moment and then said: Go away. He heard her bare feet on the floor as she went to her bed. One day he knew he would knock and there'd be no answer. She'd die in there and he and Eddy would have to break the door down so they could bury her. Every year with her seemed harder than the last since Father died. No matter his accusations, she always said, it was her blackness after her daughters' births that killed them. She'd sunk into the shadows and there was no coming up for months. She had lain staring up into the ceiling as if trying to see through the stained tiles all the way to the night.

You never wanted any truck with a girl, he'd say when they were in the midst of a yelling match. When have you ever thought about Rose and Alice?

Which daughter? The ones you buried or the one you burned?

Their accusations were always at the end of a drunken fight about why there wasn't enough wood piled up for winter, not enough food, no money, something, nothing, a dropped mug, a broken toaster, a greasy wrench left on the arm of the couch in the living room, an empty bottle, isolation or contempt. At the end, Father's voice would always rise to a cry about the girls, a sign he'd ceded the floor to her. Go to hell, he'd yell as she went down the hall. And then her words to him: Hell? Where's that? Here?

Tom tried to drive out Mother's and Father's angry words, gripping his ears in his hands, but he could see Mother standing over Father's body down by the well. Eddy had brought her down from the house the night Father died. His father was lying there, legs crooked in a pool of creek water, part of his head gone and the shotgun lying beside the pump, barrels pointing at the North Star. Misery, she said, Father in the grass by the stone wellhead, blood like iron scum floating on the creek pools, his brains scattered in the grass as if he'd wanted to think along with the grasshoppers and beetles about what living and dying were. Tom was the one who dug the hole and buried him. When he was finished, he came back from the orchard with the wheelbarrow and the shovel. She sat beside him on the lip of the well, staring down where Father had been lying with his feet in the creek and said: Blood is blood and sometimes better gone. Tom, frightened, exhausted, looked at her, but there was no tear he could see in her eye. A stillness, yes, as if she was a snake, lidless and staring, gone out of the sun to rest in the cool that darkness promises.

Tom turned from Mother's locked-down life. He walked up the hall and saw a couple there, leaning against the wall in a clench, one grunting and the other breathing out a moan. The boy's hand was under the girl's skirt, holding her buttock. She was hanging on to his neck as if afraid she might sink into some torrent and drown. They were likely strangers from town, drunk on the glory they'd gained by being at one of Eddy's parties, gatherers, hangers-on.

There was a shadow rising in him like pit water climbing up a narrow shaft and he wished it far away. He looked down at the floor, feeling again the fir splinters in his knees and palms, hurting him. He was just small. He'd stopped and was leaning his head down. His nose had been sniffing, something thick in it, a smell he'd known and not known before. It was dust and wax and heat, heavy, and polished there by the shuffle of feet, the scour of brushes and cloths. The smell was a blow so thick it gagged his throat.

He didn't want to be that child, but suddenly he saw himself upstairs on the landing crawling, eyes closed, following the soft whisper that was Mother's nightgown trailing. She was crawling too. When he opened his eyes, he couldn't find her. She had turned the corner where the stairs angled up to the attic. He rocked there on his knees and hands, naked but for a pair of tattered pyjama bottoms. It was so strange to move back and forth and not go anywhere. Tom's chest heaved now with the memory of it. He was at the top of the stairs and he could hear things breaking down below. Dishes shattered and something heavy fell on the kitchen floor. He could hear the sprinkle that was the last sound of glass. Like glare ice sliding from a roof, the thud as Father's fist hit a wall. He was drunk again. The glass sprinkle diminished until it was only a music playing on Tom's skin. He kept trying to move. He knew where Mother was. She was in the secret cupboard. He couldn't see the hiding place because it was under the stairs. He rocked harder, but his knees wouldn't budge and his toes slipped on the wood. He'd gone to the cupboard before but he knew he wouldn't be allowed in. Mother would be in there with Eddy. They were hiding and there was only room for two. No, is what she always said. He knew that's what he'd hear if he butted the door with his head.

Go away, you little bugger, she'd hiss. Hide somewhere else.

But there was no other place. Eddy would tell her to let him in, but Mother wouldn't open the door. Tom heard himself making small noises. Mother said it was the sound a pig makes. She said through the secret door: You're nothing but a pig.

> This little piggy went to market,
> This little piggy stayed home,
> This little piggy had roast beef,
> This little piggy had none,
> And this little piggy went *Wee Wee Wee*
> All the way home.

He felt the quiet for a brief moment and then he heard Father's boots crossing the kitchen below, the rasp of his rough hand on the stair rail, and Father going *clump clump clump* on the stairs. Tom's throat pushed a smell into his nose. It rested there in a ball that held like wet fat he couldn't swallow. He rocked harder and harder and then he was back in the hall, a couple of strangers beside him, one of them grunting, the other in a moan.

There are things happening to me, Tom said to them, but they didn't look like they wanted to know. He felt his hands, the sweat on them cold and slippery, and he rubbed them together as he leaned back against the wall. Eddy had told him so many times not to remember, but there was no stopping any of it.

6

the door to the spare bedroom across from Eddy's was partly open and Tom glanced in. Wayne was down on his knees in front of the girl he'd fallen over in the yard. He was trying hard to get her underpants off. He had his two hands hooked on the elastic at her hips, but she wasn't moving for him, her pale legs crossed tight. Her sweater was still on and her stained white bobby sox were rolled down, faded parrots flying inside out in a circle round her ankle bones. She had her hands in her hair and wasn't saying anything to him, just staring into the clenched cross of her legs as if what she saw there was all the world she had.

Get the hell out of here, Tom said. This's private up here.

Wayne tried to twist away from Tom. I'm sorry, Tom, he whined as he was pushed out the door. I didn't know.

The hell you didn't, Tom said.

Wayne fled down the steps, and the girl, her face fish-belly white, fixed her clothes and ambled after him, saying childishly to Tom as if in apology: I mostly just want to go home.

Tom turned and knocked on Eddy's door, the sound of "Jambalaya" coming loud through the thin wood. He opened the door and went in.

Sally-Ann, makeup spilled in black pools under her eyes, was dancing naked on the thin mattress of the iron army cot, Eddy in his pants sprawled back barefoot and sparrow-chested on his sprung armchair with a glass of whiskey in his hand and a cigarette stuck between his lips. Her lipstick was worn away. Tom looked at the needle tracks, the bruises on her arms and on her thighs, the swell of her breasts and the smudge of hair at her groin. It had only taken a month or two for Eddy to help her into a habit. Tom wondered at how his brother could stand apart from people, yet at the same time draw them to him. Men and women seemed to fall under his spell, only to be crippled by their closeness. Confusion followed Eddy everywhere, yet Tom knew there was a bond between him and his brother that couldn't be broken. It was a presence of brotherhood which Tom tried to keep clear of impediment, even as Eddy cluttered it.

Sitting on a crate, the bullet-lamp gave off a dim light, its red bulb a faint glow in the corner. Harry was perched on the edge of the kitchen chair Eddy had spirited from downstairs years ago. Mother had never missed it. After Father died she noticed little of such things as chairs or dishes, tables, forks, or mirrors. Harry had tucked himself back in the shadows, Eddy's only friend, a part-time carpenter when

he wasn't stealing, a pool-hall hustler dealing amphetamines. His belly filled him out. He looked to Tom like a
white grub hunched there. Under the bell of fat was Harry's
belt cinched tight around his hips holding what shone
below, the Harley-Davidson buckle he'd taken off a biker he
and Eddy put the boots to a year ago on the road past
Lumby. They'd followed him in their car and ridden the
biker into the ditch after the guy cursed them in the bar.
For Harry the buckle was a souvenir much like the ears soldiers brought back from the Pacific after the war. Tom had
seen them hanging like dried apricot halves speared on wire
in the basement room of a vet crazed on cooking wine, him
shaking the copper circle of ears, the whispers as they
touched each other, the skin a soft leather slip as on the
inside wrist of a child.

Tom didn't wonder why Harry was there. The only thing
Harry cared about was Eddy. They were always together and
had been since they were small. They'd shared their petty
crimes when they were boys, the shoplifting, the bullying
of others, the liquor and money they stole from cars and
trucks, the homes they plundered. Their crimes came to a
head that night they broke into the bar at the Legion Hall
and Eddy had been arrested. He never held it against Harry
that he'd been the one caught. Harry had once told Tom he
wished that he'd had the chance to go to Boyco with Eddy,
the two of them criminals together. Eddy had returned from
Vancouver to Harry's petty cunning, Harry relying on his
selling of drugs, occasional robberies, and the abuse of girls
too young to know what they were getting into, thrilled to

be given all they could drink and a few paltry pills in exchange for their bodies.

Harry worshipped Eddy as Joe looked up to Billy, wanting to have the same kind of power. Joe felt he had been thwarted by his birth. He was coldly vengeful for the wrongs, real and imagined, that had dogged his days ever since his childhood, but there was no such bitterness in Harry, who would have been bewildered had anyone told him he wreaked havoc on things. He'd survived growing up with a Baptist father and a slavish, back-country mother who loved her son and who Harry disdained for her humility, and especially her submission to a man who spouted prophecy and doom, his father, a labourer at the soda pop distributors who hand-trucked bottles of Coke and Orange Crush all day. Harry was embarrassed by the people who'd brought him into the world. He took what opportunity presented itself, a wallet left lying on a counter, a door unlocked, a young girl come from some village in the Cariboo, shivering in an empty luggage stall behind the bus depot. Eddy felt nothing when he came back from Boyco, and Harry spent his days and nights trying to feel the same.

When Eddy was a kid, he looked at Billy and saw what he could be. Tom had always known Billy saw himself in Eddy, the same cruelty and toughness. The two of them had been born to loss and visited that birthright on everyone they met. It was their coldness that drew people to them, Harry to Eddy, Joe to Billy, and others in the tribe too, each one loving the fear they felt when they got that close to emptiness. Tom had looked into his brother's eyes, Billy's too. He knew what wasn't there.

Doesn't she dance like hell, Tom? Eddy said.

Tom sat down on the edge of the bed and looked at Sally-Ann. She was Eddy's latest girl, a waitress at the Venice Café. Flirting with Eddy had carried her into a place she'd never dreamed. Tom could've told her it would happen when she first went riding in the Studebaker, but he knew she wouldn't have listened. People didn't listen to him. He could see in Eddy's eyes that he had begun the rise from his last spike. The junk had tempered in him, and he was soft at the edges as he floated up out of the laze of his nod, a lax grin on his face. His works were on the side table, beside them a paper of heroin. Tom knew it wouldn't be his brother's whole stash, but he knew it was all he'd told Sally-Ann there was.

Sally-Ann was still dancing, her movements ragged and jerky, "Jambalaya" over, the needle doing its repetitive grind in the last grooves of the record. The sound was turned up loud on the .45 record player Eddy had stolen somewhere, and Tom wondered again why any girl would put up with what Eddy asked. He knew it wasn't just her need for junk that made her dance. She did it because Eddy had told her to. Sally-Ann hung in for the heroin and the love she'd confused with it. He knew Sally-Ann could pick up her clothes and walk out of the room and Eddy wouldn't hold her back.

Sally-Ann had been hanging around Eddy for months in the hopes she'd get her chance to go out with him. Now her days and nights were measured out by needles in the bind of her arm. She was the latest in a long line of wreckage. She stayed half the time with her mother out by Coldstream Creek, in an old house on an abandoned farm. Tom knew Elvie Madden. He'd seen her at the Okanagan Hotel where she worked. Sally-Ann's father had taken off years ago. He'd never brought home a nickel to his family, just himself, and that only when he was broke or hurting.

Sally-Ann had loved Eddy from afar. She'd been serving him free coffee all spring and summer, not charging him for breakfast, and generally doing anything she could to get him to ask her out. Eddy was a prize in her eyes. Like most women she thought she could change him. Women thought that given tenderness and love Eddy could be healed and made back into a man. Tom knew women were mostly wrong about men, and always wrong about Eddy. Sally-Ann had got her chance and there she was dancing for him while Harry stroked himself, his bent cock poking out from his unbuttoned fly.

Tom rubbed his cheek and felt the stubble growing there. Things have got out of hand downstairs, he said.

Eddy smiled, his face loose with dope. C'mon, Tom. Look at Sally-Ann dance. Isn't she something else?

Norman's gone to the hospital, Tom said. Billy did some damage with that hoe.

Eddy lifted his arm, the hand languid, seeming to hang from the barbed-wire tattoo wound around his wrist. He wove his fingers through the still air. He'll be okay, he said.

He's a fucking mess is what he is, said Tom.

71

Sally-Ann stopped dancing then and began to cry, her arms crossed over her face. Tom got up and grabbed the Indian blanket hanging off the foot of the bed. He draped its folds over her shoulders, calming her enough to get her down from the bed. He found some of her clothes on the floor, tucked them under his arm, and pushed her gently toward the door with his hand between the sharp blades of her shoulders.

She stopped crying then. Fuck it, Eddy said, as Tom eased Sally-Ann out the door, closing it behind him. He handed the clothes to her, and she began putting them on.

Why's he like that? Why's your brother like that? Sally-Ann asked as she did up two of the three remaining buttons on her blouse with trembling fingers, but there was no answer other than to tell her Eddy didn't have limits and she should have known going in he was a mine shaft, not a mountain.

I don't want anyone to see me like this, she said. My purse and everything's still in there. She looked at her bare feet. I don't even have my shoes.

You can get your stuff later, he said. He took her down-stairs, Sally-Ann protesting a little. He needed to put her somewhere and the only quiet place he could think of was Mother's room. He led her down the hall, knocked at the door, and when Mother finally shot back the bolt, he nudged Sally-Ann in and told Mother to keep an eye on her.

Eddy, she said.

It wasn't a question.

Tom said: Yes.

Light from Mother's dancing-girl lamp glanced off her paring knife. She pushed the blade out the cracked door past the shadows. Just so you know, she said.

What does that mean? Tom asked, some threat coming from nowhere he could see.

Mother didn't answer, and he turned away as she closed the door.

Tom walked down the hall and turned into the crib room, expecting someone to be using it for something, but there was no one there. The old ironing board leaned against the west wall with a kicked-in wicker hamper beside it filled with old clothing. The iron crib where the girls had died was across from it, the mattress still covered with a rubber sheet, brittle, cracked by the years. The pink bars of the crib and the blue walls behind them were streaked and stained. The sun striking the floor over time had worked hard at further ruin. By the closet door was the old high chair and Tom could see himself as a little boy sitting there, his legs tied down with flour-sack diapers so he couldn't climb out and fall, the white cloth twisted at his back, knotted tight where he couldn't reach.

He had sat in it every morning, his fingers making their *slick slitch* porridge noise in the bowl as he watched Eddy on Mother's lap. How old was Eddy then, three, four? She'd opened her dress and Eddy suckled on her breast, cupping the blue-veined flesh in his freckled hands. Mother would tell Eddy to move from one breast to another, Eddy pretending to be the baby he wasn't any more. She'd lift her dark nipple between two fingers and place it in his mouth.

Mother held his head to her tightly as she hummed softly to him, "Blue Canadian Rockies." Each morning she'd tie Tom into the chair. No wonder he hardly ever talked. No wonder he didn't want to. Except to Eddy. He'd talk to Eddy, but only when Mother and Father weren't there.

Whenever Eddy asked where Father was, the answer was always the same. He's gone to work in the bush. *In the bush, in the bush, in the bush.* Tom would listen as she went down the hall, Eddy following as she murmured: My baby boy, my darling. Tied to the chair in the kitchen, Tom could hear Mother close her bedroom door. It wasn't hopelessness he'd felt when he was tied there. Nothing had happened yet in his life to tell him different. He simply waited out the hours, knowing that somehow, sometime, Eddy would come back and release him.

Then Eddy would come to untie him and help him down. Because Eddy loved him. Eddy loved him even after Boyco, though things had changed. How could they not have? After Eddy was taken away, Mother drove Tom from the house with her granite face. Every time I see you I think of Eddy, she'd say over the months. Why are you here?

Tom wandered the hills with his rifle. Some Saturday afternoons he'd walk the two miles to town and drift down the back alleys, picking through the green garbage bins behind the stores in search of plunder. If he got hungry he would go to the New Dawn Café where Winning Chow's wife would always give him food. He'd take the rice and vegetables to the Cenotaph Park where he'd sit with the old men and listen to their stories while they played checkers.

A First World War vet once told him about a soldier in France who seemed to be lost in no-man's-land between the Canadian and German lines. He said they'd see him under the star-shells in the shadows, moving among the craters and concertina wire and they'd call out to him in the hope of finding out what man he was, one of theirs or one of the Boche. When Tom asked if they ever found out who the soldier was, the old vet just looked away and shuffled off in search of a bottle to share or just to be alone. The last thing he'd said to Tom was that the world was built on bones.

Tom would come back to the house in the evening and peer through the windows until he was sure it was safe, his cold supper on a plate on the counter, Mother in her room and Father gone in the truck. Tom would eat quietly and then slip up to his room and kneel on the bed to stare out at Ranch Road and the far lights of the town. How Eddy would make it back from the coast was a mystery to him. Vancouver was an impossible city, a metropolis far away through the mountains and down the Fraser Canyon to the delta lands where the river emptied out into the sea. Eddy was there locked away and Tom wished him home each night, sure that with Eddy back, Mother would be content again, her anger toward him abated by Eddy's calming presence.

Tom pulled the curtains over the dusty glass. He didn't want anyone to see into the room. He looked around. Blankets and soiled sheets had been tossed in a heap in the corner by the hamper. Clothes no one had worn for years were mixed in with Father's things, torn shirts and pants, underwear and jackets, like bits of skin Father had sloughed off. Father's boots and shoes were piled on the floor, a confusion of worn soles and bruised leather.

Tom touched the crib and saw the scars where he and Eddy had gnawed at the bars in their time. He fingered the scratches and tiny crevices in the paint and he remembered his sisters. Little Rose hadn't lived long enough to stand and wear out her mouth against the iron and Alice had just lain there, staring through the bars, her world a cage. Every day for the six months she lived, Tom had knelt on the floor and sung songs to his tiny sister, nursery rhymes, cowboy tunes, "Mother Goose," "Big Rock Candy Mountain," "My Old Kentucky Home." After supper, when no one was watching, he'd creep downstairs and sit by the crib, each breath he took an echo of his sister's.

He could see his father coming up from the creek and throwing the shovel into the truck box, that clang of metal, and then driving away, his tail lights dwindling. He remembered the times later, on nights when Eddy was gone into town, and he'd walked out to the orchard alone, the smell of sage and willow lifting from the creek wallow. Alice's blue stone lay shouldered from the earth, and he'd kneel down and brush away the dry leaves and bits of rock as he thought of her small body. Once Tom had imagined freeing her from the earth, lifting out the small bundle, untying the knots and folding back the canvas Father bound her in. He'd sit there, the thin blue shift unveiled, the fragile bones, the fontanel spread like a tiny, lipless mouth, baby teeth floating in the cup of the skull.

Alice.

Tom looked around him now. The room seemed to get larger, and the things lying in the corners and on the floor grew as he looked at them. He was getting smaller and smaller and he knew if he stayed there he'd be a baby again, standing in the crib, gnawing on the bars with his teeth. He backed out, closed the door, and went down the hall into the kitchen.

The usual people were there, most of them he knew, but strangers too, standing around fishing bottles out of the sink, drinking and talking about the fight in the yard as they looked on at a poker game in progress. Someone had pulled the table out from the wall and sitting around it now were Lester Coombs on an apple crate with his back to the door and Billy across from him in a kitchen chair, shuffling a deck of cards. Against the windows next to Lester was a quiet guy from the mill, Gregor, his face pitted with chicken-pox scars, Rafe Gillespie beside him with his greasy hair and black-rimmed glasses. He drove one of the town's dump trucks. Across from Gregor and Rafe were Don Stupich and Andy Kimball. Don he'd known for a long time. He'd graduated from apprentice to full-time mechanic's job at Caterpillar Tractor two years ago. Andy was Eddy's age, a pool player from Falkland. He worked the money table every Saturday afternoon down at White's Pool Hall. Eight ball was his game, but he was a deadly snooker player as well. As Tom looked on with the others, Billy stopped shuffling and started dealing out a hand of five-card stud, one card down and the first of four cards up. Lester looked at his hole card and matched the five-dollar bet Gregor put down, Rafe beside him folding his hand and tossing his cards back at Billy, a smug smile on his face. Tucked behind Lester's shoulder was Nancy, tunelessly humming a song. The crowd around the sink and strung along the wall were like the lights on an old Christmas string, one bulb going out would crash the rest of them into the dark.

Tom noticed Marilyn slip out the back and he followed, stopping at the door. His hand played across the ragged screen, small points of wire brushing against his fingertips. She was so small. He thought of her standing over Norman as if he was a hurt animal and not a man. Then she'd glanced up, and her eyes had gone right through him. He'd felt her inside his body and, confused, suddenly wanted to touch whatever it was that could do that. She was a girl, yes, but she was a woman too. He felt she was someone he could hold without hurting, him or her. Marilyn, he said, and she looked back, walking toward him, her skirt switching around her legs. He felt she was a girl who needed looking after. She stepped up onto the porch and smiled through the broken screen at him. It's you, she said.

Tom asked if she wanted a drink and she nodded. She followed him into the kitchen and he gave her a gin and Seven-up in the cleanest glass he could find. They walked together into the living room, her head barely coming to the middle of his chest. People were there, some of them passed out, one couple he didn't know on the couch partly covered with the curtain they'd pulled down off the side window. There were others in corners they'd blocked off with a cushion or chair, places where they could pretend to some privacy. Not much was broken, the lamps still burned, the three remaining dining-room chairs were upright, and the ashtrays were full but not on fire. Someone had turned the loveseat around so it faced the window. Tom sat down on it and put his feet up on the windowsill, Marilyn taking his hand. He held it awkwardly, small in his. He'd kissed girls before. He'd touched them too, girls he'd met when he was still in school and others through Eddy and Harry. His brother had told him he could fuck one out at the lake two summers before, but he'd walked away when it came his turn. He knew most everyone thought he was strange around girls, but he'd never cared what others thought of him.

Marilyn's scent rose up around him, makeup and lipstick and something she called Evening in Paris cologne. You smell good, he said, and Marilyn laughed and poked her pink tongue into her gin. They sat there listening to "Blueberry Hill" yet one more time.

That Fats Domino can really play the piano, she said.

Tell me what happened to your eye.

She turned her head so he couldn't see. Oh, that, said Marilyn. That's nothing really, and then she lifted her shoulder, keeping her head turned partly away to hide that side of her face.

The house was quieter now, the poker game having put a damper on the party. He was suddenly interested in what she had under the sweater with that little necklace of plastic pop-pearls draped across her chest. He wanted to take hold of the beads and pull them just hard enough to scatter them across her lap onto the skirt that had ridden up above her knees.

What he felt was strange and new. He was sitting with a girl whose feelings were everywhere on her and all he was doing was holding her hand. He felt awkward and said, I read a lot of books, you know.

Like what?

Oh, you know, books like *The Amboy Dukes* and *Cry Tough*. I even read *Of Mice and Men*. I get most of them from the library in the basement of the Courthouse, but it's the Bible I like most.

Marilyn giggled and told Tom to close his eyes and kiss her. He felt her soft lips opening, her tongue delicately slithering across his teeth, the milk in her bad eye a small sea storming. His hand found its way under her sweater, flesh on flesh but for the cage of her bra, and her hips rose to him, that girl-smell rising. Tom felt himself get hard and he shifted his leg, afraid she'd feel it, but she didn't move away. She held herself close as the talk in the kitchen began to fade. A couple of drunken girls screamed as a car pulled out of the driveway, the horn blaring, men shouting back at them. He heard Stupich make a bet, Andy answering him, saying he'd raise ten bucks. Tom could imagine Billy sitting there as he thought about the bet, Lester across the table watching Billy and the other players for any sign of a tell.

There'd be a pile of loose bills in the middle of the table. And then someone dropped a glass on the floor. When it shattered, everyone out in the kitchen went silent.

Marilyn gave a little gasp. What's going on?

It's too quiet, Tom said.

Some guy he didn't know stuck his head out from under the torn curtain on the couch. His eyes squinted as he stared over the arm toward the kitchen, a girl's voice coming strangled from under him, telling him to get off her. The two bodies scuffled for a second and the guy's head went back under, a girl's bare knee poking out the side, brown hair sprawled on the arm of the couch. Tom listened and heard footsteps on the floor above him where Eddy's room was. His brother had heard the car pull away and the shouting, then the sudden quietness downstairs, and wanted to know what was going on.

It's my brother, Tom said. He's heard it too.

Heard what?

The quiet, Tom said. His hand lay under her sweater, still splayed across the narrow folds of skin where her waist bent. He could hear bare feet move across the landing overhead and start down the stairs, Harry's boots behind him.

Marilyn tried to kiss him again, but Tom pulled away and unhinged his arm. Her tongue retreated like a sly snail. You told me you'd close your eyes, she said, pulling down her skirt, the pop-pearls bouncing on top of her small breasts.

They got up from the loveseat and headed to the kitchen, the room feeling thin as if someone had taken a rubber band and stretched it out to its breaking. When he stepped through the doorway, he saw Mother scolding someone, telling them to move out of the way. She was at the counter between a boy and girl he'd never seen before, reaching into a cupboard, a whiskey bottle there behind a stack of plates. Mother, he cried, and then he saw Lester Coombs lean over the table and grab Rafe Gillespie by the shirt. The deck Rafe had been dealing from sprayed from his thick fingers over the litter of money on the table. Tom put his arm out, holding Marilyn behind him as Andy and Stupich reared back. Gregor tried to get out of the way, his chair tipping as he fell sideways onto the floor. At the same time, Billy was on his feet, his chair spinning away from him and bouncing from the door frame beside Tom's leg, Joe close, just behind Billy, the two of them starting to turn, but toward Lester and Rafe or where, Tom didn't know. He took another step into the room and saw Eddy by the washing machine, waving Lester's pistol crazily, yelling at everyone, saying: The party's over! Harry, who was standing with Crystal, made a move toward him and then the pistol went off.

The bullet seemed to travel so slow Tom thought he could see it, that lead gleam streaming through the smoky air. The bullet crossed the room and chose to enter into the skin above Lester's collarbone. When it came out the other side, it went looking for Nancy's throat. Marilyn peered from behind the living-room doorway. Stay there, Tom gestured. And then the pandemonium. The men and women who'd been watching rushed for the back door, a girl he didn't know screaming as she tripped and fell, everyone cursing as they tried to push through the door into the backyard. When Tom turned, he saw Billy bump into Mother as he tried to stop Eddy, Joe right behind him. Tom had time only to reach out his arm and clothesline Joe's throat, Joe falling to the floor, Tom's knee in his back, his hand pinning Joe's arm behind him. Andy and Gregor scrambled around Joe's sprawled legs, and then over the fallen girl who was trying to get to her feet, only to go down again, the breath broken from her, Stupich swearing at someone as he reached down and pulled her to her feet, propelling her out the door. Andy and Gregor shoved past the table as they told the last few people to get out of the way, Andy bumping into Lester Coombs, who was standing in shock in the corner, Nancy beside him, her hand on her throat, a wisp of blood between her fingers. Rafe Gillespie crawled out from under the table and stumbled through the door Tom had just come through, Rafe heading for the front of the house and his car parked up on the road somewhere. Tom heard vehicles starting, the sound of their tires in the driveway, cars and trucks going in wails toward town. He had Joe's arm behind him in a hammer lock, Joe cursing him as he tried to get free. Tom looked up and saw Billy trying to grab Eddy, shouting, You shot my sister, you son-ufabitch! He saw them struggle for a moment and suddenly Eddy had the pistol pressed in the back of Billy's skull. Okay, okay, Billy said: Enough. Eddy stepped back from him, the pistol still in his hand.

Mother had somehow got herself jammed into the crevice between the stove and the counter and was holding on to her side, Sally-Ann by the sink trying to get her out.

Tom kept holding Joe down, Joe squirming there. Let me up, you fucker! he snarled, as Tom pressed harder, warning him not to move. Crystal was leaning against the window-sill. She lit a cigarette and looked on, Harry beside her, picking up a fallen chair and shaking his head.

Nancy stood there silent, her mouth quivering, the blue gnarl of the bullet just under the skin on the side of her throat looking like a swollen tick that had pulled its whole body into her blood. Tom and Joe stood up, Tom releasing Joe's bent arm and pushing him toward the door. Tom told him to get the hell out of the house, but Joe only went as far as the doorway, Billy telling him to help Nancy outside and Joe then, with one last look at Tom, taking her by the elbow and leaving. Lester Coombs took his hand from his shoulder, looked at the blood on his fingers, and said in disbelief to Eddy, You cocksucker!

That's when Eddy and Harry started herding Billy toward the door, Eddy stopping a second and taking money from the table. Lester told him to leave the cash alone and Eddy said he was taking a hundred bucks for the aggravation. Eddy waved the pistol at the rest of them and said again that the party was over. Sally-Ann was at Eddy's elbow saying *please* to Eddy, Tom knowing she was asking for a hit of junk and not for help.

I think I broke a rib, Mother said, adding: That Billy should learn to watch where he's going. She leaned against the sink, still holding her side, and Eddy, never taking his eyes off Billy, told Sally-Ann to help Mother back to her room. Lester scraped the rest of his money together with one hand, stuffing the bills inside his shirt, blood staining his shoulder, and left. Crystal walked out behind him, her red shoes hanging from her hand, the high heels hard and bright, stabbed against her thigh. And then they all left, Harry following them out a few minutes later.

The room was suddenly quiet again. Marilyn picked up a chair, sat down at the table, and started gathering the cards together from among the spilled drinks. She'd been watching when Eddy put the pistol against Billy's head. Tom had heard her saying over and over in a sing-song: *Do it, do it.* He looked at Eddy who was leafing through the money he'd taken, a tight smile on his face.

I'm a ghost, Tom said, and Marilyn squeezed his wrist and said it wasn't true. Feel me, she said, pressing her hip against his thigh, his cock stirring, a blind mole in his pants, and for a moment he wanted her gone with the rest of them.

Marilyn said she felt sorry for Nancy.

She'll be all right, he said, it's just a flesh wound.

Marilyn held his hand, the two of them going down the hall to the open doorway of Mother's bedroom. When they got there, they saw Eddy sitting on the edge of the bed, Mother lying there with her hand against her ribs. Eddy said: Mother, and then told her how she should've known better than to unlock the bolt he'd put in precisely because of everything that had transpired. He held out the money he'd taken from the pot and said it would cover buying a better refrigerator, maybe even a used Kelvinator or

International Harvester, or at least one with a really good freezer compartment that worked and how she would like it because of the way the old one froze everything, especially the vegetables down below, and for her to think of the milk, which always separated and went bad when you thawed it. He went on like that, his mouth as fast as ever, trying to reduce all that had happened to something of little consequence. While he talked, Sally-Ann murmured: C'mon. Eddy, please, each word like a bead counted by a thumb.

I think we should have some breakfast, said Tom.

Who's she? Eddy asked, nodding toward Marilyn.

She's with me, said Tom. For now, he said.

Mother groaned as Eddy rubbed her left leg, the one she said always pained her. Tom stood there with Marilyn's hand on his arm, knowing that what had happened at the party would have consequences no matter Eddy trying to talk it away.

1

tom drew a cloth over my face the night I died, his thumbs on my eyes to close them. He'd watched a hundred animals die, a thousand birds. His sister wasn't going to be left staring while her eyes dried into raisins. Then he left me and went to Father, who was passed out in the cellar. He shook him awake, ducking the blow that Father threw at him. After he told him of my death, Tom went to sit on the well-head, a boy in tattered pyjama bottoms shivering in the cool of the autumn night. He sat and watched his father moan his way up to the house. It was Father told Mother I was dead. She listened, and when he was done, she rolled over and covered her head with the quilt.

Father gave me a little charm on a string. He tied it around my neck in the hope it would necklace me to heaven. Instead, it hung me here on earth, my spirit roaming. It was a dark place Mother dwelled in, a cave sealed up, no opening to be found. No matter the cause or belief, the spite or spectacle, Father stood under the apple tree, his bare feet in untied boots, nothing on but long underwear, and filled the hole, the last breath of mine still trapped here on earth or so Mother would say. Father had said I'd be gone within the year. You watch and see, he'd cried to his sons. She'll kill this baby too.

What we hate most, we love to death. What we deny, we want.

My passing was my own.

When I was born, Father told his sons my name was Alice, after his sister. Eddy had told Tom it was Alice Blue-Gown, like in the song. But why? he asked. Eddy just smiled his smile as Tom began careening with delight through the house, saying my name over and over, *Blue Gown, Blue Gown*, Eddy watching as Tom flickered from room to room until he flew out the back door.

Father came and went, and when he was away Mother would come out into the house. Sweeping down the hall or shifting the furniture in the living room, working in the vegetable garden or on her knees in the flower beds, she was a sight. She'd curse the world under her breath. When we were dead and buried, a madness was born in her. There were times her mouth was a flail, her silences a terror. The boys saw her tears and heard her lamentations. No one knew who she'd be when she was around, just as no one knew who she was locked inside her four walls, the bars she made Father put in her window an iron frieze keeping the world out. Father could've broken into her room with a well-placed boot on the door, but he never did. He said whoever was behind it was better left alone.

Once when Father was shaking himself out of a drunken sleep, he told Tom the only thing he was afraid of was Mother killing him. He said he dreamed of her cutting his throat when he was passed out. There were nights he'd come home drunk from town and swear she was an apparition. He'd wonder aloud to Tom at how any of his children were made, let alone born. He told him that he hadn't ridden their mother. It was some other man come out in him, a nightmared man he didn't know who she'd tried to kill without success.

He told me one night that the first time he saw her standing by the road back in Saskatchewan, she'd been strange. I can hear Father now: A siren is what she was. She was sent to tempt me from my path. She stood between me and sun. She still does. That day I could see right through her cotton dress to her nakedness. She knew what I looked at and displayed it so. She laughed at me staring. Every year has been marked by her crazed ways. Her mother was just as mad at the end. Some nights, she'd wander out to the barn and sit under the dangling rope, railing at the bats that hung like soiled gloves from the roof beams. Who she was when she came back to the house then was anyone's guess. Nettie was snarled wire, white water. You waded in her wronged pools at your own cost.

Tom and Eddy figured Father must've lain with Mother four times, though who knows his own father ever?

Mother would say that last with a quick smile at her boys, and it drove Father wild when she did. He'd shout at her: Little did I know that farm of yours was to be the beginning of my end. Little did I know! Mother laughed at him. Tell that to my *mother*, she said. She was the one you took to bed each night after being in the stable with me in the day. I remember the spool bed creaking, just like I remember the straw stickling my knees as you took me!

All lies, said Father, raging. What about you at Watrous with that slicker out in the parking lot? What of him?

We were only talking.

His hands were all over you. You were bad from the start, he cried.

Not so bad you didn't take up with me, tearing off my dress that night in the barn, she said.

Me? Me? You couldn't keep that dress on. And it wasn't in the barn. It was the field.

My own mother! Tell me about that, she yelled, and re-treated to the bathroom as Father went out the door.

After Docker and Father were gone, Tom would drift off by himself, disappearing for days sometimes, wandering in town or in the hills. Mother never asked where he went or why he wasn't home half the time, but Eddy would track him down. There's only me and you, he'd say. Lost wasn't the word Tom should think of. Found was what Tom had to learn. You're found, he'd say. I found you and now you're not lost.

Nettie.

Mother's mother.

Nettie couldn't stop thinking of her husband hanging in the barn. It plagued her. Some are like that. It's a sorrow she kept working on as if she hoped she'd got it wrong. The shallow caragana grave she was laid in back on the farm in Saskatchewan was uneasy. Her husband's plot was in the suicide's graveyard beyond Nokomis. Men like him, men who'd killed themselves. The silence in their lives stayed silent in that limbo. They slept it deep.

But what of Father?

He was at the farm for a year and then Nettie's cancer. It started in her breast. Elmer had stopped coming to her bed months before. He was with her daughter then. It hadn't been a sudden thing, it had crept up on Nettie. Watching them together was to get old. A kind of envy is what it was, a bitter wistfulness in seeing her daughter so young and with a grown man who'd shared her own bed, a man she'd thought was hers, such a fool she was. She'd see Lillian twirl a two-step to the kitchen window where she'd look out toward the barn. Her daughter couldn't keep her feet still. He'd be walking from the corral or standing at the edge of the fields he figured were already his. She swore her daughter glowed she was so alive, like a young heifer or mare wild with summer and the heat. The girl couldn't wait for him to come in from the fields, couldn't be content unless he was there. And then the touching, the secret laughter. It pained Nettie to watch.

Lillian never once thought of her.

Nettie hated her daughter for that, but she understood. It's what the young were, thoughtless. It didn't occur to Lillian that her mother had a need. She thought her mother's lust was past as if it never was, but it was never past, it just got denser, like alkali water, a heavier blue that sank. It was a different kind of longing to want that again, what her daughter had, what she couldn't have, not any more.

Even in the beginning when she knew he'd been with Lillian out in the barn and she could smell her daughter on his hands and chest, his belly, he'd tell her she was imagining things, but she knew, and then the trying to hold him, competing for a man with her own child. He never understood what it was like after her husband hanged himself. How could he know what it felt like to have a man fall through her arms when she cut the rope? Her husband had been a clapper without a bell, turning slow in the air. How could Elmer know how she lay awake nights, seeing her man out there in the barn, hanging from the failure of his life?

Lillian was still a girl when her father died. Nettie called to her daughter to help. Nettie took one of his feet and made Lillian take the other, the shoes he'd shined, black in their hands. Then they dragged him across the barn floor, out the doors, around the wagon tongue, and past the loose bales of old straw to the yard and finally into the house. Nettie looked back across her husband's body at the barn doors open, the dragged trail his head had left, and the ankle she held gripped crooked, braced on her hip as she leaned away from him, pulling backward, her rubber boots loose around her bare feet and slipping in the straw and dust.

Then they were at the kitchen table, the clothes he'd worn draped over two of the kitchen chairs, his pants smeared with dirt and manure from being hauled across the barnyard, his shirt and socks and underwear in the sink soaking in bleach. She'd folded the jacket after cutting off the brass buttons, the crease in the pants still sharp from when she'd ironed it into them the time two years before when he'd gone reluctantly with her to the Easter dance at the church hall in Nokomis.

She put Lillian to work. How else was it to get done, she said, the girl afraid of her father dead who she'd loved alive. Lillian, crying, brought basins of hot water from the stove to her mother, her hands shaking, her father's body naked on the table, his head bent to the side. Nettie kept trying to straighten him, a thick welt like a bruised snake coiled around his neck. His one ear had been torn part off by the rope. She told Lillian he'd likely struggled as he tried to get out of what he'd done to himself. Then she cleaned him, telling Lillian to stop whimpering and pay attention because some day she'd have to do the same for her or for a husband, a son, a daughter. She knew his body frightened her. Lillian had only ever seen his chest and arms bare, his feet when he'd sat by the stove pulling on his socks in the morning. Now she was seeing her father's sex, flaccid, a white thing grown out of the thatch of wiry black hair at his groin, the bag below a pale blue bulge, and him being washed between his buttocks where he was soiled. Her daughter had closed her eyes, not wanting to see what was being done.

What had it been like with her husband? It must have been good with him, sweeter maybe for the years. There were times she thought it was. There were times she could almost touch the part of him he'd hidden away. She tried, but each time she got close he slipped apart from her. A month after she buried him she went out to the barn to bring down some hay for the milk cow and smelled his tobacco, and him nowhere to be found. He never knew she was tired too. It was so like a man not to give a woman a thought.

Those years were bad, one after another. Winter to winter it was the old story of thin snow, wheat and oats barely come to a head before they wasted away. Little withered seeds. There were summers they couldn't find the fence posts for the dust piled up, the winters with the wind alive in the walls. She loved him talking to her when they went to bed at night, their daughter a baby in the crib he'd made for her. And then the drought years when he stopped talking, the grain he grew left to rot under the snow. He couldn't give it away. The day came when he sold the herd for nothing, the cattle bawling inside the truck. It was after that he crawled so far inside there was no finding him. She didn't go out to the barn that night. She'd set his place and left it there till dawn, the food cold on the table. She went out then because the chickens had to be fed. Was that it? Was that why she went?

Oh, I don't want to talk about it, she said to me.

But you do, you do, Nettie. You want to tell your grand-daughter.

She said the cancer was in her breast. Her mother died

the same back in Minot, North Dakota. She remembered washing her mother's body. She dressed her mother in her one good dress, the green velvet one she'd been married in at the Baptist church in Fargo. She'd had to cut it up the back so it would fit around her mother's swollen belly, pushing her mother's thin arms through the puffed sleeves, and then tucking the halves of her dress under her so it looked like she was truly wearing it in the box her father had made for her from wind-worn wood he'd pried off the wall of an abandoned chicken house and nailed together any which way. She'd folded clean sheets into the coffin for her mother to lie upon, placing under her head the souvenir pillow from the summer rodeo they went to in Fargo on her honeymoon, bucking horses embroidered there on either side as if they were dancing in her combed-out curls, all the time her father asking why she'd wanted a coffin made, given it would rot anyway.

Elmer was afraid of her disease and so was Lillian. They stood around waiting for her to die. Nettie lay in the old spool bed brought over the Medicine Line. Her mother, Elvira, had told the story of how their wagon had threaded through the last of the Sioux at Wood Mountain, deserted tent circles like ringworm scars on the barren earth, a few squaws left begging food from farms, their children thin as winter rats. Elvira said she never forgot one woman's face, the stillness in it a kind of peace, her baby dead in her arms. Her husband had told Elvira not to waste food by giving it to the dead. She'll be gone too in a few more days, he'd said.

As Nettie laid herself finally down she saw her daughter in the bedroom doorway, half in and half out. She could see it in those young eyes, fear, and the desire to have her pass on. Maybe it was then her daughter knew that her mother was a woman. Strange how it took the cancer in her breast to teach the girl a simple thing like that. Elmer? He wanted it over. At first she thought it was the callousness in him, but then she realized he was just a man, impatient, as if with an animal gone sick, a threat to the herd and so a threat to them all.

They buried Nettie beside a clump of Saskatoon bushes at the back of the house. There was no one to tell of her death. The nearest neighbours had packed up and left months before, searching for a place where water fell from the sky, where it gathered on the earth. The church was in town, but what would the church have done but talk? It cost three dollars for a grave in Nokomis. Elmer said some words he thought might quiet her, *Yea, though I walk through the valley of Death*, such words as that, a rare spring shower as if it was a help, the sun, the endless dust. Lillian seemed to cry. She looked like she was trying to find some grief, afraid yet relieved, somehow, at last to have her gone. Elmer was surprised Lillian had a tear in her at all. She thought only of herself. He believed she was spoiled, but spoiled by what or who? It wasn't the land. It didn't care enough to spoil a girl it was so busy killing things. It was like she was with the Bible. She read the words, but they didn't touch her. She could speak the verses, but she couldn't feel them.

I think there are those with something wrong in them,

and no matter the trying to change them back to good, you always fail. She was like a jar of crabapples put up in the fall, the fruit so beautiful behind the glass, but something else inside, the lid not sealed right, some flaw in the ring, something, or nothing, and then the black smut growing behind the glass and you helpless to change it. You throw that fruit away, but what do you do with a daughter?

Lillian's need was for a man all right, but a man who would take her away from the land and the life she saw her mother make, working from dark to dark until she died. But go where? Do what? She'd say she wanted to see the cities, but Elmer was uncomfortable in towns. He'd tried living in Calgary but he said there were too many people there. He'd lived outside Turner Valley, Alberta, in Dog Town where the bars and whorehouses were. The gas wells had come in and there was work to be had there. Dog Town was a place he despised, those tarpaper shacks and the men and women who lived in them a kind of damnation he never got over. He said the oil burning in the ravine on Hell's Half Acre was enough to cure anyone of living near people. East of the ravine where they burned off the oil, it stayed green all winter from the heat, snow geese, swans, and Canada's swimming in the snow melt, feeding on grass that grew in January. By spring the swans had changed colour, their white feathers black from the tarred grease that fell out of the sky. Most of the birds couldn't fly for the oil on them, men coming from the bars and killing them with clubs, a few birds running out onto the snow above the coulee, their black bodies easy prey for coyotes. Father said towns and cities were useless places where people ate each other up. A town to him was a hunting ground, a place to wile away women, and to cheat and steal from men.

He was a desert man out on Ranch Road just as he was on the prairie. He'd wandered with Lillian in those early years after he sold the farm. He told me there'd been land down in the rattlesnake country of the Triangle where they'd found only remnant fences, land so dry a post lived longer than the wire it held up. The houses and barns were already disappearing, piles of boards lying in the dirt where the people had once tried to grow a crop. They left their homes behind as testament to all who passed that theirs was the land of Cain.

The one thing Lillian loved was dancing. The Town Hall in Nokomis wasn't enough, seven steps and nine steps, minuets, and polkas. She wanted the new dances. Every two weeks she'd stared at the bedsheet nailed to the wall at the Hall in Nokomis, the projector clattering as she watched movies like *The Gold Diggers* and *Love Me Tonight*. She begged for Watrous, and Elmer finally took her there the year after Nettie died. It was just the once. They stayed two nights, Elmer doing the best he could on that horsehair floor, but it was the city boys from Saskatoon and Helena who could really dance and who took her away to the places she'd only read about in magazines, *Chatelaine*, *Modern Screen*, *Canadian Home Journal*. Slow waltz, quickstep, foxtrot, she did them all. She circled the floor with other men till Elmer hauled her off, telling her she danced too close to strangers. When was that? Nineteen-thirty-three, the Depression hard around them. Some time later he caught her out in the parking lot with a man from Great Falls. He chased the American slicker off and yelled at her by their Model A, said she was a cheap hussy, struck her in the face. She hit him back. They raged for an hour until Elmer threw her into the car, Mother howling at the indignity.

What was wrong in her was her need to be wild. It only took Watrous for her to tire of Elmer, but she was married to him then, the farm ready to be sold, and three months later they were on the road heading to a ranch near Manyberries, south of Medicine Hat, where Elmer had some deal in cattle that would eventually go bad. He lost at everything he put his hand to, cattle, grain, the land itself, his daughters, sons, and her. And always her frustration, his promises of a better life leading her deeper into the west until they ranged out of Pincher Creek into the foothills, threading their way through the Frank Slide into the Crow's Nest Pass, the Rocky Mountains swallowing her, walls of trees like blinders taking away the light. She never forgave him that. Her dream was south to Minneapolis or further, California.

Every farm back then had a story not much different than hers, maybe a man not dead, just gone, a daughter or not, a son, accidents, runaways, a family loaded on a truck or wagon going farther west or north, away from the desert the drought had made, or back east on the train holding on to the nothing they brought out with them, a couple of silver serving spoons, a handful of quilting squares, two needles tucked into a cotton corner, things small and always less than what they came with, everything diminished, made worthless by the land. Dying seemed natural to a family, they took to it so well. Most of that earth should never have been broken. It was a place best left to grass and animals.

But there were times, after her husband died, Nettie would be kneading bread in the morning and she'd look up from her floured hands and see her daughter standing at the window looking out past the windbreak to the road. The girl had only been a woman for a year. Just fourteen.

She was waiting for him. All the wrong man had to do was come.

8

afe's cards lay on the kitchen table among the crumbs and crusts of the morning's breakfast, the pack with thumbnail scars in the corners to mark the aces and faces. Patience was Eddy's solitaire game, and though he had figured out the backs of the cards, he didn't cheat. His game was simply picking up and laying down the cards, the beginning no different from the end, his only opponent himself. His sitting there was to wait for some interruption that would give him the action he needed, his freckled hands riffling the thinning deck as he slouched over the detritus of the breakfast they'd eaten so many hours ago, playing his lonely game for no one knew how long.

Tom had slept off and on through the day, Sally-Ann appearing every once in a while in the kitchen to talk to Eddy and then going back upstairs. She looked wasted, the chips of heroin Eddy was giving her just enough to keep her quiet. Tom wondered if Eddy had slept at all. His brother sat among the forgotten litter, greasy plates, bits of potato and onion, sausage tails, eggs that had dried to yellow blisters, all of it looking like the pictures of paintings Tom had once seen in a magazine. People stared at such magazines in the drugstore, seeing huge buildings, odd landscapes, and men and women so strange the people looking at them turned away in puzzlement, shaking their heads at how anyone could be so alien and still belong on the earth.

For Tom there was too much thinking about what wasn't real to touch or smell or taste in the world. When he was a boy, Father had told him that out in the far cities were people who did things beyond reason, their minds bent from beauty or from ill. For Tom, such people existed only in books and magazines and in the stories that arrived in town with strangers and left with them, no one lasting long in the valley not born to it. If they did stay, it was in the town and not the country. Tom had met them over the years and listened to them talk about where they'd been or what they'd seen, parsing words out in riddles and random tales that made little sense to him. His brother never bothered to listen to their stories. He didn't care what had happened to strangers. For Eddy, stories about the past, anyone's past, were deadly and he wanted none of it. He looked at the town and saw a place to be swept down upon and pillaged. He'd long ago learned from his father that he was from a line of people who could not live among others and saw anything not their own as plunder, the things people owned fair to be taken. Eddy's grin said it all, not his laugh, for Eddy had never laughed aloud in this life.

Even as a child he only sucked at air as if stifling on what others thought amusing.

Tom turned from Eddy and walked back into the living room and over to the couch, where Marilyn lay sleeping under the blanket that was always kept there. Mother had knit it for when Little Rose was born. Half-awake on his feet, Tom swayed to Marilyn's breathing, the faded blanket across her small breasts rising and falling in time to his body's rowing the stale air above her. At her throat, the plastic snap beads seemed made from the same colour and substance as her eye, which, even as she slept stayed partly open, watching him, curious, blind. He stared at her in wonder. The Marilyn he looked at was grown and not grown, child and woman, sixteen years old and sixty, a girl who'd lived longer than most and not long enough. What lies under the dying will have a life, he said out loud. There was no one else there to answer.

He sat down heavily on the loveseat. It was the end of the afternoon now, the day once again losing to the coming dark. He heard the *flisssh* as Eddy shuffled cards in the other room, his brother at the table, a globe of stillness surrounding him. He thought about Eddy sitting there all day and saying nothing to anyone about what had happened. His brother never said what was in his mind. What he might have thought about anything Tom could only guess at.

For Eddy, the world was without boundaries. He learned that from both Father and Mother. Tom never saw it that way. Eddy's crimes and misdemeanours, the things he did and didn't do, were just a part of his life.

He remembered Eddy telling him about a story he'd read a long time ago in *Life* magazine. It was about an old man who'd gone to sea somewhere near Florida and caught a big fish that he let the sharks eat. Eddy couldn't get over why someone would do that, as if he resented anyone making a choice he'd never make himself.

Tom was different. He could get lost in stories of other places and other lives. It was like sitting in the Empress Theatre when he was a kid. He'd be there with the other Saturday-afternoon children, all of them in their rags and patches watching cartoons as they waited for the feature. He remembered the first movie that scared him. Lou Costello, with his chubby, boylike hands, was being told by Bud Abbott to go to a door at the end of a hall and open it. Tom had wanted to shout out of the dark where he sat with Eddy: Don't trust him! Don't open the door! The monster was behind it, standing there with a ponderous, murderous stupidity, the dullness of its face a threat greater than malice. He was like the gorilla Tom had read about in *Ripley's Believe It or Not*, a huge ape that had torn apart a baby it got hold of, the keeper saying it had only wanted the baby to stop crying so. Tom learned from the movies that there was no saving anyone, only the watching and then seeing in the dim light the girls with their brooms and buckets cleaning up after the show was over, walking between the rows of seats, scraping popcorn off the sticky puddles of spilled pop, everyone else gone home, sure that if the movie wasn't their life, what was?

Tom lay back and thought about everything that had

happened the night before. He knew most others found his family strange, but what did that matter? Or Mother's withdrawal from the world, Father's violent ways, the valley gossip swirling? They all had their pride, each in their way, held together by an unspoken bond that separated them from the rest of the town and valley. It was the Stark pride that made others look up to them, yet they resented the family too, thinking Eddy and he acted superior in some unknown way, but what Tom knew to be isolation and loneliness, others saw as arrogance and contempt.

People gravitated toward the ones they thought were powerful. Tom had seen it happen. He'd watched men and women creep close to Billy or Eddy in the hope that something, anything might happen. It's why they'd come to the party, why they'd go to the dog fights on Saturday. Some people would drive a hundred miles in the hope of watching a bridge collapse into a swollen river. They'd be the first at a house fire, the first to stand over carnage on the road. They liked to get close to destruction, and it didn't take much.

He heard Mother now, moving in her room. She was tired all the time, it seemed, but said she couldn't sleep. He wondered if she would tell them that the madness of the card game and Eddy shooting the pistol was all part of one of her prophecies. She'd told them both when they were small that there were times to come that would rival any known before. She said that her two sons were destined, but she never said for what. Both he and Eddy had believed her in their bones. They were the Stark boys and therefore somehow promised, but to what they didn't know. She'd talk then of strange times, her golden glass of whiskey weaving words out of the air, bits of the Bible spilling from her tongue, but she never explained what the old days meant or what the days to come would be.

He'd been a boy, no more than six years old, when Mother whispered to him: *And of thy sons that shall issue from thee, which thou shalt beget, shall they take away.* They'd been sitting in the kitchen at the table shelling peas into a bowl when Mother said those words. It had terrified him to think that he and Eddy could somehow be stolen like the boys in the stories she read to them at night, the stories she told. He'd imagined someone coming in the night and grabbing them from their beds. He'd cried out to her: But who? Who will take us away?

Never you mind, Tom Stark. You just wait. Little kids vanish all the time. One day they're there and then they're not. You listen. There was a family lived on a farm a few miles from where I grew up back on the prairie. It was a hard-scrabble quarter-section. That land around Nokomis was rocks and brush, spare grass and not much more. The father didn't have much when he came with his family from the States and looked like he had less when he left. He had a baby girl and a boy a year or two older. His wife had died birthing the girl and a year later he married a woman he'd hired to keep his house. They had a baby the second summer she was there. The next January it got cold, forty-five below, and for a week those two kids never showed up at school. I remember they rode an old sway-backed horse to get there. I used to see them crossing the fields on old

Apple Jack to the West Line road where our one-room school was, the reins pulled under their blanket to keep their hands from freezing. It used to get so cold out there a horse's breathing would turn to crystals in the air. You could hear it fall on the snow from ten feet away, a sound just like those peas you're shelling plinking in that bowl. My father always said that horse was wrong music, but I never understood what he meant. It doesn't matter, but blizzard or cold, they always came to school, until one day they didn't.

What happened?

I'd see old Apple Jack out by their farm, but I never saw that horse on the West Line road again. I did find the blanket though.

Where?

Out on the ice of a frozen dugout a mile from their farm.

Mother was silent then, and Tom had huddled closer to Eddy as he looked up at her. She was peering down at him, her eyes slit so thin he'd thought they would cut him if she got too close. He wanted her story to be over, but he couldn't stop himself asking for just a little more. How come the blanket was there?

Never you mind, she'd said again, and then she looked at him slyly. Well, half that blanket was sticking up out of the ice and the other half was under. It looked like something left behind, not lost. I pulled it out of the ice and took it back to their farm. By the time I got there it was hard as a chunk of wood. The woman came to the door with her baby in a shawl sling under her arm. She told me the blanket wasn't theirs, but I knew different. She never answered me when I asked her where the kids were. She just closed the door without a word. A few weeks later they were gone south to Fort Yates in North Dakota where the man was from. It was still winter, the ponds and dugouts frozen. My mother told me they put this country behind them and wished she'd done the same.

Tom remembered whimpering. What *happened* to those kids?

Wouldn't you like to know, Mother had said, smiling into Tom's fearful face. She laughed at his fright and said: You just remember there's no such thing as ice so thick on a dugout that it can't get broken when a woman wants it to.

Eddy had grinned at her spooky voice and told Tom not to pay her any mind. She likes to scare you, he said.

She was many mothers. Sometimes in the day she'd walk from room to room as if each doorway was different from the last, but finding them the same, she would move on from living room to kitchen, hall to bedroom, sometimes stopping to shift a piece of furniture, a chair, an end table, the loveseat or couch, from one wall to another as if by such arranging she could change what her life was to some other, better one. But what life was it that she wished for and how to get it?

She never went upstairs. The hall landing above with its hidden closet underneath the attic must have held too many nightmares for her to bear. It did for him. Or perhaps she didn't care, the bedroom off the landing Eddy's room, and Tom's above, both lairs where he and his brother hunkered down. She stopped going into their rooms when they changed from boys to men.

The older he and his brother got, the more life they piled up behind them, and the less it seemed there was to come. Tom had always known he wasn't like Eddy and had felt proud the day Father chose him to be the executioner. It didn't matter to Eddy. He said Tom was better with a rifle than he was. Father had taken him outside one morning in early spring and placed the rifle in his hands. Tom had been ten years old. You're the family executioner now, Father had said, and laughed.

He told the neighbours along the road that his son Tom was for hire if they needed any killing done. Tom would take his rifle to this farm or that and shoot a badly lamed horse, help some farmer string up a pig for butchering, drown rats in tilted barrels, shoot lambs in the fall, wait out a fox or coyote in a chicken yard, a marauding bobcat or weasel. Eddy, who had watched Tom's quiet returns from farm or ranch, told him not to worry, that death was a welcome thing, but after Father died, Tom never killed again.

———

Sally-Ann stood at the sink, her spindly arms up to the elbows in soapy water, her bare feet slippery on the wet floor. She was drug-sick, her body shivering. Marilyn stood beside her with a wet tea towel in her hands, spreading the soapy effluvium around and stacking the dishes on the counters and lower shelves of the cupboards above her, the doors long since torn off by Father in one of his furies at the secret places where he thought danger lurked, poisons hidden, blasting caps and bullets in the sugar bowl, a butcher knife missing from a drawer.

Marilyn seemed almost to dance. She picked up a plate, scraped egg yolk from the rim with her fingernail, and tilted it up to fall on those she'd piled before it on the shelf, her arms not long enough to reach higher than the stack, the shelves above mostly empty but for a few oddments of crockery that no one had used for years, gravy boats, chipped mixing bowls, and leftover pieces of kitchen machinery. She took a mug with moose heads on it and turned it to her eye. Mother spoke up and said she'd have helped dry if it hadn't been for her sore chest and the nights without a decent sleep, drinking steady to ease what she called her restless legs.

I barely slept all day, Mother said, whining. I got these pains in my belly again. And you know how nervous I get when there're too many people around. You know that, Eddy. There's too much noise and me with a bad heart on top of a heart that's been broken so many times it's a wonder it still beats. Her voice choked. It always did when she'd had too much whiskey.

And then the tears.

Tom waited for them, the misery, the complaints, and finally the blubbering about her sorry life. Sally-Ann's arms rose out of the sink water and she went over and put them wet around Mother. Sweat was gathered at Sally-Ann's forehead, her hair stuck to her scalp, her red blouse torn at the shoulder. There, there, Mother Stark, she said. It's okay, it's okay. Please don't cry. Please.

Tom asked why women always say things twice in comfort, and only once in anger, but no one paid attention. Eddy put another Export cigarette in his mouth, took up the book of matches, lit the cigarette, and placed the match-book down beside the green cardboard pack to his right, just so, in an exact order on the table, the same each time. Smoke eased up the side of his face and drifted through his hair. The only sound in the room was the rattle of dishes and the turning of the cards.

As Marilyn moved by the counter her small buttocks rolled inside her grey skirt. Tom saw smooth creatures shifting there beneath the cloth the way animals moved, without shame or shamming, alive in their muscle and skin and bone. Marilyn wasn't looking anywhere but at the dishes in front of her, plates and glasses piled up with whatever else had been left over from the party and the breakfast Tom had made so many hours before. Marilyn looked like she'd lived in the house for years.

Oh, Marilyn, he whispered. What kind of woman are you?

Someone's calling, Eddy said suddenly from his solitude, and a second later the phone rang from the corner table in the living room. Tom didn't flinch at Eddy predicting the call, though he saw Marilyn go still and Sally-Ann put her hand up to her mouth. Then Marilyn laughed, her throat arching up, seeming delighted at this new world she was in. They waited to see if Eddy would answer as ring followed ring, Tom and Mother both knowing that the call would be for him. The ringing was enough to make Mother anxious, certain that whoever was on the line would somehow take Eddy away. She turned and went down the hall to her room. Tom knew her heart was a small fist gripping his brother and losing a little more each day.

The phone stopped.

That Joe is sorry grief, Marilyn said out of nowhere as she laid another dish on the teetering pile. He's not one to forget, Tom.

No one said anything. Your mother's strange, Marilyn added, a wet dish towel dangling from her hand. I've never known anyone like her before.

No one knows what Mother knows, Tom said.

Sally-Ann sat down on a chair and drew her hands up to her chest, crossed there as if to ward off a blow.

The phone rang again. It sounded to Tom like the word *briinnnng*, as if asking for something to be taken to its voice. Eddy shook his head, but Tom went to answer it anyway. He picked up the phone, listened, and called out: It's Harry.

His brother at the kitchen table, playing his endless game of Patience, didn't move.

Harry was breathless, whispering.

Where're you? Tom asked him.

I'm at the pay phone at the gas station near Priest Valley Road.

Tom looked into the kitchen, but Eddy just shook his head again.

You tell him to come out here. I'll be parked in the old gravel pit up by Garofalo's place, Harry said. I have to talk to him about something he needs to know. And, Oh yeah, he said, I need a favour. Crystal's out here with me.

I'll tell him, Tom said. He hung up the phone and went back into the kitchen. Eddy didn't look up, a cigarette burning between his fingers.

He says it's important, said Tom.

Eddy set his cards down on the table beside his Export pack and stuck his cigarette in the sand of the ashtray. Tom bent over, his arm around his brother's shoulder, Eddy's breath a dark sweetness like burned sugar. What's going on, Eddy?

Where did Harry say he was?

At the old gravel pit. Crystal's with him. I think he wants you to take her off his hands.

Right, Eddy said.

Tom could see Harry and Crystal parked there among the piles of stone and rubble as Harry waited for Eddy to come. Something was going to go down, Harry's message carrying the promise of some kind of scheme. Nothing was ever simple. He looked at Eddy. His brother was worn to a stub and there was little Tom could do about it.

Eddy picked up the cards from where they lay between a blackened crust of toast and a tarnished kitchen knife, one of a set Father brought home from collecting a debt he was owed by a man who had a cherry orchard in the high desert country near Omak down in Washington. Only Father would take a family's eating tools to cover money he was owed, Mother had said as she counted the knives and forks, irritated for a moment that there were no serving spoons. Father said he walked into the man's house with his shotgun and picked up the cedar chest that held their Joan of Arc silverware. Father liked telling how he told the family they could eat with scoops of cherry bark when they got hungry.

Tom knew that most everyone in the valley had believed Elmer Stark would break a man's arm because of a sack of rotten spuds, a box of bruised peaches. They just had to point out Jack Perrault, the mechanic down at Eston Motors. Jack had a crushed hand after Father had struck him with a wrench in a rage over a bad truck tire. Or Marge Perslock. He'd forced her into his truck and driven her into the hills to spite her husband who'd cheated him on a load of logs. Father put the fear in her. She never told her husband, but Father knew. He told Tom and Eddy about it when they were small so they might learn from it. He said when he saw Marge and her husband together all he had to do was grin at her. He said he liked to see her quail. He told Tom and Eddy sometimes the better is your knowing and your enemy not.

Suddenly, Eddy swept the cards left in front of him into the deck, the *clack clack* of the full pack in his hands now, tapping the table, sharp in the room. He stood up then. His fly was undone, and Tom told him so. Eddy went over to Sally-Ann, who zipped it up for him, her face glistening, the skin on her hands puckered from the dishwater. She glanced sullenly around the room to show them she was the one who was with Eddy now. Then she shrugged her shoulders, her body small. Eddy, she said, can you help me?

Go get your stuff, said Eddy. He ran his hand through her shock of brown hair. You're going home, he said. Sally-Ann begged for just a little chip of heroin, but he told her to wait. After she collected the rest of her things from up in Eddy's room, Eddy took her arm and led her into the bathroom, closing the door. When they came out, she was smoothed over, floating light on the bit of heroin he'd allowed her. Her purse hung from her wrist, a soiled sweater pulled through the straps, one arm dragging on the floor. I don't know why I have to go home, she mumbled. What'll I do?

You'll figure it out, Eddy said. He leaned over the table, tucked cigarettes and matches into his jacket, slapped his hip pocket, his wallet there, hooked to a belt loop with a stainless steel chain, and then his front pocket where the car keys scraped against his buck knife. Satisfied, he went and took the leather bomber jacket from where it was hanging by the door, and put it on. Scarred and worn, the jacket was the one Father always wore when he went down to the Royal Canadian Legion for the meat draw. Tom moved a step away. If he stood too close when Eddy was wearing the jacket, he could smell Father, the same sweat, tobacco, gunpowder, and liquor soaked into the leather.

Tom?

Yeah.

You take your truck over to the gravel pit. I'll meet you there. You take Crystal wherever she wants to go. I'm taking Sally-Ann home.

Tom turned to Marilyn and asked her if she'd be there when he returned. She nodded, her back to him, a wisp of hair falling across her cheek. It was Vera brought me out here, she said. It'll have to be you takes me home.

Tom got his denim jacket and followed Eddy and Sally-Ann out of the house. Eddy started the car, each tick, creak, and whistle of the motor a language to him. He revved the engine, the grumble of the Hollywood mufflers loud in the night. Then the car reared up the incline and out the driveway to the right, heading east the back way through the ranchlands and orchards.

Hand on the door of his truck, Tom watched the cloud of Eddy's dust drift out over the fields. Mother always said that they were a family, and to her that meant the Starks looked after their own. What happened in the family, stayed in the family.

Tom got in the truck and sat there staring through the crack in the windshield. He reached out and brushed the dust off the sun-blistered dashboard. His father had bought the truck in 1939, the year after Tom was born, with money he'd got setting forest fires for logging outfits that needed to put their equipment to work.

The far mountains had become shadows among pale shadows. The forests on their flanks seemed to go on forever. He remembered the years his father had driven away in the early hours, not to return until dusk and sometimes not then. Father had loved the truck, the flat dashboard with its round gauges, the stick shift with the black bulb, and the engine, especially the engine. He always said the V8 was the best motor Henry Ford ever built. They forgot how to make one after the war. The truck was a three-quarter tonner with an oval grille and an empty rack on the side running board, the tire long gone from it, torn off on a tree limb, Father used to joke, when he was chasing a moose to see how far it could run down a bush road before its heart gave out.

Tom turned the key, the engine sputtering through its changes until it caught. He pushed down on the gas pedal, feathering it as he waited for the motor to mumble its way to smooth. Then he put the truck in gear and rolled up the driveway on the nearly bald tires, taking the long way across the east side of town to Priest Valley Road. He thought of the times he and Eddy took turns on Sunday mornings driving the truck when they were kids. They were barely old enough to see over the dash when they'd drive it across the creek by the well and out into the orchard where they turned and counter-turned, in a skid on the hardpan or cutting deep ruts in the soft earth down by the creek. Week after week, Father had driven it into the mountains to work and over the years the truck body had gone from shiny black to streaks and dents and rust, the grille cracked and the headlamps hay-wired to the fenders to hold them straight, but the motor thumped along as it always had, Father changing the oil and spark plugs, working on the brakes, tinkering with the transmission and carburetor whenever they needed tuning. It was the first Tom knew how much machines meant to his father, and to Eddy too. When there was a problem, Eddy worked on the car and truck, the tractor too, when it was still useful. Now it sat rusted against the fence, a nesting place for mice, the sun-hardened tires perches for magpies.

When Tom went to work summers picking in the fields on valley farms around that time, bringing his meagre pay home to Mother, Eddy always refused to go unless he could work machines, driving fruit sprayers or tractors. Tom picked beans and peas and tomatoes, and then, when he was a year or two older, he picked apples in the orchards. Later, the green-chain. Five years now at the sawmill. With Father dead these past years, the money Tom made put food on the table, his brother little help at best.

It was dark now, the headlights sweeping along the bare yards of the Hundred Homes. They'd been built after the war for the returning soldiers and the families they'd started. The houses were all the same, the paint peeling away from most of them, a few small trees trying to grow in the dense earth.

He cut down north hill to where Priest Valley Road began, Silver Star Mountain looming ahead of him. He and Eddy had hiked up there each spring when they were boys, so they could look down upon the world they came from, and there they'd buried themselves in the alpine meadows, the flowers so bright it hurt their eyes to look at them. Those were days when they ranged the back country, animals no less or more than coyote, hawk, or cougar. They'd slip out of the house at dawn, chunks of bread and baloney in a ruck-sack, the .22 in Tom's hand and Eddy with Father's hunting knife. They'd be gone for the day, returning late for supper, Father pushing his plate back and Mother dishing out whatever she'd made to her boys, slices of overcooked venison or mutton, white flour gravy, and summer spuds exploded from their jackets. As they sat at the table and ate, she'd complain about them, saying there wasn't enough wood in the stove box, the garden wasn't weeded, something, any-thing, Father reaching out to whichever son was close with a slap up the side of his head. The next day they'd duck out again at dawn, heading east into the Coldstream Valley to shoot gophers in the orchards, out to the lakes or up some nameless creek to fish for cutthroat trout. The crumbling stone escarpments high above the valley held everyone he knew, each of them born like himself to the valley under the same blue shoulders of stone and snow, ice and cloud holding hard above the desert floor, gullies and arroyos like old wounds cut into their sides.

The darkness stretched ahead, mountain folding back into mountain, his brother and him living in a land without history. The trees and stones were without stories, the hills a vacancy, the creeks and rivers a white water sound he knew the Indians had always listened to. The Indians were strange visitors to town. They rode in on buckboards and wagons, their horses short-roped to trees at the end of Main Street, the animals waterless, standing in the sun, their chil-dren sleeping under the horses' bellies for shade while their parents went to the bars. He remembered taking water to those horses, carrying buckets to them from the tap behind the New Dawn Café, the animals burying their noses in the cold. Sometimes he'd beg a half bag of wire-cut oats from Winning Chow, who'd scoop handfuls into the dented hubcap he'd brought, some horse under a dead tree lipping at it, nothing in its eyes but a brown waiting. He knew some of those people ended up getting placed on the Indian List by Judge Smythe. Barred from drinking, they bought beer from the taxi stand and drank it under lilac bushes and elms in the park down by the railway tracks.

He wound through the farms, here and there a yard light on, a window pale with yellow light. Just before the big hill on Priest Valley Road was the gravel pit. For years the town had mined it there, digging into the hill until they exhausted it all, turning the land into crumbling sidewalks and cracked basements, driveways and walls. All that was left were piles of loose stone, rocks too large to be of any use. The piles dotted the huge cut like burial mounds.

Tom turned in and drove over the broken chain that had once prevented anyone from entering, and saw the cars. He pulled up behind Harry's Coupe. Crystal was standing beside it, its dented fenders and cracked windshield the measure of Harry's driving. Next to it was the Studebaker. Eddy and Harry sat separately in their cars, two outlines in the dim glow coming from their muted parking lights. Beyond them was a derelict, rusted-out car and a scavenged dump truck, discarded, forgotten, parked among piles of rocks. He looked back the way he'd come. It was quiet, the road behind him deserted. There was no one else around, the unused field on one side dotted with porcupine grass and fescue, on the other a dying orchard, under the trees a tumbledown cabin, windows broken, the door hanging from a hinge. No one could see them here. He watched Harry's arm push out his side window and flick at his cigarette, a worm of ash falling to the road, its flare a momentary light. Eddy and Harry stayed in their cars.

Crystal nodded at Tom, but said nothing. She had one arm folded across her chest while the other hand tapped a cigarette, the red coal slashing. She looked like she wouldn't be getting back in with Harry anytime soon. Eddy's head was leaned back against his seat, one hand up and hanging off the steering wheel with its braided leather cover.

Tom had seen this a dozen times: Harry and Eddy sitting in cars, separate or together, figuring things out while some girl or another stood around waiting to see whatever they were going to do. Tom knew nothing would happen here until Eddy said it could.

The three of them were a picture. He'd seen photographs of the Dirty Thirties that Mother kept in a shoebox in the crib room. Here they were, like the people in them, beaten down or beaten up, each of them alone in a mined-out gravel pit, the blue desert hills and the mountains, the edges of their world.

Crystal walked over to Tom's truck, opened the door, and got in. Take me home, she said, as she dragged her skirt down over her knees. They told me you would. She pushed at the waves in her blonde hair and said: Well?

In a minute, Tom said. He got out, went over to Eddy's car, and leaned in.

So, what are we doing here, Eddy?

Eddy stretched, cracked his door, got out, and walked to the front of his car. Harry did the same. Shadows mottled their cheeks and chins. Eddy took out his Exports and tipped a cigarette into his lips. Harry slouched as he took one from the proffered pack, and they lit up.

Just up over the hill, there's a house, tucked away into an old orchard, said Harry. It's across from Garofalo's butcher shop.

Don't talk so loud, Eddy said. Crystal doesn't need to know what you're saying.

She's in the truck with the windows closed, Harry said. She can't hear a thing. Anyways, it's some old man's place, Harry said. He's supposed to have money hidden in there.

Who says? asked Tom.

Wayne.

When did he tell you this? Eddy said.

At the pool hall a few hours ago, before I took off with Crystal.

Eddy and Harry smoked, the red sparks of their cigarettes carving the same curves in the air. Eddy flicked his butt at a cracked boulder jutting out of a pile of stones. It caromed off into a tangle of wild rose.

Wayne says he heard the old man's gone to Kamloops, Harry said, to visit his sister in the hospital up there. He stared moodily at his butt as it missed the boulder Eddy had hit. I even drove by the place a little while ago. There's no lights on. Like I said, there's for sure money in there.

How does Wayne happen to know? Tom asked.

Joe told him, Harry said, rolling his shoulders and tucking his chin into his jacket.

Wayne, Joe, what's the problem? Eddy said to his brother.

Tom stuffed his hands in his pockets and stared up into the night sky. I don't like this. There's something wrong with it. Why would Joe tell Wayne of all people?

Eddy ground his heel into the gravel.

It's no big deal, Harry said, and he took a Sweet Marie bar from his jacket pocket and peeled the paper back. He took a bite and began to chew. Why're *you* so worried?

Seems strange to me Joe would be telling Wayne about this and not Billy, Tom said. If there's money in that house, then Joe would tell him and they'd break in and get it. He sure wouldn't be telling Wayne about it.

Harry looked down at his boots, hunching there as if he was thinking his way into things. He pushed the last chunk of chocolate into his mouth, his jaws working steadily as he wiped the back of his hand across his lips. According to Wayne, Joe was drunk, he said.

That makes no sense, Tom said. Joe's not a drinker. He turned to his brother. What do you think about all this, Eddy?

Seems to me that shit, Wayne, wouldn't lie about it. He wouldn't dare. Not to us.

There's no lights on, Harry said again, rubbing his hand on the bullet nose of Eddy's car. You drive by there and you'll see.

You wouldn't catch me going in there, said Tom.

Who's asking you to, he said, as he tilted his head at the truck. Eddy smiled. Anyway, I can always use money, he said.

When Tom didn't move, Eddy just looked at him. Tom kicked at a stone and said: What the hell. I know you'll do what the fuck you want.

Look, Eddy said. You take Crystal home. I'll see you later at the bar, and saying that, he walked around to the back of the Coupe, Harry following him. They stood together whispering.

Tom stared into the gravel pit at the rusty old truck, the small bits of forgotten machinery. Tom thought he'd seen the house they were talking about. He'd been at Garofalo's before. When there was extra money around back when he was a kid, he would be sent on his bike to pick up meat. Jim Garofalo was famous in the valley for having frozen his toes off on a hunting trip one winter up in the Cariboo. Tom once asked him about it and Jim told him he'd been still-hunting for a whole morning and had forgotten his feet were sitting in slush. Jim had taken off his boot and showed Tom how he had only two toes on his left foot. Tom could picture the tired canvas awning over the front window and the red plywood cutout of a side of beef hanging from the iron post by the door. The different cuts were outlined in white paint, a map of the animal made to show a man where to place his knife or saw. Back then, he used to think it somehow had a meaning.

He walked over to his truck and slid behind the wheel. As Crystal sat there, her fingernails clicked on the door handle, her look telling him what had happened before he got there, Harry probably getting a hand job in exchange for a few pills, Crystal likely thinking it was a bad bargain, given Harry and his ways.

Tom started the truck, pulling out of the pit and heading back the way he'd come. Across the ditches, broken fences and wild rose stretched out in staggering lines down the long hill. He slowed to take a hairpin turn, bats flickering like cinders in the sky. Moths fled from them toward the moon, wings endlessly turning toward the light. A cat howled somewhere deep in the sagebrush and another replied. The cats sounded weary of battle, heavy-necked males slinking along the ditches, some female in estrus, hiding, wounds on her nape, her nuptial scream guttered in her throat. Casting his eye across the moonlit field, he saw a bicycle, the back wheel without a tire, its front forks stubbed into the dirt, the handlebars ratcheted up like horns.

Crystal was quiet. Tom moved the steering wheel with the heel of his palm as the truck tossed in the potholes. You okay?

Just get me home, she said. When Tom didn't reply, she said: I'm not scared of you. She said it like she thought she was. She took a cigarette from the pack in her purse and lit it. The radio Father had installed two years before he died was playing "Peggy-Sue," the station tuned to Spokane. Tom figured she believed like every other girl in the valley that Buddy Holly was singing only to her. Her foot tapped on the floorboards and he imagined her dreaming of a love both rare and true. She twisted the rear-view mirror and prodded her hair into a shape she knew by heart. She glanced at him watching from the corner of his eye and said that after she got home she was going out again. When he asked her who with, she gave him a smug smile, and told him it was none of his business. Someone a lot more special than Harry, she said.

There wasn't another word from Crystal. He dropped her off, the look from her one he'd seen before, a kind of magpie glance as if she'd caught some deeper scent in him. He eased the car away from the curb. The road wound under the bare acacia trees, maples beside them slumped inside their worn leaves. The town's graveyard with its many stones slept in uneasy peace as the truck rumbled on, iron gates locked, the hill dry with its pines and red-tipped junipers struggling in the gravel, tilted white crosses and pitted angels waiting for a sign, the startle of salt growing on headstones as plastic flowers glowed dully on the plots, shoved like broken sticks into the ground.

The road slid past the high fences of the rich on the hill as the pavement sloped toward town, everyone getting ready for bed or already sleeping, curtains pulled, doors locked, shutters closed. Even the gardens by the sidewalks looked exhausted.

Closer into town the houses got smaller and meaner. The truck had crossed the line between the old rich and the old poor, there being next to none new to either, and no one in between. The trees on these streets had been stunted by axes and saws, girdled by blades. He'd seen children throw hunting knives and hatchets into the trunks as they practised their art of movie death, their imitation of the war their fathers never spoke of, Nazi and Jap deaths in every throw, John Wayne slogging forward on the sands of Iwo Jima, or riding the desert plains to Fort Apache, Henry Ford somewhere out there waiting. Elms pushed at the sky, their tops crowned, long scars up the trunks. Lilac hedges twisted below windows, leggy and bloomless. The town began to die as the truck neared the core. The last poor lived there. Fences leaned unpainted with missing pickets like the teeth of the veterans who sat on the Post Office steps, yard gates leaned open, cats sliding through the gaps on their nightly rambles.

He pictured Eddy breaking into the dark house, Harry somewhere ahead of him, Eddy stoned, mumbling to his friend to go slow. Tom had seen Eddy shoot up. Each time he'd watched, helpless, as Eddy tied himself off, finding a vein, the needle slipping in, and then his head dropping to his chest as the heroin obliterated him. Resting on his knees, he'd stare at Eddy's fluttering eyelids and try to think himself into his brother, but he never got deeper than his skin. Eddy said the moment the heroin hit was like a warm explosion inside his skull, soft arms holding his brain, a thick quilt wrapped around his heart. No one can touch me there, he said. His body would sag away, nothing left in the muscles, nothing in his bones.

He remembered a month or so ago when Eddy had gone to town to make a buy from Billy. He'd shot up in the toilet at the pool hall and Sergeant Stanley had cornered him as Eddy was shambling along in search of his car. He came home pale and angry, a tight grin on his face. He went outside again some time later and when Tom didn't hear him come back in, he went to look for him, finding him in the root cellar, his belt loose across his arm, the needle leaning by a bruise like an icicle fallen from a rain gutter. When he laid his ear against Eddy's chest, he could hear his brother's heart beating slow, his lungs screaming for a breath. Tom blew into his brother's mouth, the air battering the sacks behind his ribs, until Eddy's mouth whimpered a reply. Tom raised him to his floppy feet, and walked him out into the orchard. As they stumbled over the grass and stones, he told Eddy that he'd grown in the basket of his mother's belly, listening to blood songs, saying to him: *For thou art thy father's son, tender and only beloved in the sight of thy mother.*

He remembered how the creek had muddled its way as a cock pheasant peered from behind a clump of bunch grass. Confused by the end of the moon, blue light breaking above him and his brother, the bird began looking for food in the shadowed grass around its nest. Tom's eyes were wet with salt. He'd trudged beside Eddy in the great circle they had made of the field, trying to talk to him, hoping that words might be enough to keep his brother alive.

Tom's hands trembled on the wheel. He pulled the truck over and parked it under a twisted elm halfway down the hill. Thinking of Eddy like that left him with little to hold on to. He took a few long breaths, filling his lungs as if surfacing from deep water. He needed air.

The lawns were dried out, the night cool as he started to walk by the houses, stopping only to peer through a window now and then before moving on. He was invisible in the dark. At the last house on the block he stood and parted a tangle of branches. A woman was sitting in the dim light of a kitchen, no cup of coffee in her hand, no plate before her. The table was bare, but for a salt shaker spilled over. She was staring beyond it at a cold wood stove, no fire in it he could see. He watched her for a long time, but she didn't move, her hands folded in her lap, nothing he could find in her blank and steady gaze. The wind stirred in the leaves as he lowered himself to his heels and like a pale criminal stole away under the trees.

He got back into the truck, put it in gear, and drove down the hill. At the bottom, the truck tires rumbled on the rails as he crossed the tracks and rolled to a stop by the curb. In front of him was the train station, its red brick walls streaked by coal smoke from the old steam engines. The ancient clock in the tower above the station doors measured no minutes, the hour hand frozen, pointed halfway between ten and eleven. He looked at the empty train platform and thought of the people who'd come to the valley. They were the men from the war, the ones who missed the marching into guns and the ones who'd marched through them. They were also the immigrants from Europe who wanted to put war behind them and find work in the valley, families who'd drifted north from the States, west from the prairie, and from the crowded cities of the East. Tom had seen them arrive when he was a boy, speaking languages Tom couldn't understand, showing up confused in their strange clothing with their frail belongings or in dilapidated trucks piled high with mattresses and children, only to stand and stare in amazement at their dream, the high hills, the valley with its lakes, its green orchards and fields.

Across the street was the decrepit Mission Hotel with its cracked windows, its rooms empty now, their existence only to justify the licence for the beer parlour below where vagrant workers and old soldiers spent their treasured nickels and dimes, nursing their twenty-cent beers for hours until they were kicked out to sit shaking on the sidewalk.

Getting out of the truck, Tom stood in the crackle of railway cinders. The noise of men and women in the street outside the Okanagan Hotel on Main Street was a block away. There were only a few hours left before closing time. After that, Main Street would be mostly deserted except for a few abandoned vehicles parked slant. He'd seen them there, bits of paper and clothing strewn across the seats as if someone had searched through what little remained of their life, and finding nothing worth keeping or holding or wearing, left odd objects behind, a single baby shoe hanging by a lace from a rear-view mirror, a woman's torn blouse on a back seat, a pair of logging boots, a glove.

9

the worn floor of the Okanagan Hotel beer parlour was smeared with dim light, clusters of tables jammed together, ashtrays smouldering, a nimbus of smoke hanging above a clutter of glasses, and the faces around the tables moving in and out of the shadows, a hand here and there reaching into the tepid glow to lift a beer or put it down, arguments and shouts. "Don't Be Cruel" thundered from the jukebox against the wall, Elvis importuning his reluctant lover, the guitar eating into everyone's imagined, broken heart. The wall that used to run through the middle of the room to separate single men from women had been long ago torn down, but the scar where the wall plate used to be was still there, the nails that held it bent over and beaten by hammers, nail heads gleaming, iron stubs in the floorboards grinding into shoes and boots.

The room was full, the women held close by watchful men. Waitresses, their beer trays held high by their shoulders, eased their way between chairs, stopping at table after table to place down yet another order of draft beers. Empties loaded, they picked up bills or coins from the pile in the middle of the table and made change, men keeping an eye on their quick hands, women watching their men, empty glasses clinking on the tray as the waitress moved on, a two-bit tip slipped into the side pocket of her apron, the dollar she'd filched back-folded around her little finger.

Tom sat perched on the edge of the tender's chair at the end of the bar. Beside the barman's knee was the stubbed-off baseball bat he kept for quelling fights, the handle ringed with black tape for grip. The clock over the bar said twenty after ten. Where the hell was Eddy? Tom surveyed the room, the men and women he knew from the bush, the back country, and the valley, all of them riding out the hours until closing time when they'd stagger out to the street and the parking lot to find their cars and trucks. Deals were going down among the men, a possible job at the fruit-packing plant, on a highway paving crew, or at one of the sawmills promised, talked about, considered, and rejected. That, and an impossible wife, mother, lover, or child being vilified, regretted, or damned, friends lied to, found and lost, moments left over, an hour or two remembered, then forgotten in the dregs of another glass. Men didn't move from their chairs except to play a game of pool or head to the toilets. The women went in pairs for the same relief, staying there for what seemed forever, brushing their hair and repairing their faces, the gossip and the back-biting drifting between the cubicles. Tom watched Deb McVittie and Irene Scutts, both stocky brunettes with backcombed hair, traverse a complex trail through the maze, men nudging and winking at them as they passed by, the *he said* and *then she said* like broken glass stirred by a fork.

Across the room he could see Billy and another guy playing eight ball, the bet five dollars, two blue bills resting on the rag at the end of the table under a square of green chalk, Billy winning, given the sour look on the other player's face, the way his hand with its skull-and-cross-bones ring gripped his blunt cue. Around them was the same old crowd, Weiner Reeves raising his glass to whatever corpse was lying in the basement of his father's funeral parlour, Vera with Norman beside her, the side of his face taped over, his brown hair curling over his collar, talking too much to anyone who'd listen, his words garbled. Wayne was off to the side, as always, grinning eagerly at Joe who was sitting a table away ignoring him. Tom watched close as he wondered again at Wayne telling Harry about the house, Eddy walking into danger and not giving a damn. Nancy was sitting close to Billy, who was whispering in her ear, his cue by his side. Lester Coombs was nowhere to be seen. The ones who were there cast quick looks at Tom sitting over by the bar. They knew he only came in to look for Eddy.

Tom watched Nancy staring dumbly into the mirror on the wall. Joe was tilted back in his chair propped against the wall behind the pool tables, a full glass of beer in front of him. He was watching Billy win. Every few minutes Joe turned his head to Tom, his eyes opaque, nothing showing

on his sallow face. Tom looked long at him, knowing Joe
was deep into his and Eddy's lives.

His fight with him at school had been years ago, but Joe
remembered it, his grudge nursed through the years. Joe was
staring through the crowd, his eyes cutting through the pall
of blue smoke. Tom knew it was an old revenge Joe wanted,
but not just for losing some long-ago fight at school. He
couldn't stand it that anyone had seen the weakness and fear
in him, and it was something he'd never forgiven Tom for.

Joe had arrived in 1949 from the Ukraine, his father and
mother bringing him over with them after the war, his
name changing to Joseph. He came to school in gumboots
and odd-looking clothes, older boys pushing and tripping
him, laughing at his bowl-cut hair, his bare feet in rubber
boots stinking with sweat in the hot classroom. Tom never
went close to him except the once when he tried to help
him up after Joe had been knocked down the fire escape.
Joe had screamed at him to be left alone, but Tom wouldn't
listen, and Joe turned on him, the fight beginning. Tom
remembered hitting Joe's head over and over with a rock
at the end, wanting to stop and not knowing how, Joe taken
home bleeding to the wrath of his father. Tom was dealt
with by the principal, Mr. Bruno, a man who was supposed
to have a silver plate in his skull from the war. He had stood
in front of Tom spitting out his rage, flailing at Tom's hands
and wrists with a leather strap. He hated both Eddy and
Tom, for what reason Tom had never understood, other
than they were Elmer Stark's boys from up Ranch Road.

Eddy had told Tom how Joe's father used to punish him.

He and Harry had watched Joe's father take him out to the shed after church and make him kneel on dried peas while he read the Bible over him. One Sunday morning, Tom had hidden in the back alley and, peering through the fence palings, he had seen Joe there on his bare knees. As if he knew what Tom was thinking, Joe glanced at him now and turned away. He said something quietly to Billy, got up, eased through the tables like a slender blade, and went out the hotel doors into the street.

Tom heard hard laughter from some men nearby and saw a woman on her hands and knees under a table trying to find something, a fallen quarter, a lost earring, a purse mislaid or dropped. The man with her had his boots resting on her back, two others with him laughing at her squeal of outrage at the man holding her down. Nothing ever changed. The bar was there with its relief from boredom, its excuse for beauty. He got up and headed for the doors, people watching him go, Eddy Stark's little brother, and he stepped out onto the sidewalk past the usual crowd of Indians and kids, crossing the street to sit on the steps of the Post Office.

From there the neon lights of the hotel hissed and sputtered as moths threw themselves helplessly against the cold glow of the glass tubes. Wherever Eddy was, at the old man's house or shooting up in a cul-de-sac, nothing good could come of it. There'd been times he'd got involved with Eddy's escapades, cartons of cigarettes and chocolate bars their booty, Eddy selling them for half-price in the alley behind the bar, but no more. When Eddy told him about killing

Stanley's dog the week before, Tom said he didn't want to hear about it.

Across the street the interdicted Indians and penniless bums were begging beers from passing men. Teenage boys stood to the side of the hotel entrance, lights fluttering on their peach-fuzz cheeks, their skinny bodies promising the men they'd be someday. They were waiting for someone they knew, someone older to go in and buy them a case of beer, no questions asked. In the lot at the back were the cars and trucks they'd spent the summer fixing up or the newer ones borrowed from their fathers, some girl they'd brought into town in the front seat looking into the rear-view mirror and adjusting her makeup while her girlfriend struggled in the back seat, her nylon legs crossed, elbows guarding her breasts, the boy with her untiring as he made his moves toward what he thought love was.

And then he saw Joe come out of the alley behind the bar and move along the hotel to the edge of the neon glare. He stopped and stood in the flickering shadows, his narrow back against the wall, ironed pants, his bent knee cocked, a foot braced on the bricks, black boots shining. Tom thought of Joe in the kitchen at the party, the card game stopped, Tom's knee in his back. He thought of that and how he knew Joe would travel from there all the way to the frozen playground dirt at school, the floor of his father's shed where he knelt and listened to the wrath of Isaiah. Joe was looking right through whoever passed by, his eyes seeming to be fixed on the granite wall across from him. Josie Cameron, the grade-school teacher with the birthmark on her neck, came out of the doors into the night. Dishevelled, confused, she moved slowly, her hand tracing the wall of the bar as she trailed down the sidewalk, black purse dangling from her loose hand and bumping against her ankle. When she passed Joe, he nudged her, and she stepped wide around him only to reach out again to steady herself. At the end of the wall her hand waved as she leaned upon emptiness, staggering sideways and gone for a moment before reappearing, crossing the street, and vanishing among the caraganas in the park.

The doors to the bar crashed open, and two men Tom knew from the sawmill, the Cruikshank brothers, pushed out onto the sidewalk and walked off down Main Street, laughing, beer bottles in their hands. He wondered what time it was.

The granite was cool against his thighs. He leaned back on his elbows as he watched Joe pull away from the wall, cast a quick look at him, then saunter down the street. The door to the bar opened, a woman's bare arm holding it there a moment, the sound of "Heartbreak Hotel" weaving out, Elvis plaintive, wailing, and then the arm pulled back and the door closed as if whoever had been holding it open had wanted the song to leave.

Someone shouted in the park. For a moment Tom thought it might be Joe, and then there were two sets of running footsteps, Josie Cameron appearing alone up the street, the sound of her shoes growing smaller and smaller, diminishing to nothing in the dark. He stared down Main, late cars pacing wheel to wheel, engines rumbling,

Hollywood mufflers with their roar, girls talking to each other from open windows, their boyfriends urging other drivers toward the south road so they could race to the cliffs above Kalamalka Lake.

Tom listened to the cars careen down the block and then they were gone and the street was strangely quiet. He looked toward the station and saw Eddy and Harry coming up the sidewalk. They turned at the corner across from him and went into the hotel, the doors closing behind them. He got up off the steps and followed on his brother's heels into the bar. Inside, he saw them heading toward the pool tables. Tom noticed people looking at them and whispering. Light danced around his brother, something electric flickering across his shoulders. It reminded him of the ghost lights he'd seen on rotted stumps in swamps. He could tell by the way Eddy moved that he was hungry for a fix. And Harry seemed jittery. He twitched as he walked, leaning down to one table or another, and talking fast, a whisper here, a handshake there. Eddy crossed to where Billy was shooting pool, Harry waiting by Billy's table against the wall, picking up a glass of beer and chugalugging it. He put the empty glass down and peeled the paper from another Sweet Marie bar, taking a bite, all the while moving his head nervously. Tom wasn't even sure Eddy knew he was there or, if he did, that he cared one way or another.

Billy took a long look at Eddy, racked his cue, and moved into the corner, Eddy beside him, standing there like he knew what he was doing. Their backs were to the room, their shoulders hunched. Money changed hands, a square of paper was slipped into Eddy's pocket, and then he headed toward the toilets, Harry behind him.

Tom crossed the bar and caught the Men's Room door as it was closing, following them down to the last stall.

So what happened? Tom said.

Eddy stood in a dark shadow against the wall, shaking his head. I can't talk right now, Tom. I need to get fixed.

His brother's hesitation gave him what he wanted to know. I told you something was wrong with this, Tom said.

Eddy took a shallow drag from a cigarette, smoke dribbling from his nose. Forget it, Tom, he said. I'm hurting here. Eddy held his hands loose at his sides in damp fists, salt beads on his forehead.

Tom turned and started to walk away.

Okay, okay, Eddy said. Jesus. We went in the back door, sure, but the place wasn't empty. The son of a bitch was hiding in the living room. We never even saw him until he tried to shoot us with a bloody .308. Not once, but *two* times.

I won't bother asking why you didn't check the house out first, Tom said.

The fucking place was dark, okay? Eddy said.

We didn't know he was in there, said Harry, unapologetic, just trying to keep it simple.

I shot the fucker, Eddy said. Tom just shook his head. Yeah, with the pistol I took off Lester Coombs.

Harry shoved his hands in his pockets. Shit, Tom, he said, what the hell did you expect us to do? Anyway, Wayne was right. There was money there.

Eddy looked over Tom's shoulder. Fuck off, Joe, he said.

Tom turned and there was Joe standing at the urinal, running his hand over his hair. For a moment Tom wondered how he'd got back so soon from wherever he'd been outside. You heard what he said, Joe. Take off.

Joe just stood there smiling as he pissed.

Tom put his hand on Eddy's arm and leaned in close as Joe stepped down, shaking his cock and tucking himself in his pants.

I said get the hell away from us, Tom said. Don't you see us talking here?

Joe pointed at Tom, a smirk on his lips. Fuck you too, he said, as he turned and went out the door. He didn't look back.

You're a mess, Tom said to his brother.

Eddy ignored him, turning to his friend. Harry?

Harry pulled open the toilet stall door and Eddy slipped into the cubicle, Harry and Tom blocking the door, a dull light above them shining down like a muddy moon. Tom could see the house they'd broken into, some old man on the floor with a bullet in him, and the two of them walking away without a thought for anyone.

What about the body, Harry?

Get out of the way, Harry said. Tom leaned back against the door, helpless as Eddy struggled out of his leather jacket, dropping it on the floor, slumping down. It's okay, Harry said as he knelt between Eddy's knees and undid the button at his wrist, pushing his shirt sleeve up. Knife scars appeared like snail slicks as Harry rolled the sleeve to Eddy's shoulder. Eddy, rising from his slump, urgent now for the shot, lifted his hips and fumbled down inside his underwear, pulling out the cotton sack that held his works, his hands shaking. He slid the thin leather belt from his pant loops and tried to wrap it around his bicep, but the belt kept slipping in his sweat. The valley of Eddy's elbow was blue with bruises. The closer he got to a fix, the more desperate he seemed to be.

Eddy laid his works on his clamped knees. His hands were shaking. He looked up and Tom stared at him, wishing he could call his brother back from the abyss he'd fallen into. Not me, Tom said. You know I can't.

Harry took from Eddy's hand the paper Billy had given him, opening it carefully. Use half, Eddy said, eager, and Harry took the spoon and matches from Eddy's thin fingers.

Harry wiped it with his thumb and dipped for a bit of water from the back of the toilet, then shook a quarter of the brown heroin into it as he whispered to Tom: He always uses too much.

Tom watched as Harry held the spoon over a wooden match but the match burned down to Harry's fingers, sputtered, and went out, Eddy humming urgently as he saw the flame go out in Harry's fingers. Harry lit another, the heroin starting to bubble in the spoon, the powder seething in the boil. Eddy's eyes seemed to reach out like fingers to the needle as Harry sucked the junk into the syringe through a tiny spill of toilet paper.

Eddy was slapping at what was left of the vein in the crook of his elbow with three flat fingers, then with his knuckles as he tried to bring a vein up, but his blood stayed buried, burned cold under the scabs. He moaned at his arm.

There's one, said Harry, as a small vein appeared halfway between his wrist and elbow crease. Harry took the syringe and after a try or two, slipped the needle in.

C'mon, Eddy said, c'mon, and Harry drew the plunger back and pulled the barest of Eddy's blood into the syringe. He waited a second, no more, and pushed the plunger gently down, the bubble of junk a tiny bloat under his freckled skin.

It's okay, Tom, Eddy said, his eyes pleading.

The breath Eddy held went out of him. Harry put the syringe down on the back of the toilet and caught Eddy's skull in his hand as it flopped to the side. He smiled as he stroked his friend's cheek.

We'll go out to my shack, he said to Tom. Until things cool off.

Tom reached down, picked up Eddy's jacket off the floor, and handed it to Harry.

You guys do that, said Tom. Stay in touch is all.

10

the dead came crowding in, each with a story, what happened and when, who was there and why. Most faded into fragments, faint mutterings and murmurs, the stories rising as if from narrow caves, the sounds distorted, vowels drawn out into echoes, consonants clipped and rattling like a snake's tail whirring in the sagebrush, the same kind of warning, the dead telling me things they thought I needed to know, tales from so far back they no longer had any meaning except to the ones who told them. I heard, I didn't hear.

The house where I was born and died nudged up against Ranch Road. No whisper of smoke lifted from the chimney. The day had been hot, the doors and windows shut tight as Mother waited alone at the kitchen table, gazing at the mountain. A thin breeze came in the window off the lakes and hills. For me there was no heat, no sleep, no cool of night. Swallows flew through me; Sulphur butterflies fluttered through my eyes and out my mouth.

I told Nettie to quiet. Her spirit was seething still. She was Mother's mother and she'd told me yet again how Elmer Stark came to the farmhouse out in Saskatchewan following on the heels of her daughter who'd stopped him on the grid road and asked him to come in and share their evening meal, a flirty girl at the fence line watching the road for a man. Nettie told me how she regarded this man, younger than her and older than her daughter, his hands resting on the kitchen table, the large knuckles and the burnished hairs on the backs of his fingers and hands, the curl of his red hair, wet with sweat, stubbled out over the collar of the blue cotton shirt she'd given him after he washed at the sink, one of the two shirts of her husband's she'd kept in the trunk in the bedroom chiffonier.

She told me how she'd stood, gripping the back of a kitchen chair while he washed, his naked shoulders, the gleam of his skin, and the lines of charred bronze where the sun had burned his neck and wrists, the faint red-gold of the hairs that edged from under his belt at his waist. Nettie had wanted to brush against them, feel that softness on her wrists, her belly. She'd not touched nor been touched by a man in the three years since her husband hanged himself, leaving her and her young daughter, Lillian, alone on the farm. Now her daughter was seventeen and had spent spring and summer afternoons at the window or standing at the fence line looking out along the grid road that led down from Prince Albert and up from Fort Qu'Appelle.

Nettie had stood with her back to the same window with its flour-sack curtains she'd dyed orange with willow bark and chokecherries. She told me how her daughter sat at the kitchen table and watched the man she'd brought in from the correction line. Nettie said she knew her daughter thought she was the only woman in the room, her mother to her a dry leaf, a forgotten stone. They both gazed at his naked back and the hairs leading like a wedge of late-summer wheat down under his brown, sweat-stained leather belt.

She stood there and watched her daughter suddenly become a woman. Her own need was heat between her legs.

As Nettie quiets, gone back to brooding, Elmer shouts into the dirt, his story blundering among the roots. He starts in again about the sister he left behind south of the land of the little sticks, the mother who stared into his back as he walked away, knowing what would happen when his father woke. Elmer said nothing to her when she gave him a bag with a part-loaf of day-old bread, a turnip, five eggs in a jar of vinegar, and strips of smoked venison she'd had hidden away. He'd rolled an extra shirt in a scrap of blanket along with three fish hooks, fish leader wound on a stick, and his father's short knife stripped from his father's belt as he lay sleeping. The sheath was stained with sweat, a salt line running like a lake edge across the leather. What was there to say but that he had to go, the bruise on his cheek a mottled blue from his father's back-handed fist thrown at him when he'd forgotten to tie up the dog. His father had been herding cattle into the pen and the dog had spooked the stock, half the steers veering off and gone into the dusk, not to be found till the next day, and then that fist again, hard across the side of his head, Elmer calling to the dog to come back, all to no avail.

The fist was nothing to what his father did three hours later when he finished a jar of moonshine, hauling him out into the bull pasture and beating him as he cursed his son. His sister, Alice, the one I was named for, had burst from the kitchen door and run across the stubble field. She had begged her father to stop, but he wouldn't listen. Elmer found out Alice was gone when he woke up in his cot in the lean-to at the back of the house. His mother was washing the cuts in his skin. She knew where Alice was and so did Elmer. She was where he always took her, out past the barn to the empty grain shed beyond the dugout.

Elmer had lain awake in the lean-to until he heard the early howl of a coyote. The moon was gone and the hours were running to the dawn. Alice wasn't back, his father sleeping loud behind the half-wall that separated their bed from the kitchen.

When will he let her go?

His whisper to his mother. She squatted beside him and told him not to fear, that his sister would be back later in the morning when father fetched her. Elmer looked at the chapped skin on her hands as she gave him his father's old boots and a can with a skim of dubbin in the grooves. Take care of your boots, she'd said. They'll save your feet on the road. She told him he had to go north before he could go south. Leave the road, she said. He'll try to find you.

Follow the creek. The creek leads to the river and the river leads to people. Remember that. Follow the upstream. The Saskatchewan River will find you a home.

It was the fear in his mother and sister that frightened him the most, what he couldn't accept. He was afraid that it might live in him some day, that woman-fear stopping him from becoming a man. He was afraid that it might grow inside him until he became like his mother, like Alice. It never occurred to him that by leaving the farm and family it would be his father who would grow in him, like a moth grub in an apple that waits for the fruit to ripen before eating the heart.

At the fence line where it met the northwest road he almost turned aside. He'd looked into the dark where he was headed and saw it in shreds among the western clouds, the first light coming out of the east behind him in a brittle band. He knew where his sister was and he almost turned away from the road to go to the alder-log shed by the dugout, but he couldn't, wouldn't go. He knew what he would find there and he knew, finding her, he would have to do something. But what could he do? He lifted the barbed wire, and ducked through, the fence between him and what he knew. His mother had told him he had but an hour to run before his father woke.

He'll not forgive you taking his knife, she said.

He started walking again, his feet loose in his father's old boots, the bound blanket slung over his shoulder. He was thirteen years old and would not look back, not ever.

I know, Father, I know.

Father was just a boy when he first wandered the plains. That summer he found himself in the southern foothills down near Pincher Creek where he lived a short year in an abandoned sod hut with a Métis woman and her baby, the woman a stranger kind of mother, her language a mix of Stony, Chippewa, and French. When he left, he stole his first horse from a ranch near Fort Macleod and rode east out of the spring storms into the Cypress Hills where he worked the ranch and wheat country of Palliser's Triangle. The border meant nothing to him, Saskatchewan and Alberta, the Dakotas, Montana, Idaho, and Washington, they were all one country in his mind. He didn't think he belonged to any one place. He was a wanderer and called nowhere home. When he was fifteen, he hid out in a cave on the Big Muddy down in the Badlands, piling grease-wood and sagebrush to block the blizzard winds. He lived there a winter, shooting wolves with a stolen Enfield rifle, selling their hides in Havre. In the spring, he drifted past Old Man On His Back to the Frenchman River near Eastend where he got a job on the railway for the summer. Later, he cowboyed on the McKinnon ranch, worked thresher crews near Medicine Hat and Olds, then quit and hit the trail again. He worked a season here and there, moving on from farm to ranch, from village to town, Sweetgrass, Climax, Wolf Point, Cut Bank, footloose and drifting through his younger years. He was a "stopper," riding in alone, working a day or a week in exchange for a shed to sleep in and food for whatever horse he'd traded for or stolen.

The next year, he laboured dawn to dusk in the fields in a desert camp on the river benches near Walla Walla north of Grand Coulee. Every four hours the workers were allowed a break and found what shade there was in the lee of onion wagons where they ate their spare food and passed among themselves a tin cup dipped from one of the buckets the water-carrier, old Albertine One-Time-Song, had hauled with her yoke from the river down below. Father sat apart from the men, the women, and their curious children. He was young enough to be wary of their affections, the women because he knew the kindness they showed was only for the season, the day, and sometimes just the hour, and the men because they were jealous of anyone who might try to get close to what they owned. Father knew enough to stay to himself, far from the rags and patches of the Indians and itinerants who worked the fields before finishing the year by heading upriver to the fruit country for the autumn harvest.

The days were safe enough, but he slept careful in the dark, not knowing who might come crawling to find him. One night an early cold came creeping down from Canada and he hauled his blanket and kit over to the wagon where Albertine and her man, Seymour Dubois, slept. He curled up to the coals of their dwindling fire and lay huddled in his blanket with his knees pulled up to his chest. He lay there not sleeping as he watched two scorpions come from the sand to dance at the edge of a hot stone, then Dubois came out of the dark of his wagon and sat down across from him, a blanket pulled around his shoulders, his greasy hat tipped low on his forehead. Elmer couldn't see his eyes clearly, only the glance of light in them, a glitter as of mica flashing under his dense brows. Elmer had filled onion sacks near Dubois for the past week and trusted him enough not to get up and move back to where he'd been before in the cold by the sagebrush. Dubois spoke out of the glow of his beard, his voice a rattle.

Looks like they're dancing, Elmer said.

They're not dancing, said Dubois.

The scorpions circled each other, their claws raised up and their tails curved above them, the barbs catching the fire's light. They circled for a long time and then they grappled, claws clicking on legs, the tails jabbing down as each tried to find an opening in the other's scales. The fight lasted only a few minutes, the larger one stinging the smaller, the dying one stretching its legs out, its barbed tail losing its high curl. The big scorpion started to drag the dead one under the shadow of a flat stone, but Dubois pushed it away with a stick, picked up the dead one, and threw it on the coals in the fire pit. He said nothing, just rolled a cigarette, Elmer watching the scorpion's body crack open in the slender flames.

Father drifted east into Montana. It was the early Twenties and these were days he would remember as the best years he'd had, riding the rodeo circuits, winning a few dollars on bucking broncs in towns across the west. Get him drunk enough and he'd talk about a horse he'd ridden named Devil's Child. Where had he been, Fort Qu'Appelle? *Who calls.* That town a question without an answer. Father said it was a rinky-dink rodeo, but what did that mean? He'd just turned seventeen, and was ready to be a hero, heading up from Chocteau, on a worn-out gelding he'd picked up outside of town. He was looking for a chance to shine and when they asked for his moniker at the rodeo grounds he gave them The Chocteau Kid, knowing the good rodeo riders had names like that.

He would always remember the horse he won on in the rodeo, Devil's Child, and the way that stallion trembled under him, the shudder when he laid his hand on his neck. He could hear the shiver, the horse talking with his skin before they opened the gate and let them loose. Seventeen years old and riding his ten seconds on a horse that had thrown every rider that season, each man in the stands wanting to be him, riding like he was against time.

Ten American silver dollars, all of it spent in the bar that night, a hero for an hour or two as he stood drinks for the house, farm girls hanging off his arms, and then the Rambler Café the next morning, eggs and bacon, spuds and bread, and the coffee cup he could barely hold in his shaking hands, the waitress giving him seconds for free, thinking he was a cowboy down on his luck. He sold his Montana mare for next to nothing and rode the bus, following the rodeo horses to Alberta, coming in first at the Calgary Stampede, having drawn Devil's Child again and riding him into the dust. He stayed three nights in the Palliser Hotel, riding girls in his top-floor room, their names left behind each morning in the bottom of a bottle.

Elmer knew the colour of the land in all its moods, felt the heaviness of the South Saskatchewan River, its great brown heave. He squatted in an abandoned shack one winter by the Qu'Appelle lakes, camped in the Badland coulees and in the wasteland at the edge of the Great Sand Hills. He heard the call of the loon and saw the fall of the snow geese onto the sloughs, the Canadas and curlews as they came in their millions down the sky onto the desolate prairie lakes. Going north or south, blade after blade of birds cried down until the water was so weighted by their breasts he thought the lakes themselves would rise above the earth and drown the land forever. He'd seen the dust walk the plains, a thousand-foot wall of earth moving across the fields. He lived the drought years. It seemed at times all he talked of was dust and roads.

Turner Valley was where Father found himself again, early one November. He rode in on a spavined horse and saw the snow geese come down through the blizzard sky in the wrong season, the great Alberta coulee a vast flame with black clouds rearing up and the land green in the heart of the foothills winter, men like charred sticks in the coulee as they burned the oil. Mary Bellman's whorehouse out in nearby Dog Town was his home for six months. He worked there part-time when he wasn't trying to put a dollar together out of nickels and pennies, sweeping floors, hauling wood, and going to one or another bar to get whiskey for the ladies. Eloise was his favourite whore, a girl with long black hair and an easy laugh. It was the way she teased him early on about how he wasn't really a man, not yet, and him bristling at her for the way she laughed at him, the other girls going along with the gag and saying: *Ain't you just the prettiest boy,* calling him Carrot Top, loving it when they made him blush with their fast ways, a glimpse of Eloise's white breasts enough to drive him mad, him wanting to touch them and without money enough to try. Mary got angry at him for hanging around the girls too much, telling him to get back to work doing whatever it was she wanted done, a floor wiped down, garbage hauled to the nuisance ground, bottles taken to the men in the rooms upstairs who wanted to get drunk with their whores before heading back out to the gas fields to work or to some rooming house, tent, or tarpaper shack they were living in. If they were without shelter, they'd walk the long trail back to Turner Valley and head out to the ravine to roll up in a blanket as close as they could get to the burning oil in Hell's Half Acre, waking up winter and summer to geese and ducks that stayed year-round to feed on grass that wouldn't die, no matter it being thirty below out on the prairie. Mary Bellman rewarded him that summer by giving him a Sunday night with wild Eloise. In the false dawn she said she wanted to run off with him, but after a breakfast of crackers and corned beef, he packed up his bindle and headed into Calgary once more, for the Stampede and a chance to ride for money on the bareback broncs.

Father, The Chocteau Kid, hitting the circuit again.

I turn in the memory of his tellings.

But what's a father's witness to a dead child? What meaning was there in his hoard of words? Adventures, not confessions, his stories not a life.

There's a leaf floated down through the air. It rides the autumn current of Cheater Creek. Boulders have washed down through the years and lie strewn across the waters below the clay bluffs beyond the bridge. The spare rains and the winds blowing up the valley have eaten the clay away and the creek has chewed the foot of the bluff, glacial gravel sliding down from the seams. The leaf follows the current through the rocks and is thrown by a brown wave into an eddy bound by stone. The current runs close by and the leaf turns and touches faster water, its crinkled edge turned back and circling there, the leaf a small boat caught. Like that leaf, his life.

I've listened to it a dozen, dozen times, how he sat in the bar in LaBret and heard talk of the woman on the farm with a lonely daughter. Some drunken drifter told him how the woman's husband had hanged himself in a barn. It was the old story, the woman going out and finding her man seven-stepping the air, then her cutting him down, the weight of him falling through her arms. He'd heard it many times in those days, so many he thought there must be a hanged man in each barn or house he passed, a lonely woman on every quarter-section from the Dakotas to Alberta. There was always a daughter who lay on a narrow cot each night, her hand between her legs as she imagined a man who might save her from feeding pigs, collecting eggs, and milking the cows she dreamed someday of owning, a hired man, lean and hungry hanging his arms over a corral fence, smiling at her as she passed by.

He'd heard the story and the jokes. Did you hear the one about the farmer's daughter? Men drinking their beer and laughing. It was the same in every bar, someone sitting alone and looking for company. After a few beers he was told of the farm near Nokomis and the women living there alone.

Why did he believe the story? What made him cadge a ride on a passing truck and why did he get off the truck at the road where it swung east toward Nokomis? Why didn't he keep riding all the way to Prince Albert? Or into Saskatoon? That's where he thought he was going. He'd been told he'd find work there on the bridges. Why not go there? He said a man goes naturally toward trouble and it's always a woman. He told me he didn't know.

What happened, Elmer?

She witched me wild, he'd say. I lost my mind the day I saw her there.

She was standing at the crook of the correction line just as the drunk in the bar back in LaBret said she'd be. She stood near naked in a threadbare dress by the barbed-wire fence with her hair adrift in the wind and he followed her to the house. Sometimes she walked backward, asking him questions about where he'd been and what he'd done. She said she was going to be a dancer someday. She turned once in a spin upon her bare brown feet and stood between the sun and him. He saw her body inside that white cotton dress, the fall of her young breasts, the shadow at her groin. Lillian knew what he was seeing, spinning there on her toes.

Nettie was in the house making bread, her mother. He knew, seeing them both in the kitchen, they were hungry for a man and he knew he was good for both of them until the daughter swayed him apart with her talk of his owning the farm, the smell of her crotch rich as the crush of new-mown hay. He could have just had Nettie and the farm, but he couldn't have both. Not in the end.

Lillian knew that, young as she was. She waited for him in the field behind the barn and lifted her dress, brazen and wild. He says his brain was between his legs back then. When was it other than that? But back then how could he turn down something sweet as her? And the farm was a good one. He knew he'd get a price for it no matter the drought.

The rope her father used was still hanging from its beam. Nettie wouldn't have it down. The end of it where she'd cut her husband loose hung frayed like a shock of antelope hair caught on a barb of wire. Nettie told him her husband's hair was the same colour. Elmer thought it's why she left it hanging there. He'd watch it catch the breeze coming through the open doors. It swung there as if waiting for another man to hang himself. He told me he should've taken to the road the night the rope danced with blue fire, a storm passing over, lightning walking on its spider legs across the land, the thunder a fitful groan.

11

It was just past eleven-thirty when Tom left the bar and drove back up Priest Valley Road, turning down the driveway through the trees to the clearing and the old man's house. Tom pulled in with his lights off. There was a beaten-up logging truck parked in front of the house, its front end up on blocks, old cables hanging down from the log-stakes in rusted coils. It looked like it hadn't moved in years. He parked between it and the house. When he'd passed by Jim Garofalo's place, it had one dim light glowing above the awning over the door of the shop, everything else had been dark.

Tom stared through the windshield at the old man's house with its shallow roof, nothing above the main floor but an attic. There was a body in one of those rooms. He listened, but there was no sound to be heard other than the crickets. He imagined Harry opening the trunk of the Coupe and taking a hammer from his toolbox, Eddy beside him with

Lester Coombs' .22 in his hand. He knew the power his brother must have felt as he'd held that pistol. It was for close-up work, a machine for killing a crippled animal, a man. Father had let him and Eddy use an Enfield once, out by Cheater Creek when they were kids. He was teaching them to shoot and they'd had to hold it with two hands, it was so heavy. The first time he fired the huge pistol, he knew what such a gun was for, the clutch of steel like a fist in his hands, him aiming the pistol at a chalk circle Father had drawn on the wall of a deserted shack, feeling in the jolt of the recoil what John Wayne must have felt when he was taking down some enemy facing him. He remembered how much Eddy had loved shooting the handgun and how angry his brother had been when Father lost it in a card game at the Legion.

He opened the truck door quietly. Tom knew Eddy would have made Harry go in the house first to break trail and take the danger. He knew, he didn't know, what had happened next, and as he stared at the scarred front door he imagined the old man's rifle shot, a *crack* so close it split the night. He gazed at the house and thought he heard something fall, something break, and his brother's voice coming from one of the rooms, his outcry: You fuck! You fuck!

A fox passed through the tall grass at the corner of the house. Tom sniffed the Reynard's raw scent, saw the bronze tail vanish behind a tangled brush pile. He took the flashlight from the glove compartment and flicked it on, the light weak, the batteries almost dead. He stepped away from the truck, looked through the trees at the empty road, and went to the back of the house. Going up the steps, he tripped on a sprung plank and fell, his left hand skidding on the boards, a nail-head ripping the skin of his palm. Shit, he muttered, and made a quick fist.

The door was ajar, and Tom drew a long breath. But he wasn't afraid of what he would find. He'd seen bodies before, horses, bear, moose, and deer. He'd seen his own father. He went inside and closed the door behind him. The kitchen smelled like an old book left in the damp too long, the odour a clutch of mould, a smell that clogged his throat and stopped his nose. He felt with his feet on the cracked linoleum, moonlight slanting through the window panes. On the table was a plate with two gnawed pork chop bones, a scraped potato skin, and three black peas in clotted grease. An empty bottle of Old Style was by the plate, drowned flies floating in the dregs. He picked up a dish towel and pulled the cloth tight around his hand, knotting it with his teeth. He glanced down at his feet. There were spider motes and dust everywhere. Tom moved his light on the floor and caught a blink of brass by the door. He picked it up, a .308 shell casing, and put it in his pocket. One bullet then, fired when Eddy and Harry were somewhere down the hall.

His eyes followed the weak glow of the flashlight around the room. This was where Eddy and Harry had come in. He glanced down the hall to where the bedroom had to be. They would've gone to where they thought the money was. He could see his brother standing there with the pistol in his hand, moving it around, pointing it at shadows.

He played the light across the rusty stove and the counter, the faint beam catching on dirty dishes, stepped past the refrigerator to a door, opened it, and went in. His flashlight caught on an easy chair by a window in what he saw was a living room. It's where Tom would have sat if he'd been living there, a clear look at the driveway so he could see anyone approaching from the road. He might have been sitting or sleeping there when he heard the cars, or maybe he woke when he heard a noise at the back door. The old man would have got the rifle then, or he had it with him already. But why didn't he yell when he heard them? Maybe he was relieved they'd come in. Maybe he'd wished for some kind of trespass, an old man's dream of revenge against a world that cared nothing for his plight.

Against the far wall in the room was a green couch, its plush worn thin on the arms, and a pine table with a chipped leopard lamp standing on it. The cat's ruby eyes flickered red in the flashlight's passing. Around the easy chair were piles of old magazines, on a side table a crumpled pack of Sportsmans and an ashtray full of butts. The room had the same stink as Father, an unwashed, rancid haze, cheap tobacco, a bad lung smell, charred breath. There was a Queen Heater with a cone of ash on the floor in front of the vent. The ashes had to have been there since spring when the stove had been last lit.

The room looked as though it hadn't been cleaned in years, the old man sitting alone in there, day by night by day, his house draped around him like a funeral shroud. Tom clenched his eyes, opened them slowly, and followed the flashlight back through the kitchen and down the hall, briefly illuminating rooms, one cluttered with rotting cardboard boxes, discarded clothing, heaps of old magazines and newspapers, another room empty but for stacked crockery in a corner beside a damaged chest, the drawers pulled out and piled under a window, a single grey work sock, the toe missing, hanging from the lip of the top drawer, and then a bathroom, the toilet rank, the sink cracked, the tap dripping. The closet halfway down the hall was empty except for a woman's winter coat on a bent hanger. Moths fluttered into the beam of light.

In the room at the end was a bed with a crumpled mass of sheets, a worn blanket on the floor, partly under the bed, and a pillow resting against the headboard. The bed had been pulled out and sat crooked to the wall behind it. The old man smell was everywhere. It brought Father back and Tom didn't want him there any more than he wanted his brother.

On one wall was a photograph framed in carved wood, the picture slipped down inside the glass. It was of a man and woman standing by a Model A Ford. The woman was wearing a dress with what looked like beads sewn on it, her hair combed back on the sides as if creamed with oil. She was wearing a necklace, jewels glinting in the woven chains, one stone larger than the rest, a teardrop hanging at the top of her breasts. She had a teasing look, one pretending to a wildness she didn't have but for being with him. The man's stance, arms crossed upon his chest, said he owned what was his: the woman, the car, the dirt road he stood on, his fists, his lidded eyes. Behind them the flat land rolled away toward a high storm of dust, a ragged fringe behind them dropped across the sun. Mother had a picture like it of her parents. She'd been a little girl in the photograph, small beside her mother's long dress, the land receding, little or nothing in their eyes. It was the farm near Nokomis, far north of the Dakota badlands and Montana, the clapboard house behind the three of them, where Mother was born, the dwelling small against the sky. The picture on the wall had to be the old man when he was younger, and the woman with him, likely his wife, once alive, was now dead or simply gone. The woman and the man in the photograph were forever lost. All that remained was this picture on the wall or others in a book somewhere, an album hidden away, the past reduced to bits of seized memory, rigid images and nothing more, reminders of other days that made the old man all the more bitter for looking at who he'd been once, what he'd become.

This was where you dreamed, he thought, and he turned off the flashlight and lay down on the bed, his head resting in the furrow left behind in the pillow. Tom saw through the old man's rheumy eyes, and imagined another photograph, two children and a woman sitting on a blanket on an alkali beach in a wallow between low hills. The children, boys, wore knit bathing suits tied to their middle by cotton belts just like he and Eddy had worn when they were kids. The boys' legs and hummingbird chests were bare. They shone with soapy salt. They were laughing, excited by their picture being taken. The woman's eyes seemed guarded as she looked at the camera. As Tom lay there he felt like a seed swimming inside the old man, the anger he'd held at a world he thought had wronged him. The rage swirled inside him, what the man had wrought upon them all, his woman, those boys, himself.

He wondered who had taken it, the picture, that rock-strewn beach so barren, not a bush or tree, not a soul in sight but them. But someone had, a stranger, a boy maybe, drifting past in old boots and threadbare clothes, the sack over his shoulder limp but for a few gnarled potatoes and a half-eaten turnip in the bottom, banging against his skinny back. Some kid like his father had been, one who, for a penny or two, would hold the box camera and look down into the finder, a finger's blink on the button, and the boy continuing on as his father must have gone on when he was himself adrift on the vast plains.

He remembered one of the few stories his father told him. It was about a woman with a little girl, someone who had watched over him for a few months when he was a boy. Had he been with them near Drumheller or was it Medicine Hat? Or had they lived nowhere and just wandered the road allowance begging from passing trucks and wagons, the back doors of farmhouses. He couldn't remember if his father said. What he did say was that she'd found him hungry by the Old Man River, crouched beside the stringy legs of a sagebrush, some woman wearing a man's boots and with a child trailing along behind her. Back at her fire under the edge of a coulee she fed him dried horse meat, half of a huge carrot, and two raw grouse eggs sucked out of holes she poked in them with the nail on her little finger. It was the first time he'd eaten meat or eggs in days. How old was Father then? Tom didn't know, nor did he know how long Father had travelled with her, only that one night he had taken what coins the woman had secreted away in her rawhide purse, and then disappeared into the dark, only to appear in Fort Macleod where he cleaned stables at the rodeo there and earned a dollar catching a greased pig, people laughing at him as he bore the squealing animal to the judges by the corral fence. Stories, none of them making sense but for the telling of them, Father taking a few drinks more from his bottle and never finishing the tale, Tom sitting there with his fingers gripped together, rapt.

Tom lifted up off the pillow and swung his feet down, suddenly something more beneath his shoe than the ragged wool of the blanket. He moved the blanket back with his foot, and looked down at a hand, the fingers bent. He stood and pushed the bed back against the wall. The old man lay there on his side, one fist against his chest and the other arm sprawled. Blood was streaked down the side of his head, a small pool spread around his cheek.

Then the rifle fired again, the sound of it huge in the room, and Tom heard bare feet moving, the sound of a lever-action, the *snick-snack* of oiled steel pulled back to eject a spent shell and push another into the chamber. He could see Harry duck into the corner as the man came down the hall and turned at the doorway, firing blindly into the room. His brother shot him where he stood.

No, Tom said, unable to stop anything.

The man stood there stunned, the rifle lowered to his waist, his hand still moving, jacking out the spent shell. Tom could see the worn hand tremble from clutched fingers to wrist. His blood blubbered in the grey stubble beside his ear and his locked jaw.

Father.

Mother had said nothing to Tom when she came down to the well that night in the fall when his dog was killed. There was no anger in her, no punishment. What concern she had was for him to hide Father away. There was to be no trace of him. She said to dig a hole and bury him, and they dragged him into the orchard. What terror was there as he struggled with Eddy to pull that body through the grass? Father had left two ruts in the dirt with his tired boot heels, Eddy hauling from one wrist and him from the other. When they got to the apple tree by his sisters' graves, Tom got down on all fours and stared into Father's skull. What thoughts Father had were hidden too deep to save anyone.

They say the brain lives longer than the tongue, Tom said aloud now. It was as if he was explaining some mystery to himself. It's like hair, he thought. Mother says hair keeps growing after the dying. And he saw Father then in his grave, his hair like thin roots growing through the soil, parts of his brain scattered in the grass by the well, ants and beetles collecting it, taking his thoughts into their tunnels where his father's dreams nourished the garden's worms.

He spoke to his father. He was sure he had heard him, though his words were only vibrations of his breath, a story told to the part of Father that moved his right arm, another story told to the part that moved his eyes, his hands, his lungs. Eddy had sat there leaning against an apple tree, turning back the cuffs of his shirt. Tom had dug the grave. It wasn't shame that drove him, it was fear. He wanted him gone. He wanted him not to come back.

Where was Mother? Gone back to the house, or was she in the garden among the vines and tendrils of the runner beans as they climbed the summer corn? He could hear the corn talking as it grew, the sound of wet sand grinding in the leaves. Or was she at the kitchen table pouring a glass of whiskey as she waited for them to return? What were her thoughts, Father dead, the silence around her, her hand on a young cob of corn, her mouth tasting the smoke in the whiskey. Or was she in her room on the bed, the first hour of a next, another life?

Quiet sometimes is a whole universe. It's a huge thing held in without pain. Tom remembered sitting beside his father in the dry grass. Eddy had come down from the house and touched him. It was a caress that a girl would give when she's curious what a boy might be thinking, a touch that asks him to leave the far place he's in and come back to the world. And he had come back, Eddy telling him to forget what he had done.

The old man's eyes were wide open, staring up at the window. He was looking at what was his, an orchard gone wild, a rutted driveway, a strange car under the apple tree, the side of his logging truck, the rust streak on its passenger door, the one broken headlight he'd been going to fix for the past two years, the ribs, spine, hooves, and horns of a deer kill he'd made in spring just beyond in the dusty grass, and the hills across the valley rising brown toward a waning moon they couldn't reach, not yet.

Tom could see the pistol in Eddy's hand and Eddy standing there over the old man's body as the sounds of the rifle and pistol receded to echoing whimpers, Eddy surely thinking the shots were nothing at the edge of town. A pit-lamped deer feeding on windfall apples or a coyote crept too close to the house in search of rats was just another night-kill. Night shooting just made anyone hearing it from afar huddle down a little deeper in their beds. And then Harry covering the body with a blanket, pulling the bed out from the wall to hide the body, and then going through the chest of drawers, him hissing his excitement, a white pill clenched in his teeth.

Tom knelt on the floor beside the old man. A single splinter of pine leaned into the man's nostril. It was a small and perfect thing, a tiny, remnant tree sticking up out of the worn floor. A clot of nose hairs curved around the pale of the wood needle. A bloat of blood welled from the hole where the bullet had gone into the old man's temple. He rested there, one foot on top of the other, the sole Tom could see, a hard orange. The calluses were ridged moons on the bottom of his foot, the one big toe with a nail curved over, cliffs and valleys in the deep lines of horn runnelled with dirt.

He stood up and began looking for the rifle, but couldn't find it anywhere, not in the bedroom or in any of the other rooms. The flashlight played across the floor as he hunted for the other shell. There had to be one. He got down on his hands and knees, finally finding the last one in a corner. He put it in his pocket with the other one, the clink of the brass a tiny bell. He didn't know if the pistol Eddy used ejected its shells. He looked hard, but couldn't find any.

He heard a truck go by on the road. Hands shaking, hurried now, he ran down the hall and grabbed a towel from the bathroom. He lifted the head, a gout of blood swelling in the hole, congealing there. He wrapped the towel around it and dragged the pillowcase down over the face. Then he rolled the body in the bedsheets and the blanket, binding it all with butcher string he found in a kitchen drawer. He tied it tight around the ankles, the soles of the feet sticking out below the knot. He wanted it all to be over. He went to the kitchen and came back with some damp rags and cleaned the floor as best he could, jamming the soiled cloths into the winding sheets. Then he dragged the body down the hall to the front porch. He walked back down the hall with the flashlight, leaning over, making sure there were no smears of blood left there, and then he went out onto the porch and closed the front door behind him.

He backed the truck to the porch steps, turned off the engine, got out, and humped the body down the steps to the truck box. He lifted the head and shoulders onto the tailgate, struggling awkwardly with the hips and legs, finally hefting them in, the body heavier than he'd imagined. He shut the tailgate and covered the body with the tarp from behind the back seat, mounding branches from the brush pile he'd seen at the corner of the house on top of it. He gripped his fist tight as he got back into the truck, his hurt hand pounding.

He drove down the undulating road past the gravel pit, his lights out, navigating by the moon, passing by the boundary lines of fences, and the gaping cellar of a burned-out, abandoned house. He could smell the old man's body on his hands. He drifted past mown fields with their scattered bales of late alfalfa. The air whistled through the branches piled in the back of the truck. He turned left at the crossroad, taking the back road to Black Rock and home, and then he saw headlights coming up the road he'd just turned off. He wondered who'd be driving that way so late. Uneasy, he pulled over. Through the rear window and the fret of branches, he made out the white and black markings of a police car as it went past the corner, heading toward the hill he'd just come down. He broke into a sudden sweat.

He had to see for himself what he feared. Tom did a fast U-turn and went back the way he'd come, driving by the moon and the feel of his tires on the road, weeds and ditches going by on his left, then the gravel pit with its ghostly vehicles, the red tail-lights of the police car far ahead of him, guiding him back to where he'd been. At the top of the hill, he slowed and watched the car turn into the driveway of the old man's house, the trees swallowing it.

He coasted partway down the hill and turned off a few hundred yards from the butcher shop where there was a break in a farm fence, rolling through the high grass and coming to a stop behind a pile of ruined apple boxes.

Getting quietly out of the truck, he ran across the field and clambered over the fence that bordered on the old man's property. He crept through the trees off to the side and lay down behind a loose stack of cut wood, the smell of the fox he'd seen earlier redolent on the split rounds, the smell stinging his nostrils, belly churning, his heart pounding against his ribs.

In front of the truck was the police car, and Sergeant Stanley was standing by the front fender. Tom stared at him, this man who had wreaked torment upon his brother. He brought malice with him wherever he went and Tom wondered what his being there would lead to.

Stanley was looking at the house, no uniform on, his off-duty belt buckle shining. He was on his own sweet own with his bare arms, his jeans and cowboy boots, his black brush cut and pencil-thin moustache. Then the dome light went on in the car and he saw Crystal sitting in the front seat fluffing her blonde hair and looking bored. Was it Crystal who'd brought Stanley here? And why? She'd seen Eddy and Harry talking in the gravel pit earlier, but that was all. She hadn't heard them talking. No, someone else told the police to come out here. She'd just gone along with him for a night ride into the hills. What kind of dream could she have that she'd go anywhere with Stanley?

The Sergeant's boots stubbed up the porch steps, and he knocked on the front door. He waited a second and then knocked again, his hand on the doorknob. After a few moments he opened the door and went in. Those snakeskin boots were walking the same rooms Tom had walked, but Tom knew there was nothing in the house to tell Stanley any of them had been there. All he could know was that for some reason the old man was gone. Go ahead and poke among pork chop bones and blackened peas, Tom thought. Look under the bed. There's nothing there to find.

He unclenched his fist, the tear in his palm pulling open a little. Stanley's flashlight flickered in the window of the living room where the old man had waited for his intruders to come in. And then the light disappeared. Tom imagined Stanley going into the kitchen and down the hallway to the bedroom where the old man had died. Then, for a moment, he saw the Sergeant pass by the bedroom window, a shifting glow and shadows. After a few minutes, the front door opened and Stanley came out onto the porch.

The crickets stilled. Tom glanced over at Crystal in the interior light of the car, looking in the rear-view mirror as she put lipstick on, her blonde hair curled around her face. The Sergeant came down off the porch, and got in the driver's seat. He said something to Crystal, she laughed, and the squad car pulled out on the road and headed back toward town.

———

When Tom was finished digging, he rested the blade on the floor of the grave. His hand had started bleeding again, and he pulled the makeshift bandage tighter. The piled dirt on either side rose over his head and shoulders, the grave's lip at the midline of his chest, his pick part-buried by the last dirt he'd thrown out. He pushed the shovel blade into the side of the pile, pulled himself up and out. The last boulder had come out of the grave like a tooth from a jaw. It teetered on the edge of the hole as the sky bore down on him. Orion hung in the dark, the great hunter wheeling on his back as if he were falling into the southern horizon.

After he got the old man's body out of the truck and into the wheelbarrow, he pushed him toward the orchard, the iron wheel of the barrow grating on the path. Father floated in the air just beyond his eyes. He tried to banish him with thoughts of anything, the sky, the stars, but when he got to the well he stopped and stared at the spot where Father had lain. Eddy's words came back to him, Eddy saying over and over that Tom had to stop remembering. He closed his eyes and thought of his sisters. Alice, Little Rose, and his half-sister, the baby he never saw, but for a towel and a fire burning.

He was angry at his brother and the mess he'd got them into. Eddy had lost whatever control he might've known. He had passed through some door and there was only destruction in the room he found himself in. He trundled the wheelbarrow over the uneven ground, past the water of the creek to the orchard. When he got to the grave, he lifted the handles high and the old man slid headfirst into the hole.

Tom rolled the tooth stone in, and then the shovelling of the gravel, clay, and clods, and last, the desiccated grass which he had carefully cut square by square, replacing it now in the same design. He tamped the grass down lightly, not wanting to bruise the frail roots. The first spring rains would green the grave.

He put the shovel and pick in the wheelbarrow and started back to the house, stopping at the well. This is where he'd sat after Father died, on a night that felt the same as this night, but for the coolness. There were the same stars in the sky, the same moon. Tom breathed in deep as if there wasn't enough air in the world to keep him alive. *Blood is blood and sometimes better gone*. That's what Mother had said that night.

He looked down at the few apples withering at his feet and remembered how once Father had showed him the star hidden inside the apple's flesh. He had plucked an apple from a high branch, one that hadn't been touched by scab or worm. He held it in his palm and took his knife and sliced it across the centre the wrong way. Father parted the halves and held them open, the flesh white against the rim of red, a star in each half, the bronze seeds buried in the heart.

He was walking again, steel handles in his hands, the iron wheel grinding. He rested the barrow against the porch at the back of the house, bracing the handles up under the wind-worn siding. He stretched and looked up at the dark window of Eddy's room.

At the water drum he took off his shirt and draped it over the end of the dead raspberry canes near the corner of the house, and unwound the filthy cloth from his hand. He bent over and pulled water up in gouts, washing it over his face, his shoulders and chest. On a cedar shingle by the barrel was a chunk of soap, its dried pores scored with dirt. Tom rubbed it into his hand, the bits of clinging grit a scour in the ripped skin where he'd been hurt, a bit of blood seeping there. He leaned deep into the drum, pushing his head under the brackish water. A dead frog drifted by his eyes as he went under, its outspread limbs supplicant. He looked past it and swung his head from side to side. Suddenly, he felt two small hands coming gently around him, circling his waist. They brushed across the bare skin of his belly. He went stiff against the steel of the drum, a wet cold against his heat. The hands moved up, pulling hard on his nipples, then went to his belt. He felt it unbuckle and the buttons of his jeans come loose and then Marilyn's fist was tight around him. She stroked once, twice, and at the third Tom faded away, his head lifting from the drum, his knees buckling, water in a shower flowing from his thrown hair.

12

Who named me?

I named you. Listen, I've told you this story so many times. Father came out of the bedroom with you wrapped loose in a towel. He held you high as Mother cursed him. Her outrage was thick in the room. There was a strange woman in her bed. She was your mother. Her brown hair was splayed across the pillow in heavy tangles and her white hand was by the sheet, plucking at the cotton, worrying itself there. Tom was by the door staring at two tiny feet sticking out from the towel. When Father saw him, he herded Tom down the hall with his knees. You were the wrapped baby above Father's head, a wet thing flying there. He shouted at Tom: Get out! Get the hell outside!

Was she pretty?

Your mother? She was beautiful beyond the pain she had.

Who was she?

She was a woman who lived in an old cabin under the hills below Silver Star Mountain. She had moved to the valley a year or two before she met Father, a woman who'd come from the ashes of Europe. She'd known men before in the war, but here she'd stayed by herself away from others until Father came along with his smile and his red hair. One day he was passing by and offered her a ride in his truck. She was carrying two small canvas bags of eggs and a clutch of wildflowers, all to sell door to door in town. How she got the chickens is anybody's guess. She told him she walked the five miles every Monday and Friday. The next week Father was there waiting for her on the Monday morning, his truck parked by the ditch, the side door open like a gift. She was dirt poor, but then so many were. I don't think she had any family here. She never said. The cabin was a deserted one left over from another time, some prospector down on his luck built it, or it was a line-cabin from the ranching days when the miners came south to try their hand at cattle after losing most of what they had in the gold fields of Barkerville. It was pine logs and rotting shakes. She patched the roof with cedar she split with a hammer and froe and put in panes of glass where they'd been broken. There was a two-plate stove bound with haywire and sitting on field stones, the stove fed with dead wood she gathered in the hills. The Indians from the head of the lake had helped her through that first winter. They gave her meat, fish, salt, and flour, and dried Saskatoon berries and blueberries from the meadows. She'd lived there for three years when Father first saw her.

What did she look like?

She was tall for a woman back then, her long brown hair woven into a single braid, the feathered end curved up as if trying to be a wing. Brown eyes set deep, dark as wild chestnuts, and cheekbones so high you'd think there was some Eastern blood in her. She had an easy walk, long-legged as she was in the drifting woollen skirts she'd made from cut-up army blankets she'd begged from the Salvation Army down on Tronson Avenue. She was pretty in a country kind of way, her skin fresh as the spring water she washed in. Troubled, yes, for who knew what grief she'd seen during the war. What she saw in Father was only hers to know. Perhaps she thought she'd found some love in herself for a man in what to her was a new place.

And Father?

Maybe she was someone he imagined from the days when he wandered the prairie, living as she did in that cabin up under the mountain. Maybe she was beautiful to him. But what she was doesn't matter. In the end, Father always broke whatever was close. Men get impatient with things they can't get around.

I never knew, said Starry Night.

Mother had started to clean the woman, wiping her thighs with a towel she dipped in a basin filled with hot water from the stove. The afterbirth had come, and Mother was wrapping it in a piece of old newspaper. She'd yelled at Father when he put the woman in her bed: You bugger, you damned bugger!

She'd helped in your birthing, all the while cursing Elmer for what he'd brought down on her and her house. To

Father, an illegitimate child, a bastard, was a miserable thing, but to bring the very woman to Mother's bed and ask for her help? And her his wife, the mother of his sons. Still, she was washing the woman clean. She remembered her own birthing, and no matter her anger at such a betrayal, his bringing your mother into her own house and throwing one of his get in her face, she couldn't leave a woman in a man's hands. Not at the last. She said that night that Elmer had never helped her once in all the days and nights of their lives. It was such an effrontery, such an insult to her who had birthed her own, Tom and Eddy, Little Rose and me. Yet she'd accepted the woman when he drove in from wherever he'd had her when the pains came. Mother had told him to take her into the house when Father appeared at the kitchen door, your mother moaning as he held her up. Eddy sat in the corner of the kitchen, watching as his father helped her through the door. At the first sound from her, he fled to the stairs and his room. Tom kept asking who she was, and Father, desperate, drove Tom out of the bedroom. He crept back down the hall to watch and listen as your mother cried out on the bed, the pains coming hard and fast.

Father just shifted from one boot to the other at the end of the bed, staring, his cap with the broken bill stupid in his hands, wanting what was happening to never have happened, wanting the birth to be over so things could be as they'd been. It wasn't so much that he wanted to be free to gallivant about, but that he knew the woman on the bed loved him and he didn't understand her wanting him and then wanting the baby too, one of his, and what that would do to them all, to him. No, he wanted the baby gone. He'd learned how to put things behind him the day he walked away from the sister I was named for. He was good at denying things.

When your mother was in the bedroom, Eddy came back downstairs and sat near the front door on the couch in the living room, his fingers twined together in a knot. He wanted no part of what was going on. Your birth was to him yet another madness of his parents' ways. Eddy was afraid of his own fear. He could hear everything just as Tom could, the cries of your mother as she bore down, the curses from Mother, telling him he had to get rid of the baby when it came. I'll not have your bastard in this town to shame me. You'll get rid of it or else!

Did she mean for him to take me to the orchard?

Mother just wanted you gone. She was so angry at what he'd done.

Your mother lay on the bed and told them in her broken English not to take her baby away when it came, but what could she say or do, Mother holding her down, telling her to push. When you came in that blood flow from her womb, Mother lifted you onto a towel, tied you off with a bit of twine, the cord that bound you to your mother cut with a paring knife, and then Father took what she had birthed and left the room. Your mother cried out to him, but Father never turned.

What did she say?

She said: My baby, my baby!

That was me.

Tom ran ahead past the bathroom and out the back door onto the porch. The fly-swatter was on top of the wood-box and he grabbed it as he went by. There were one hundred and eighty-two dead flies lying on the floor. Your brother had counted every one like he always did. Kill the gawdam flies, Father had told him in the afternoon. He had counted them out loud when he slapped with the swatter, sometimes two, three, or five at a time. His record was nine at one blow. Their bodies crunched under his feet as he ran, the fly-swatter in his hand.

Bright stars glittered in the heavens. Get in the damned truck, Father said, following behind, and Tom did. He ran to the truck, opened the passenger door, and scrambled in as Father banged the door shut with his knee. Stay to hell in there, he said.

Your father slid past the shed and down the slope to the well, the light-blue towel flapping as he disappeared over the creek. When he was gone into the orchard, Tom slipped out of the truck. The gravel under his bare feet was still warm even though the sun had fallen. He whipped the fly-swatter at the moon as if with a whisk he could put it out.

I watched as he walked slowly on the grass along the shed wall past the root cellar and down to the well. He was so little to be seeing what he did.

The well cap shone, the grey boards silvered by the stars. Tom was huddled down there watching. Father was piling dry branches, wilted grass he tore from the ground, and blackened straw he'd busted out of a discarded bale, loops of binder twine twisted in his blunt hands. When he was done, there was a mound and he placed the small bundle he was carrying on top of the pile, covered it with more straw, and lit it, jumping back when the flames licked their way up the stems.

I don't remember if I cried, said Starry Night.

Never mind now.

When the fire rose up, Father went for another bale and cut the twine with his knife. He threw mouldy straw on the crinkled flare of blue cotton burning and the flames went dark, smoke billowing out like one of Mother's dresses on the clothesline caught by wind. The moon was orange. Father circled the fire like some animal both attracted and repelled by its light. He watched it burn. Every few minutes he left to gather sticks and bits of broken flume and fallen fence posts to add to the pyre. When he did, the flames burned cleaner. Father was beyond thought. He was rippled through the flames.

Tom whispered the one word: Fire. He was burrowed into the tall grass by the well, a mouse hiding from the sky.

That's when Eddy came down from the house. He found Tom and took him by the arm and led him back. Tom said that Father told him he had to stay in the truck, so Eddy put him there. He closed the truck door, went around the house, and was gone toward town. The sound of his bike tires was a dry hiss on the packed clay road.

What about my mother?

After the fire died down, Father stood by the ash and coals until he heard Mother call him from the yard. When he came up from the orchard, she asked him where the baby was. He told her and she struck him with her fists. What have you gone and done? And she said it again: What have you done? He went past her into the house and brought the woman out to the truck, Mother helping her down the back steps. He put her on the seat beside Tom, who was crouching there. The last thing Mother said to the woman was to forget she ever had a child. There was no baby, Mother said.

Where did they go?

Away. Back to the place she came from. Your mother wasn't a girl, she was a woman alone, a foreigner, living in an old cabin up in the hills under the mountain in the between place where the pines stop and the hemlock starts. It's all meadows there. She was a stranger, and Father said she went back to a strange place. Tom couldn't tell because he didn't know where they went except to say it was north up the Spallumcheen. They were night riding, the truck careening down the back roads and up the valley into the far hills. He sat between the two of them, frightened, tapping the fly-swatter on the dashboard until Father tore it from his hands and threw it out the window. It was night and the woman was there in the truck beside Tom, crying. She didn't speak, Father cursing as he drove wild into the mountains. And her, your mother? She didn't know where her baby had gone. She asked only once, but Father wouldn't tell her. How could he say to her what he had done?

13

he big saws screamed, steel teeth biting into the log rolled onto the head-rig by two gaunt men with peevees, and the drive belts whined, high and distorted by the heavy grunts of the diesels. Cants slammed into the edger, the bite of the saws eating through wood, the sawdust behind them a fountain spray, and the new log on the head-rig set and jammed into the great saw, the slab carved off, its bark scabbed and shredding. The sawyer pulled the drop lever for the bin and the slab fell onto a bed of raw sawdust in the metal trench below, the chain bearing the refuse to the beehive burner and the flames. The piston dogs flipped the log over and it was pulled back past the saw and thrust forward again, the bite of the saw-teeth a sound beyond sound, and everywhere chains and belts shoving logs and cants and lumber through the mill, the trim saws with their insect whine, men at their machines, the horrible *clank clank clank* beating steady under the screams and whistles. Raw wood, heavy and green with sap, two-by-fours, sixes, and eights, spaghetti lumber to be sent south into the maw of the States, trundled down through the trim saws and clattered onto the long chains that carried the wood out into the heat of the sun where the men in their draw slots, shirts off, boots braced in dirt and dust, pulled the boards across the chain and into the lumber stacks, rows and piles growing. The forklift thundered as Carl Janek lifted the stacks away, the half-naked men on the line beginning another pile. The lumber poured from the mill, and, hands in gloves or bare and calloused, the men on the chain reached out and pulled the boards off, a continuous, almost desperate task that had no end, the men's curses unheard amid the moans and misery of the shift, the edger howling and the head saw howling as the blade tore into another log.

Chooksa Three-Horns worked the head of the chain, straightening out awkward pieces of wood when they came down crooked, all of the boards bumping along the creak and crank of hauling metal, the spoked teeth of the iron wheels pulling the lumber down the thirty-foot bed. Tom stood across from the new man, Wlad Kirkowski, at the tail end where the two-by-fours were stacked, the Cruikshank brothers and the other men working the bigger dimension piles ahead of them, Chooksa stepping in here and there when he was needed to sort out a mess when they got behind.

There was no roof over the chain and the morning sun ate its way into the aluminum hard hat on Tom's head, the heat heavy on his skull. Sweat poured down his face and across his bare shoulders, his chest filmed with ash and dust as he pulled the two-by-fours into their piles. The boards rolled toward Tom in their hundreds and he'd long ago taken off the leather glove on his good hand so he could work faster, his skin sticky with the bleed of sap. His torn hand with its new bandage was sore, but he could still hold a plank, the fingers bent into a curl, his leather thumb pressing down on the wood. His arms dragged boards and shucked them into the piles, four feet wide and four feet tall. When a pile was finished, Carl would come on the forklift and take it away, the machine's gears grinding. Then another pile and another, Tom never slowing down, and Wlad, who'd been hired out of the bar just before the shutdown, bitching breath after breath, *fuck, fucking Jesus*, the cries of a new man at his terrible work.

Tom's head was thick and churning slow. On the chain, his body repeated itself, not as a machine does but as bone and muscle do, each move he made identical and not, each board coming down the chain a variation upon every other board whether cut from the rim or the heart of a tree, his portion the quota set for him, the volume seemingly twice what a man could reasonably manage. At the end of the chain was a metal bumper where the boards he had rejected, split, knotted, warped, and broken, clattered and tumbled against a wall of iron.

The forklift hefted a pile of lumber and backed up, Carl's shout lost in the cries from the mill, his arm raised and waving as he grinned and rode away. At that moment, Carl looked the same to Tom as the day he had first seen him.

Tom had been a kid then, out hunting with Docker. He'd passed by the farm many times before and heard dogs barking. The hayfields behind the barn would have been a good place to find birds, but he'd always gone on by, not wanting to be caught trespassing. Then one Sunday he was on the trail in the trees above the farmyard and heard a noise, metal clanking, then someone cursing, and he'd come out to the field and looked down the hill. A tall man in overalls with brown, funny-looking hair, kind of long over his ears, was lying on his back under the engine of a red tractor, his tools laid out on a square of canvas, and Tom had crouched behind a bush and watched, his dog beside him. After a while, he went back down to the trail and crossed up to the road and headed home.

A troubled whistle burned the air and the diesels lurched for the briefest moment, an almost silence, and then the chain in front of him, which had barely halted, jerked and began again its grind of metal, the lumber tumbling, and the scream of the saws on the mill floor reiterating their complaint. He rested the end of a new board on his gloved palm and his good hand pulled it in one smooth motion, the blunt wood running across his glove and disappearing behind him as it found its place on the stack. As it rattled into place his injured hand was already cupping the next board and the next, two, sometimes three at a time, all pulled back in a single motion, a perfect dance done only with his hips and upper body, his legs spread slightly. His boots were planted in the grooves he had made in the deck over the four years he'd worked there. The foreman had told him he could get off the chain any time and onto the mill floor, but he'd turned him down so he could stay where he was in a job that was mindless, without thought or feeling.

As the boards slipped through his hands, he found himself again on Carl's farm, in a clearing back in the trees where there was a graveyard with stones marking small mounds. The stone Tom liked best had a word incised in the stone, DOBRA, with two dates below, 1948–1952. Under the numbers was carved: BRAVER HART NEVER WAS.

All of a sudden Docker barked and Tom heard someone behind him. He turned and saw the man who'd been working on the tractor the week before. He leaned down and took hold of Docker's collar and the dog quieted. He knew he shouldn't be there, but the man didn't yell at him. Instead he began to talk softly to Tom about a dog he'd raised, one who'd died in a fight two years before. It sounded like he was speaking as much to himself as to Tom, pointing at this grave or that, each animal buried there a story that needed telling. Tom had stayed in the shadow of an old cedar and watched as the man paused in front of one of the graves and called Tom over. When Tom sidled up, the man told him the grave was the resting place of Wintered Jim, a dog named, he said, for the saddle of snow-white hair across his shoulders, a brindle pit bull who'd died the year before, fighting up in Kamloops.

He spoke quietly as Tom, unsure, came closer. The man patted the grave with his hand in much the same way as he might have patted the dog when it was alive. Tom thought for a brief second that Wintered Jim might come alive again and rise out of the ground to lick the man's hand. Beside Tom was Docker, his dog's small body straining to be let go. And then the man glanced at the four fat Blue grouse hanging from Tom's shoulder, and said to him how the hunting must have been good, talking to him while Docker circled them barking in play, his dog trusting this man. He told Tom his name and asked Tom what his was. Tom said his name and then he told him what he'd seen that day in the hills and up the mountain: black-bear tracks in the mud above an irrigation ditch, coyote scat on the trail, a goshawk stooping to take a gopher. He told him too of his family and where he lived, but that was later on that fall.

Each Sunday he'd climb the mountain to hunt in the high meadows, returning in the afternoon to sit quietly on the hill, Docker waiting beside him, half-crazed with love for Carl, who always had bits of dried venison he kept to treat his fighting dogs in the kennels behind the barn, a few small strips and chunks secreted away to give to Docker when they came. Sometimes Carl and Tom would talk, but it was mostly about the weather or a crop, a machine broken down or a dog Carl thought would do well in some fight coming up. Carl showed him where coveys of quail took dust baths and pheasants hunted beetles and bugs, a clearing at the mouth of a nearby gully where Spruce grouse fed on fallen seeds and berries. Every time Tom came, Carl asked how he was doing and Tom always told him about something he'd seen or done.

Most Sundays, Carl would be out by the barn working on the tractor or the truck, his wrenches laid out beside his toolbox and in his lap some part he was working on, a generator or starter, some piece of the motor or drive train. Tom would come out from the trees and let Docker go and Carl would stop what he was doing when he saw the dog. He'd give Docker a bit of dried meat and then Tom would walk toward him, over his shoulder the grouse or pheasants he always brought as gifts for Carl and his wife, Irma. Carl would take the offered birds, telling him what a good hunter he was and then they'd walk to the house, Carl carrying the birds, Docker whining at their heels, wanting to go around back to the kennels where the other dogs were barking.

Carl and Irma's lives were bound by simplicity, their clear belief in things they could touch and smell and taste. They were by themselves on the farm, their children grown up and gone, but they never seemed to be lonely. They became people he learned to almost trust.

Later that first autumn, Tom began to come to the farm at dawn before he started to hunt the mountain. He'd arrive at sunrise, and find Carl in the kitchen putting crumpled paper and kindling into the wood stove and lighting it with a stick match from the red and white tin box on the wall, the one with little painted roses on it Irma had mentioned that she'd bought at Mac & Mac Hardware. She told him she liked it because it was so cheery.

Carl would set a kettle on the stove plate to heat up for coffee, busying about, putting out cups along with a small jar of fresh cream from the new refrigerator he'd bought when the money came in from the last hay crop. Turning to the cupboard, he'd take down the silver sugar bowl that used to belong to Irma's mother, then open the wooden chest that held the set of South Seas silverware he said he'd won at the regional curling bonspiel in 1949. He told Tom they liked to start each Sunday with their best spoons.

Then Tom would head up the mountain, only to return in the late afternoon with his gift of birds. He'd see the smoke coming from the chimney of the house from far off, and know that Irma was there in the kitchen, a batch of fresh bread cooling on the windowsill. He'd sit on the porch and she'd feed him slices of warm bread and strawberry jam.

The break whistle cut off the saws abruptly, and the green-chain shuddered to a stop, the mill floor silent, the thin keening left in the air a diminution of sound that dwindled to nothing, the sudden whine of a black hornet cutting through the air by Tom's ear. He straightened his back, trying to find the original curve of his bones. He pressed his fists against his hips, and then reached for the canvas water sack hanging from the nail on the shadow side of a post. He took a long drink, dropped his hard hat on a pile of lumber, and held the bag over his head, the cool water pouring onto his skull, cascading down across his shoulders and torso. The water scored the ash and dust on his skin in dirty rivulets to his belt where it soaked into his pants, a dark stain spreading down his groin.

Tom wiped his face on the sleeve of the shirt he'd left hanging from a nail on the post. A fifteen-minute break. His hand was throbbing now, the bandage wet inside his glove. He looked up as Chooksa waved his thermos at him, pointing into the shade behind a lumber pile, but Tom ignored the offer. He walked instead across the mill yard toward the lake, charred sawdust and ash sifting out of the air and settling on his skin. He could hear a last slab fall into the burner, a heavy thud as the long chunk of wood and bark hit the fire. The flames in the beehive never stopped, the mill refuse running up the bunker chain to the square cut in the sheet metal high in the iron sheathing. What wasn't consumed rode the plume of heat and smoke out through the cracked and broken shelter screen. Charred motes of wood rode the wind and settled upon the fields that surrounded the mill. The end of the lake was adrift with it. It floated there, a mottled sludge of partly burned wood until, finally water-logged, it sank to the bottom. Across the lake was the outfall from Carson's Creek.

He'd fished there with Eddy when they were kids. They'd head up the creek into the piney hills. Royal Coachmen were hooked to the collars of their shirts, their leader wrapped around pine sticks. He remembered how Eddy would cast into the pools under the dead-falls. Tom would sometimes hang his arm into the current by the bank and wait for the trout to lie up in the shadows against his wrist. He'd stroke their bellies with his fingers, rainbows and cutthroats in his hands. Tom stared down into the murky water, thoughts of his brother muddled in his head.

He remembered the night Eddy came home from the coast, how the year before, Father and Mother and he had come back from the train station in silence, Mother going into the kitchen and standing there at the sink as if cast in stone, and Father staying outside and lifting the hood of the truck, a case of beer cooling in the shade of the fender, greasy wrenches and screwdrivers strewn across the gravel. It was as if his brother had become a ghost, someone made up, a lost brother Tom had dreamt. He remembered the tense quiet of month following month, no word said, the silence so thick it buried them all. And then, the next summer, he had woken in the late hours of a warm night and knew Eddy was coming home. It was a feeling so deep in his blood that Tom felt if he reached out into the darkness of his room he could touch his brother's skin.

He remembered crawling naked from his bed and creeping downstairs, his feet finding their way on the edges by the wall where there were no creaks to warn his father that he was awake. Once out the screen door, he ran up the driveway and climbed the old fir tree, his hands and bare feet moving limb to limb, pulling his body higher and higher until he reached the last huge unbroken branch and laid himself down on it.

The far hills were a heavy blue, the pines in the arroyo shadows, their green so deep it seemed they were underwater. He could see the hills and below them the squat glow of the town. He lay there on the tree limb for a long time, and then just before dawn Eddy walked up over the hill on the road a half mile away. His brother had come back, the life that had stopped a year ago starting again.

Tom gritted his teeth now, angry, as if such thinking was a weakness in him. He undid his pants and took a piss, water frothing at his boots. Out on the other side of the lake he saw a flock of mallards among the cattails in the shallows.

The birds were feeding through their last days, their migration just a week or two away when they'd track the stars on their night journey down the mountain trenches and through the vast deserts to the coasts of Texas and Mexico. Go on now, he muttered. The mallards ignored him, turning tails up as they tore at the soft bulrush shoots buried in the mud below. He did up his pants and stared into the brown, baked hills to the south and west.

The whistle blew its warning and Tom turned away from the lake and walked back to the mill. The green-chain jerked into life and began its long, steady clanking. It was mid-morning, six more hours of work before he could finally go home. Lumber that had been piled up at the barrier began to rattle, a tangle of cracked and broken two-by-fours. He stepped up, placed his feet in the grooves, and heard Carl come up behind him in the forklift.

Hey, Tom, he shouted.

Tom straightened a few wayward boards in the pile beside him and waved. Carl was heavier than he used to be when he'd first seen him years ago at the farm.

He watched him climb down off the machine and take off his hard hat as he came over to the chain.

Carl stroked his damp hair back on his head. You're looking kind of troubled, he said. You okay?

It's nothing, Tom said as he pulled and stacked the lumber.

There's been some talk in town, Carl said, about that party out at your house.

Things have been a little crazy lately, said Tom, grabbing a wayward board.

So I've heard, said Carl. He told Tom people had been talking about some guy getting shot.

Tom pulled two more boards off and slid them onto the pile. Yeah, yeah, it wasn't that big a deal, he said, more lumber stumbling toward him down the chain.

Carl looked sombre as he climbed back up on the forklift. You take it easy, he shouted, and Tom nodded as he bent to the chain deck.

We're okay, he said to himself, almost believing it, as Carl moved away with a full stack of two-by-fours, his hard hat tipped back as he waved.

14

marilyn pushed the bucket full of soapy water forward and leaned into the rough cloth she held in her fists, scouring the floor to the side of the stove. The flensing knife she'd found in a drawer to scrape off the greasy dirt from the cracks in the old linoleum stuck out of the pocket of the apron she'd found in the closet in the crib room. The apron had hung in there probably for years, the edges where it was folded gone yellow from time. It was embroidered with bluebirds, two on either side, each one bearing in its faded beak a twist of ivy, leaves twining under their wings. When she'd tied it around her waist in the morning, it had been clean.

She'd already taken the dishes out of the cupboards and wiped the shelves and then under the sink, the floor soft where the drain went down, a thick smell of damp rising. She'd scoured it there as best she could, leaving the doors open so the wood might dry a little, and then started on the floor. She ignored Tom's mother, who had come out of her room, covered in a shapeless dress. She seemed so much older than her own mother, the skin on the woman's hands and face lined and worn, her hair with so much grey in it. She sat now on a kitchen chair, a mug of coffee clasped in her hands as she watched Marilyn drag the cloth across the floor.

I put those birds on that apron when I was a girl a lot younger than you, she said, her voice loud. I cut and sewed and hemmed it and then I embroidered those birds.

Mother went on as if talking to herself, her voice adrift. It was a bird I'd seen before, she said, not like the ones in *Ladies Home Companion*. My mother always borrowed the magazine from a woman on the farm down the road. The bluebirds in it were nothing like the ones we had around our place.

She was still for a moment as she sucked on her cigarette.

They're pretty enough, Marilyn said.

Mother seemed to her to hesitate then, as if wondering why this girl was talking, least of all to her. Marilyn watched her puff at the stub of cigarette that was stuck in the corner of her mouth. I used to be good with a needle and thread, Mother said. She picked up her mug and swirled the coffee around. This coffee's watery and it's barely warm too. Why don't you push that pot over onto the front of the stove. It won't get hot where you've got it sitting.

Marilyn wrung out her cloth in the pan beside her and began scrubbing again as she tried to ignore the woman, but Mother kept on.

I wanted that apron to be nice. Marilyn looked up and

nodded, but Mother's gaze was turned from her to the window as if she was speaking to the mountain looming there. If my girls had lived, I'd have given that apron to one of them, she said. My girls are dead, you know. She hesitated and added: A darkness took me up when they were born. I couldn't see for it.

The coarse weave of cloth ground down in endless circles in front of Marilyn, the woman on the chair going on, in her voice a vague reflecting Marilyn had heard before when her grandmother was alive and talked of the old days. Marilyn looked down at her hands as they scrubbed, a pattern on the linoleum rising from the grey froth, flowers repeating themselves, red ones, roses it looked like, the outline of them worn away by the boots and shoes and feet that had stood at the sink and stove over the years. Here and there a flower appeared, an outline only, the colour mostly gone.

Mother lifted her mug, looking like she was trying to follow the brown geese flying around the rim. Stupid birds, she said. They never get it right. Not these geese and not those bluebirds either. The ones we had on the prairie were pure blue and not ones with rosy breasts. She continued to look out at the fields.

I don't remember my girls much. I just wanted to be left alone in my bed. I think it was Father told me they passed on, or was it Tom? He'd have known. He was in that room with Alice night and day. Tom's always wanted to be around things that can't be fixed. It's just like that dog he used to have. He sure loved that dog, she said, and started fussing with her dress.

Marilyn stared at her, the cloth in her hand.

What're you looking at me for? That dog of his died a long time ago. She pushed at her mug, the coffee slopping onto the table. Things just went wrong, she said, no help from anyone.

Marilyn took the knife from her apron pocket and began scraping at the floor.

Oh, forget it, Mother said sharply. She stopped for a moment and fanned her face with her hand. I liked the meadowlarks best. When I was a girl, boys used to sneak up on their nests and shoot them with slingshots. There was this one boy from down the road who was always doing that. His people were foreigners. They're like that.

There aren't hardly any bluebirds around here, said Mother. They've all died off from something. People from town keep putting up nesting boxes on the fence posts along the road, but it doesn't bring them back. That boy now, I remember him. He had a mean look around his eyes. I think they were from Germany. There were lots of Germans around after the war, but you'd never know it.

Marilyn sat back and looked at Mother's narrow blue eyes. She seemed wily now, some kind of cunning in her.

Mother rubbed her cheek with the back of her wrist, opened the tobacco can, and started rolling another cigarette.

Marilyn leaned back down and started scrubbing the floor again.

Keep scrubbing like that, Mother said, and you'll wear your way through that floor right into the dirt, wolf spiders and god-knows-what under the house in the crawl space coming up to bite you. Likely snakes too.

Marilyn got up and pushed two more pieces of wood into the stove. She glanced over and saw Mother staring out the window again. Nothing was different out there since the last time she looked, Marilyn thought. The mountain was still there, just like it'd always been. Who knew what she was thinking? She carried the bucket to the back and threw the dirty water out onto the gravel. A breeze shivered the needles on the old fir tree at the head of the driveway. The mountain was blocking the early light, the rising sun still hidden from the side of the house, the driveway in shadow. Tom and me are going to be fine, she thought. It's going to be different around here. I'm going to be living in this house. She'll just have to put up with it. She turned her head and looked for a moment at Tom's mother sitting with a new cigarette wedged into the corner of her mouth, smouldering there.

I don't know why that mountain hasn't got a name, Mother said, distracted. That's the trouble with things around here. Nobody knows what anything is called.

Marilyn pretended she didn't hear her, leaned down, and picked up a shard of broken rock lying on the edge of the step and turned it in her fingers. She remembered when she was a little girl and her mother was cleaning houses for the rich people up on the hill. There was that time she'd been given a sweater by the mother of one of her classmates. The daughter had thrown it on the floor and the girl's mother said she didn't deserve to own the sweater if she treated it like that, and Marilyn had worn it to school the next day. It was a nice sweater, powder blue with short sleeves that puffed out at the shoulders. It was too big for her, but she wore it anyway. And then in the lunchroom the girl told everyone it was hers, saying Marilyn's mother had stolen it. Marilyn never wore that sweater again, not even at home. She threw the rock out onto the gravel reach, the bit of stone bouncing twice and then vanishing among the other rocks, indistinguishable from every other pebble around it.

She went back into the house and filled the bucket with warm water from the tap, heating it up from the seething kettle on the stove.

A drink of whiskey would be nice, Mother said. Just a sip or two to settle my stomach and calm my nerves. I get so tired all the time. I worry too. Where's Eddy? He didn't come home last night.

I don't know, Marilyn said.

It's damned hot, said Mother. Don't you think it's time you stopped feeding that stove?

Marilyn ignored her now, her arms straight as she pushed hard with the cloth, the job almost done. She'd finished the floor in front of the stove and was working at what was left of the linoleum by the cupboards. It was cracked and broken, bits of food worn down into the pine boards that showed through. She scraped the blade of her knife into the seams between them. A curl of stiff grease twisted black along the knife blade like a wild morning-glory vine. She placed the curls into the bucket beside her. This house is dirty, Marilyn said. She looked up briefly, judging Tom's mother and her careless ways.

What was I to do? Mother asked, and she lifted the coffee to her lips and took another sip. It's not as if I can get down on my knees and take care of that kind of work any more. I've been telling Tom to help with the cleaning up around here, but does he ever get around to doing anything? Oh, he'll throw dishwater at the floor once in a while and sweep the water out with a broom, but what good does that do?

Marilyn didn't reply, and Mother sneered and brushed a piece of hair off her cheek with her fingertips. Why have you got that fire burning so hard? A body could cook in here. It's a waste of good wood.

I need hot water for this, said Marilyn, nudging the bucket a little farther on.

Marilyn almost felt like the house belonged to her. She thought some fresh paint on the cupboards would do wonders. Look at this, she said, holding the square of dish-cloth out to Mother. This dirt here is from a meal you probably cooked when Tom was still a boy.

Tom always liked porridge in the morning, Mother said. I used to make it for him. He'd sit in his high chair right there, she said, and her hand waved vaguely. He wasn't like Eddy. Tom never spoke till he was better than three years old. It was Eddy did the talking for him. She put her mug down and poked her cigarette butt into an ashtray full of sand. She folded her hands. Eddy never ate porridge, Mother said. He'd only eat soft-boiled eggs and store-bought bread. Just like his father. I don't know what ever happened to that high chair. Elmer likely broke it up for firewood some night. It would've been like him to do that. She glared at

Marilyn. You should tie that hair of yours back, you know, Mother said. It falls in your face when you're scrubbing.

Marilyn frowned as she saw Mother fumbling, pulling a wrinkled red bandana from her pocket. The woman got up, seemed to steady herself a moment, and then she came over to her. Sit still, she said. Marilyn felt her pull the kerchief tight across her forehead and tie it under her hair at the base of her neck.

See, Mother said, straightening up. That's called a babushka. A woman from Ukrainia showed me how to do that. Her family lived in a cabin out past Black Rock. She'd come to the house to pick the leftover raspberries in the patch out back. She was a DP like all the rest of them come over here after the war. You couldn't hardly understand her. Mother stepped back, suddenly awkward.

I made that apron you're wearing, she said. I was just a girl. When Marilyn turned away, Mother said: Maybe you think you're something special being with Tom and all, but what do you know? You're the first girl he's ever brought around here. I thought you were with Eddy when I saw you. Eddy's the one for the girls, not Tom.

Well, Tom likes *me*, Marilyn said.

Mother pursed her lips as if struggling to understand something that had escaped her. She stopped playing with the buttons on her dress. You don't look old enough to be anybody's girl, Mother said. You should be home making a quilt for when you get married. A Honeymoon Quilt, that's what you should make.

But Marilyn didn't rise to what she saw as meanness. She

was tired and told her to move out of the way. Mother touched a stray lock of hair by her ear with the heel of her hand. Go on outside and get some sun, Marilyn said.

Mother walked out the back door and stood on the cement stoop. Marilyn could see through the open door the woman there, the gravel reach, and the shed. She thought of Tom. She smiled to think how she'd been with him when they woke up. She'd felt shy, as if what she'd done with him in the night was somehow wrong, her wildness, the way she'd been with him out by the water barrel and then in his bed. She liked tending to him. Her own mother's ways around wounds had taught her how to care for them. She'd found a roll of gauze and a bottle of iodine in a drawer in the bathroom. She'd bound his hurt hand tight.

Winter's coming, Mother said, as if she was dreaming. She turned then, came in off the stoop and stood in the doorway, her face in shadow. There's a storm coming any day now, Mother said, cold too. When's Eddy coming home?

Marilyn shook her head and pushed the table and chairs back over onto the clean floor and got down on her knees.

That boy, Mother said, her hands loose. What can anyone do?

When Marilyn didn't say anything, Mother went back to the table and looked down at her. What're you doing here anyway? Who asked you to start messing around in this house?

Marilyn settled on her heels, took the bandana off, and wiped her bare arm across her forehead. You can talk to Tom like that, she said, but not to me. I don't want to hear it. Now, shift over so's I can finish this floor.

Mother glared at her again as she went to the stove and poured herself more coffee, dropping into her mug the chunk of dried-out brown sugar she'd chipped from the bowl sitting on the counter. She sniffed at the milk bottle as she passed by the counter, walking across the wet floor past the bathroom in her wrecked slippers. Marilyn heard her close her door at the end of the hall. She thought of Tom's mother and her own and what the years had done to each of them in their way, what they'd done to themselves. It didn't seem right they'd let that happen.

Tom and her could make a life in this house, she thought. He didn't know it yet, but he would. She could raise chickens maybe and sell eggs from a stand out on Ranch Road, and for a moment she saw herself throwing grain out to a flock of chickens, the hens pecking around her feet. Eggs, and they could grow fresh vegetables and fruit and sell them too. Tom could even have a few sheep out there in the field. There were lots of people who liked to eat lamb. They could even raise a pig or two. And they could maybe fix up those old apple trees in the garden. She'd seen fruit stands along the road north of town. She and Tom could save up and buy a roll of new linoleum and some paint and make this into a real kitchen. A breeze came through the open side window, its screen brushed and clean. That's better, she said, wringing her hands dry on her apron.

She didn't want to think of her own child dying. If she had a baby girl, she'd look after her like nobody's business.

She went to the porch. There were no more flies. She'd swept their dead bodies out with the broom after breakfast. When she finished eating her toast, she'd tacked a piece of cardboard in the door frame, large enough to cover the space where the screen on the door had been ripped away. She let the screen door close quietly behind her so it wouldn't wake Mother in case she was sleeping now, picked up an empty pail from under the clothesline stand, and walked into the garden.

I'm a woman now and not a girl, she said to a flicker pecking at fallen fruit, little chips of red flesh disappearing into the bird's long beak. We all got to eat, she said to the bird. She looked to where scarlet runner beans hung down in their dry pods from the yellowed corn stalks. She knelt in a furrow of dead bush beans and began picking off the slender pods, dry beans rattling inside the husks. She took one and cracked it open with her thumbs. The white beans clicked in her closed hand.

Tom.

She said his name into the small cave of her fist, her breath warm, the beans there cool as creek pebbles on her skin. She lowered her hand to the bucket and opened it, the beans dribbling through her fingers into the galvanized pail. Her hands disappeared then among the desiccated plants as she stripped and cracked open the pods, dry beans dropping one by one into the bucket.

15

I'm only Marilyn Bly, she said, the valley below her like a dress thrown off, unfolded at her feet. It's who I am.

Tom laid his head on her thigh, his eyes closed, Marilyn's voice a small, sure thing.

I'm from up the lake. All my life we've been poor. Sometimes my mother would bring home clothes from the houses where she cleaned, stuff the rich women gave her that their daughters didn't want any more, sweaters and dresses, things like that. I wasn't like those girls. When they were out swimming, I was working at the packing plant. I was twelve when my mother got me a job there. I swept floors and helped old Mr. Gondor mix glue at the box labelling machine. I worked in the fields and orchards too, and my mother let me keep some of what I made.

Early evening light glanced off the lakes in the distance, a trembling as of glass moving, the wind touching the bright mirrors between the hills. Marilyn took a deep breath. No one ever saw me before, she said. Not like you did. I'm not pretty, not like other girls, and when Tom looked at her, she took her hand from his cheek and struck him lightly on the chest. Don't you laugh at me, she said. I know I'm little and I've only got one eye, but I can see things as clear as you. I'm ordinary, you know. She leaned back against the outcrop of stone. I think what I've been doing is waiting, she said, but Tom wasn't sure if she'd said it to him or to herself.

He stared past her quietness, wondering at how she seemed to have entered his life. He could see her standing in the back of the house gazing down at Norman lying on the ground, her face flushed. What he remembered most was that she didn't seem afraid, and how he knew that her fearlessness would need watching over. The breeze lifted off the fields below and rose against the cliff, a Red-tail hawk circling in the updrafts. He thought of Eddy leaping through the door into that bedroom at the end of the hall as the old man shot at him, the bullet passing through the air he'd just been breathing.

He closed his eyes again, staring into the blood of his eyelids. What was Joe doing hanging around with Wayne, anyway? he wondered. He'd finished the shift and had driven to town. He'd been buying groceries at Olafson's and was about to head out when he stopped and told Olafson to throw in a can of tobacco for Mother, and that's when he saw Joe through the window of the Venice Café, standing at the counter talking to Lucky Johnson. Beside Joe was Wayne, eager, laughing. Tom got back in the truck, watched as Joe lifted out his wallet and leafed a bill from it, Lucky nodding his head at something he'd said. The two of them had come out then, Joe pushing his wallet into his back pocket. They turned away from where Tom was parked and went down toward the Okanagan Hotel, Wayne shifting beside Joe as if unsure exactly where he should walk. Joe's collar was turned up under his duck tail, his shoulders hunched. He was kicking at small rocks, chipping them off the fenders of cars, the small shards glancing into the gutter. Tom could see the anger in Joe and wondered how far it led.

When Tom had got back to the house, Marilyn set about preparing the food. While pork chops crackled in the fry pan, she took him to the bathroom, cleaned his hand and put on a new bandage. Then, sitting at the table he'd felt feverish, his mind fuzzy. When he finished eating, he took a plate to Mother who'd said she hadn't felt well enough to eat. She sent him away from her room, telling him her stomach was upset.

When he returned to the kitchen, Marilyn had the dishes stacked in the sink.

I've got to get out of here for a while, he said, and so they'd headed up the road to the fields, stopping at the bend of a little creek where wheel ruts wound toward the mountain. He stepped over a low fence and turned to Marilyn, who was close behind, and he lifted her above a strand of barbed wire, gripping her under the arms so she flailed her legs in the air, laughing, Tom not wanting her to be severed from him even as he slowed and she descended, her feet brushing a cluster of dry grass, until finally her toes found the ground.

The day was sliding away. It was well into autumn, apples starting to fall from the trees, most of the gardens and fields they passed picked or mowed clean, the butterflies and dragonflies vanished, their eggs hidden in creeks or in the wedged crevices of trees. In another month the last frogs would bury themselves in the mud to live out the cold. He and Marilyn had continued on into the land, their trail through the grass a steady, progressive wandering. They stopped here and there, to watch a rabbit slip into the brush, to look at a rattlesnake's shed skin, the abandoned nest of a pheasant, ivory-green egg shells like fractured pottery. They waded through an untended field. The farmer who lived there had been sick these past months, a man who'd let Tom hunt his land in past years. Elsie, his wife, sat in a rocker on the porch, waiting patiently as she had every day since early spring. Marilyn waved at her and Elsie lifted her hand as if to wave back and then dropped it into her lap, the rocking chair under her moving slowly on the porch boards.

The grass had dropped its last seeds, the summer pollen long gone, leaves and stalks dry and withered. Marilyn said: Listen to the grass, and Tom swept his arm through the bent heads, a faint crash of sound swimming around them as of glass falling in an accident far away. Herefords stared at them from the shade of a chokecherry bush, a horse whinnied as they passed by.

They'd crossed through a Lombardy poplar line between two fields where a few last apples blinked in the trees. Streaks of red draped down the sides of the Foxwhelps and Northern Spies. The Gideons and Redchiefs were past ripe, a few trees unpicked, fruit hanging heavy in their autumn skins. They were old trees that had somehow escaped the great freeze a few years after the war, when so many orchards had been destroyed, like the fruit trees at home, their blossoms that spring wrapped in ice. A farm dog barked under a barnyard pole and Tom stopped Marilyn, holding her to his side as he waited for the dog's rush. The brindle hound with its scoop belly and barrel chest raged at them from the end of a tether. I love dogs, said Marilyn. Yeah, Tom said, that one looks like it'd run for a year if you ever let it go.

Your mother told me you used to have one, Marilyn said.

Yeah. Docker, Tom said. His name was Docker. I found him at the dump.

How come you called him that?

Eddy did. Because Father docked his tail. He cut it off with a hatchet so it would look like a real spaniel.

That's terrible, Marilyn said.

Tom pushed his hands into his pockets and kicked at a clump of grass, then started walking, Marilyn running a little in order to keep up. They passed along the edge of a hayfield, the low brush on the side leaning away from a line of trees as it tried to reach the light. He stepped over a fallen poplar limb and told Marilyn to be careful and she was, when suddenly a cock pheasant exploded from cover, the rush of its wings startling them both. Marilyn sat down on a rock jutting from the grass, tied her shoe, and began picking burrs from her socks. He followed the flight of the pheasant as it coasted on its wings down the field and then swerved away into the trees.

Father could not abide killing a pheasant. Tom remembered one winter morning when he and his father went out to feed them, Father scattering grain across the crust of hard snow. The pheasants came up from the creek thickets, tentative, delicate, the cocks with their red-feathered eyes, moving like jewels across the ice and the golden hens close behind, clucking nervously, chittering their way to the seeds. They're like no others, he'd said. Tom had always remembered that, and his father's huge hands strewing seeds on the white snow. His father had touched him only once with what seemed care and that too late. That early winter morning, with the pheasants pecking the wheat off the ice and snow by the frozen creek, he'd come up behind him and placed his hands on Tom's shoulders. Look at the birds, he'd said. They are rare beauty.

Rare beauty!

What did you say? asked Marilyn.

It was something my father said once. It doesn't matter now, and he took her hand and helped her up, the two of them going on.

When they got to the cliffs at the foot of the mountain, he'd turned her toward a rock chimney where they climbed the laddered stone. They had come out on a ledge and looked at the valley, the fingers of trees jutting into the edges of the fields and farms like pieces of a puzzle fitted together, thin lines of road binding them like stitched wounds. Beyond was the town, buried deep in the valley bottom, three lakes pointing their heads toward that hidden place.

The hawk floated above them now, its small shadow an eyelash on the woven grass of the fields. They gazed up at its soft, grey belly almost lost against the sky. The far hills gone behind a stray cloud, its shadow on the lake drifting. The wind blew Marilyn's hair back, a tangle across her forehead. He looked up at her leaning against the rock, her small face peering at him. You never told me how come you're blind in that eye?

Marilyn cupped her hand over that side of her face. What's there to say? My father used to get angry at me when he was in one of his dark moods. I don't know what I did one time to make him so mad, but he rolled up the hall on his chair with his cane across his lap. I remember my mother screaming at him not to hit me. But he got up and balanced himself as best he could, and tried to strike me with the cane. He slipped when he was swinging and it hit my eye. He never meant to do it. After that I was different than other girls.

Tom reached out to her.

Don't you go feeling sorry for me.

Most everyone's got some kind of sorrow, Tom said slowly. But what can be done about it?

She pointed at the smoke rising from the dump on the hill to the north of town. I've lived up the road from that smoke most of my life, she said. Just for a second, I thought I could see the light bouncing off the side of our trailer.

He followed her pointed finger, but couldn't find what she was looking at. Look harder, she said, and he squinted his eyes, but still couldn't find the spot Marilyn wanted him to see.

—

He woke startled in the middle of the night, a sound breaking into his dream of being in the dark root cellar searching for his dog, rummaging through old potato sacks and crates, and not finding him. It was a recurring dream, each time leaving Tom awake and sweating. Night sounds came through the window screen, the far-off roar of a distant truck, a Pygmy owl with its soft double hoots, and then quiet again. He heard the faint scratching of the wasps as they crawled on their dusty trails between the studs of the walls and into the room. The old house was full of cracks and patches, splintered holes. There were breaks in the stucco and fascia boards, splits in the roof shakes. The great hives in the poplars and cottonwoods had felt the long sleep coming, the nights cool lately, the wasps crawling into the south wall where the stucco held the heat. The wasps were sluggish now, hungry, weary from a season of scraping wood from the grey boards of fences, chewing it into the wet pulp that they'd built their nests with.

He remembered sitting on the well-head earlier that summer, rubbing the palm of his hand over the wooden cover. The boards had glowed, having been flayed by the wind and sun into a soft fur the wasps harvested for paper. He'd watched them so many times, their jaws carving thin alphabets in the wood, insect words they took back to their home. In the apple tree above the well now was an empty nest. It swayed in the breeze, a deserted nunnery, the last un-tended grubs in their covered cells, withered.

With little or no food, the wasps were slowly dying inside their armour plates. There was little left to hunt, too many to feed, and they'd abandoned their hives. In the hours while Tom and Marilyn slept, wasps had crept through the interstices in the donna-conna wall-board of the bedroom, and clustered now in clumps and complex chains on the walls, each wasp hooking herself sister to sister in a delicate wattle, as he'd seen them do every year since he was a child. In another few days there would be a great death, but for now they crept on stiff legs toward anything that gave off warmth.

Moonlight flooded the room. Marilyn lay sleeping beside him, the sheet loose on her collarbones, her one arm across the worn cotton, her hand gripping it as if by holding it she could protect herself from whatever nightmare loomed. There'd never been a girl in his bed before and now there was. She could stay for a while, he decided. It looked like she needed to. She seemed fragile there, dreaming he knew not what.

They were lying under one of Mother's quilts. Marilyn said she'd found it in the wooden chest at the back of the closet in the room with the crib. It was the Heavenly Puzzle quilt. He hadn't seen it in years. The quilt was one Mother had made when she was a girl. He'd tried to imagine such days, a kerosene lamp burning at the kitchen table and his grandmother, Nettie, teaching his mother the different stitches, the way to lay out the squares and triangles, the evening radio playing its tinny songs.

Sometimes, when Father was out of the house and she was in one of her moods, Mother would tell him and Eddy one of her prairie stories. One time, she sat him and Eddy down in the crib room and pulled from the closet her knotty pine chest. She told them that it had taken her years to fill what was going to be her gift to her future home and the man she would marry someday. She said she was only a little older than they were when she began to fill the chest. He had felt he had to listen even as Eddy squirmed, his brother wanting to break free on his bike and go to town. There was a sadness in her at those moments that drew Tom to her, as if in witnessing these stories he could make something up to her. She called it her Hope Chest and gathered him in with her words.

He'd seen the chest before in the back of the closet, scratched and worn from the years. Mother told him how she'd carried it with her from town to farm to ranch during the wandering years with Father. In the chest were two nightgowns, the smocking stitched by hand, and underwear she said she'd bought with egg money back home in Nokomis, one pair made from red silk, too pretty to ever wear. She told them she used to love to pull the silk over her hand so she could see the sun through its thin weave. She had stretched it over her spread fingers and showed them by holding it in front of the sun coming through the window. Look how pretty, she'd said, and Tom remembered seeing her fingers struggling as if inside a flame. Eddy had asked her to let him do it, but she shushed him and put the red silk aside. Pillowcases, sheets, and towels were there too, some of them given to her by a neighbour who was leaving the land and going back home to England. There were doilies and antimacassars, things with names he'd never heard before, things he didn't know: taffeta, appliqué, bodice. There were two teacups with flowers painted on, and a single saucer, the other broken, she'd said, years ago. Father had dropped the chest when they were moving out of Medicine Hat and driving south into Idaho, heading to some logging outfit up the Teton River near the Wyoming border. Some job that never worked out, two weeks, a month, and then catching a ride on some passing truck, back on the road with Father's promises of better times to come.

She told them how she'd sat in a painted pine chair in the clapboard house by the correction line and stitched the patches together on what she called her Heavenly Puzzle, one of many quilts she'd made in those years. In the bottom of the chest was her special quilt. She said she'd made it from bits of cloth she'd got from women on the outlying farms where there were still a few people left. When she told the women it was for her Trousseau Quilt, they gave her what they had, velvet and satin and silk, little scraps they'd saved. The women wished her luck, though Mother said there was a look behind their eyes as if they knew something they weren't telling.

The nearest house to their farm was an old soddie where a man lived alone, the wife he'd sent for from some coal town in Ohio never arriving. Mother said the roof and walls were made of dirt and grass, and that she'd gone inside with her father one day when he'd been dickering with the man for a brood sow. All she'd remembered breathing in there was darkness and dust. Tom tried to imagine his mother in such a room, or walking the narrow prairie roads, going from farm to farm in search of bits of pretty cloth, but all he could see was the thin silhouette of a girl walking against the light.

Some of the wasps had now crawled up on the bed or fallen onto it from the ceiling. They drifted across the quilt like beads of amber. The heat of his and Marilyn's bodies had drawn them, or it was not their heat, but only that they were living things like they were, breathing. Perhaps they remembered their earlier life when in their hexagonal cells they'd slept as the wind moved their nest. He'd seen the huge, grey brains dreaming in the trees.

He turned over onto his side and settled the quilt over his shoulder, the wasps holding on, the tiny hairs and hooks on their legs fixing them to wisps of thread rising from the pattern of complex stitches. He felt hot, and sleep wouldn't come. He couldn't get Stanley out of his mind. Why did the bastard go to the old man's house? He wasn't there just for the hell of it. He thought of Eddy in Harry's shack with who knows what going on in his head about what had just gone down and probably not caring.

God damn you, Eddy, he said out loud.

Marilyn stirred beside him. What?

Open your eyes, he whispered, sitting up, turning on the bedside lamp. She opened them and looked down at the quilt with its spots of yellow and black. He felt her startle and told her not to be afraid.

Where did they come from? And as if to answer herself, she said in a small voice: There were only a few when we went to sleep.

She held herself tight to his arm as he turned her head to him.

Each year they come into this attic room, Tom said. It's the warm side of the house. They come when they've run out of food. It's like they know the cold is coming down from the north. He pressed on a square of colour that rested on her belly and the wasps shifted as his hand slid under them, their hooks loosening momentarily until they grasped each other tight again on top of his hand. Slowly, he raised his hand and laid it on his skull, then drew it carefully from under them. Marilyn took thin gulps of air. She clinched her eyes and stared through her lashes.

Why don't they sting you? she asked.

They're tired. In times of fasting there's no sting.

Marilyn said: Sometimes you speak like the Bible.

They're a wonder all their own, he said, hoping she'd understand.

The wasps licked the light sweat from his temples as they crept upon his forehead, opening and closing their fretted wings. A single wasp fell across the sight of his eye, and then another, the chains of their woven bodies coming apart as they dropped from his face and hair. Others crawled down his neck and across his shoulders to the bed where their sisters waited. He said their legs were a trickle on his skin, a tickle as of water drying there.

Sometimes I think I should be scared of you. Other girls are.

It's because you're not, you're here.

She played her fingers down his arm to his wrist and laid it on his hurt hand. You're hot, she said. Your hand is burning.

It's nothing, he said. Wasps moved on the window screen above him, their passage over the rusted wire slow and measured.

I'm going to get up and go down to the bathroom now, she said, and lifted her arm, rolling away, suddenly shy to be naked in front of him. Close your eyes.

He did as she told him, his eyes almost shut, and saw her stop in the middle of the room, picking up his shirt from where he'd dropped it. She draped it over her shoulders, the shirt hanging from her small body almost down to her knees, turning the cuffs in folds up to her wrists. A single wasp rode on the lobe of her ear, a spot of gold, an earring that seemed to contain in its presence both threat and blessing.

When he heard her going down the stairs, he got out of bed and pulled on his clothes and shoes. She'd be all right staying here, he thought. Mother would have to get used to it. They'd go to her trailer so she could pick up some of her things, but that would be later. First, he needed to talk to Eddy.

16

tom wound through John Hurlbert's orchard, the truck lights low as he neared the farmhouse, a black-patch dog standing under the yard light barking maniacally, crazed by a strange truck arriving. He stopped beside John's pickup. He watched the house and saw a flashlight come on in the side kitchen. He knew he'd woken them up and hoped whoever was holding the light wasn't Maureen. Her days were long, not so much because of John, but because she made her hours that way, the house, the orchard and garden, chickens and goats, the milk cow, her children and grandchildren out there in the valley somewhere. He thought of John getting older, and him waking up to his dog barking, a strange vehicle in the yard.

Tom got out and went around to the front of the truck so whoever was there would see him clear when they came out of the house. The dog raged a few feet away. The flashlight flickered across the kitchen window, thin curtains parting a fraction as someone looked out. Then the door opened and he heard John shout at the dog to shut the hell up. Not Maureen then. Tom could see him, the flashlight's glow on the frizzled grey hair on his naked chest, his body half in and half out the door as he looked at the truck and Tom standing there.

What in christ's name are you doing, Tom, coming out here this time of night?

John came further out, leaning a gun of some sort against a porch post. I could of shot you where you're standing. This here shotgun's loaded with slugs, you know.

I came to see my brother, Tom said. I'm real sorry I woke you.

It's that gawdamn dog woke me, said John, and he came down onto the bottom step of the porch. He pointed at his feet and said: C'mon over here. I'm barefoot and I ain't walking out there. There's every manner of nail and bolt lying around.

Tom crossed the yard and came into the light playing on the dirt. Hurlbert lifted the flashlight and stroked it quickly across Tom's face. You came to see Eddy, eh.

I thought he was here, down at the shack. I don't see his car.

Yeah, he's here. Harry put Eddy's car in the shed over there. Harry left a while ago. He's in and out, you know. He's never been much for staying anywhere too long at a time. John hesitated a moment as if thinking about what he was going to say and then said: Sorry about your brother. He's not looking half good. Speaking of which, what'd you do to that hand of yours?

An accident out at the house. I cut it with a chisel. It's nothing, said Tom. John was standing there in a pair of corduroy pants cinched tight under his belly. I'll go down there then, Tom said. You better get back into the house. It's cool out these nights.

The dog had sidled up, growling, its ruff flaring, and John leaned down as if to pick up a rock and the dog scuttled away, its tail tight between its legs. That one's a good dog, John said. It's just he's old is all. The stupid dog doesn't know the difference any more between a stranger and a friend. The wife calls him That Damned Dog. I don't call him anything but Shut the Hell Up.

He's doing what a watchdog's supposed to do, I guess.

Yeah, well, said John, I suppose you're right there. At least it's a reason to let him keep on living.

So I'll just get on down to the shack, Tom said, twisting his foot in the dirt. He looked at the dog skulking by the truck, pissing on the front tire.

John hitched at the buckle of his belt. Shit, he said, looking down. My gawdamn fly's open. He fumbled at the buttons a second and then said: The hell with it. If that dog bothers you, shoot it.

Tom held his hands up. I don't have a gun, he said, grinning.

Lucky dog, said John as he crossed the porch and went back into the house, the light wavering in the window and then gone.

Tom leaned down and picked up a couple of pebbles from the dirt at his feet and tossed them at the dog who was sniffing now at the other tire. It shied away and slipped back into the darkness by a shed where a rusted John Deere tractor squatted by the chain-locked doors. The dog crawled under the tractor engine and sat down on a swale of straw.

Tom looked back at the house for a second and thought of Maureen. He'd been out there off and on over the years and liked her. She was Okanagan Indian from the Reserve at the head of the lake. She was a kindly woman who'd long ago learned to tolerate John's rough ways. They'd had four boys, all of them nearby in the valley, married with kids. Harry and their youngest son, Elijah, had been friends until Elijah moved onto the Reserve. Maureen had told Tom once that it was best so for Elijah. She said he was the one needed to know his own people most, no matter he was a half-breed. Tom hadn't seen much of him in the past few years. It was Harry's friendship with Elijah that got Harry the shack in the orchard. John let him use it for nothing. Eddy staying there now was a part of those other days.

Tom started the truck and turned the lights on, small blue moths coming out of the night. He drove slowly, the moths bellying out in a cloud and vanishing along the doors as he cut the wheel and took the turn down to where the path led to the shack. Tom loved the quiet of the night out in the valley and wished he was there for any other reason than he was, but Eddy was down in the shack and, his brother sleeping or not, he had things to tell him.

At the far edge of the orchard, he turned the truck around and parked it by an irrigation ditch. The shack was down a long trail by the creek. It looked like apple picking was finished here. The trees seemed relieved the fruit was gone, their branches slowly lifting from their autumn sag. He could hear the creek purling ahead of him. It came down from Hadow Lake behind the Kalamalka hills. It was good water. John was lucky to have such on his place.

There was enough light for him to see the path. He followed it down to the creek and to the abandoned picker's shack that was Harry's refuge, a place where he brought runaway girls he found at the bus depot, a place where he could hide out when things got rough back in town. Tom wondered if John and Maureen knew about the girls Harry brought out there and then thought they probably did and didn't care to ask questions about it. Harry was to Maureen a kind of wayward son, he'd spent so much time there as a kid. She'd forgive him the girls or just accept it. It was what Indians did, something his own people had a hard time with, forgiveness, acceptance.

Tom made his way along the path by the creek, starlight and the moon enough so he could see. Head down, so he wouldn't trip on an errant root, he noticed fresh deer sign in the damp soil. He followed the delicate hoofprints, seeing where the deer stopped to take a mouthful of grass, a bite from a fallen apple, the marks of its teeth clean in the white flesh. The hulk of the shack loomed just ahead. He could see the smokeless black tube of the tin chimney in the slanted roof. It would be cold in there the way the shack was stuck back in the trees by the creek. He stepped onto the cracked porch boards and said his brother's name.

There was nothing but night sound around him, a cricket or two creaking in a brush pile. The creek chuckled over stones off to his left. He waited, but there was no answer, so he turned the peg on the flimsy door. He pushed it in, the door grabbing for a second on the sill. He stood in the doorway, his hand on the bent spike that served as a handle. Eddy was sitting in an old chair close by a window, his feet up on a crate. A grey army blanket was pulled over his legs and tucked around him. Beside the chair was what looked like half a bottle of rye whiskey and on the arm an empty glass perched precariously. Eddy was staring out the window at the moonlight falling in fragments on the brown creek water. Hey Tom, Eddy said, without turning.

Tom let go of the doornail and went all the way in. He'd been in the shack over the years, and as he looked around in the weak moonlight he saw that nothing much had changed. There was still the rusty Queen heater propped up on four uneven bricks, the upholstered chair with Eddy in it, a table and a wooden chair pushed against the wall, a calendar with a naked girl on it that said it was still 1953 in spite of five years gone past. On the table were cold candle stubs in various stages of melt, pooled wax spread in gouts on the worn wood, Eddy's works laid out, and a deck of playing cards with their faces up, kings and jacks in their finery staring up at the ceiling, four aces in a line, separate from the rest. In the backroom was the three-quarter bed with a couple of straw ticks on it. Or at least there used to be.

You know, said Eddy, turning to Tom for the first time, you look at a creek long enough you can almost figure everything out.

How you doing, Eddy?

Eddy turned back to the window. I'm okay, he said. I didn't count on seeing you out this way, you back at the mill and all. Before Tom could answer, Eddy said: What the hell, I guess I should ask what you came out here for.

Tom took a breath and then another and began to tell his brother about hauling the old man's body from the house. I cleaned the floor, he said, and put things in order as best I could. I found the two shells but not the rifle, so I'm counting on you having it. Fuck it, Eddy. I buried that old man. This's a bad situation you've got us into, you know? For christ's sake, you just killed somebody. People are going to be looking for him. They might already be looking for you.

There was a silence and then Eddy said: I was sitting here thinking about that time Father was out in the shed with those two deer he shot up the Commonage that time. He had them trussed up to the hooks on the rafter there in the back. You know how he used to like to hang a carcass for a few days before cutting it up.

Eddy, said Tom. Did you hear what I said?

Shutup a second, Tom. Just listen. I was telling you about that time.

Tom stood there and thought he was going to go out of his mind. *Which* time? he said. There were dozens of times Father did that. He'd hang deer and sheep and whatever else that needed to season for a day or two to get the meat to set. Shit, he even hung a moose there once and damn near pulled the roof down on himself. Which time are you talking about?

We were both there. Remember how we thought Father slaughtering deer was such a big deal when we were little kids. That old drunk was quite the hero, wasn't he? When Tom just looked at him, Eddy went on. Anyways, we were watching him wash out the cavities and he called us over. There was that old tin basin on the bench and in it were the livers and hearts. Remember how Mother used to love a stuffed deer heart? They were a real delicacy, she used to say.

Where's this going, Eddy?

Anyway, he leaned down and took those two hearts from the basin. Remember? He held them out, one in each hand and told us that it was the strangest thing but when he gutted those deer he found two hearts in one animal and none in the other.

Eddy gave an odd smile then and when Tom pulled out the wooden chair from the table and sat down, he said: Remember how we believed him? Hell, we were stupid back then.

We were just kids.

Anyway, it's what I was thinking about.

Eddy, pay attention here. What happened at the party is all over town. You shot a guy and pissed off a lot of people too.

You think Lester and Billy are going to go to the police with their stories? What, and lay charges?

Stanley's on to something already. He drove out to the old man's house. I saw his car on the road that night and followed him back there.

Something fluttered across the window.

Eddy looked out again. What's one old man less in the world anyway?

Anger flared in Tom. He choked and cleared his throat, spitting on the floor between his feet. Do you know what it's like hauling an old man's body out of his house and then having to bury him? Do you know what that's like?

Do you know what it's like killing one? he said.

They were both silent suddenly, Eddy pulling the army blanket over his feet. Tom was cold all over, his heart beating fast. He couldn't remember being so angry. Not like this. He looked at his brother, thinking there was nothing under that grey skin but bones and heroin.

Eddy sucked in a loud breath and let it out as if it were the last breath he'd ever take. I shouldn't have said that. Ah, who cares, he said, his hands rising off the chair and then falling back, thin plumes of dust rising through his fingers. The glass on the arm teetered and fell, the small tumbler breaking. None of it matters a damn, Eddy said.

Tom got to his feet, the blood running crazily in him. I'm going to go, he said, his head full of weaving shadows.

What's going to happen is going to happen, said Eddy. There's one thing I know in this world and that is there's nothing you can do about nothing. Go on home, Tom. I'll see you at the dog fights Saturday.

Out in the dark the dog barked. The sound came faint

from the farmyard and when it died there was a deeper quiet than there'd been. Eddy turned his head to the window again and for a moment Tom tried to fathom what he'd just seen in his brother's face. It was a kind of sorrowing, but who it was for, he couldn't tell. Him or Eddy or just the trouble he was in, this stupid shack in an orchard, him hiding, waiting for Harry to come back.

17

there are many kinds of water. Mostly I like the one at the end of winter when everything's half-frozen. The creek grows strange ice in the spring, sometimes in hollow columns full of air. When the sun hits them, it casts a fractured light, bands of colour breaking every which way above the water running below. If you put your ear to the ice, you can hear it talking. There are voices inside those hollows. A bobcat drinking in February will sometimes leave a trapped sound there. So will a coyote or a deer. On a melt day, you can hear what happened weeks ago, the creek talking, a pheasant's cluck, a sparrow's chitter. Everything crowds near water in a desert. It's where the living go to live. Out on the dry land is where you find the dead.

I remember once seeing Eddy at the bones of a cougar. The skeleton was out in the Bluebush hills where there were no trees, just the rare Ponderosa alone and brooding. Eddy was up there by himself, Tom off somewhere with his dog,

hunting birds in the arroyo thickets at the foot of the mountain. Eddy went out alone sometimes on Sundays, there
being nothing much in town to interest him, the stores
closed, everything locked up. He never carried a gun, just
an old hunting knife that Father never used any more, the
scabbard split where the web was torn away. He carried it
as much for show as anything. There was little he could do
with just a knife up there. When he came upon the cougar,
bits of hide and bones were all that was left. The critters
had got to it, beetles, crows, and buzzards, the never-ending
flies. Eddy was still young then, thirteen years old, and
finding a dead cougar was something big to him, dreaming
like he did of someday killing one.

He crouched there among the pebbles and rocks, little
pincushion cactus like upside down spoons, pink flowers
growing among their spines. It was late spring and the
snow melt and thin rains had given the cactus enough
strength to blossom. It was like he wanted to put the big
cat back together from where the scavengers had scattered
it. The prize, of course, was the skull, the big incisors
worn down, an old animal and far from water. It was
strange how the big cat had died like that, out in the
open. Most animals when they're old and sick find a
place to hide away. But not this cougar. I don't know if
Eddy thought about that, so preoccupied was he in
bringing the ribs together, arranging them in their order
along the dried ligaments and tendons of the spine. The
tail was mostly gone, the bones small, lost among pebbles
and rocks.

But he got it done as best he could. Lying there when he was finished, the cat bones looked like they were flying, the legs spread out like wings, and perched on its lower jaw, the skull, the cougar staring through its empty sockets at whatever it had seen that it hadn't got to, maybe the lakes. Up on the mountain's side you can see all three of them and the cougar was high enough up for that. Maybe that's what it wanted, not just to get there, but to look at where it had hunted once, the places it had waited out the deer coming down through the coulees to drink along the beaches.

I thought he'd take the skull home to show you, Tom, but he didn't. He left it up there, staring sightless at what its paws had known, its hunting ground, its home. Eddy was there and then he was gone, a boy cutting slant along the mountainside until he passed into the bush near the bottom at the edge of a farm, nothing left to show he was ever up there, but for those cat bones flying. Vanishing is what Eddy did best. He was always the blink of an eye, there and gone even when he was small. Remember?

Everyone has a tale to tell, but if Eddy had one it stopped for him the day he was sent away. When they released him, he entered a place without a story, for he believed there was nothing that could happen more than what already had. He caught a ride to Hope and then another in the back of a potato truck. He rode behind the tailgate under a canvas tarp all the way to Salmon Arm, the truck dropping him off and then going on to Calgary with its load of black-market spuds. He hadn't tried to hitch a ride south from there, just walked the gravel verge or down the cut of the ditch. Near

Enderby, where a cliff of stone juts up and where it's said that years ago some squaw betrayed by a white man set fire to herself and leapt in flames to her death, he turned from the roadside and walked east into a field.

A pheasant must have cried to him from the wild alfalfa or maybe he saw a bobcat prowling for mice in some farmer's rock pile. That might have been it. A bobcat was enough to make him turn, or a pheasant or a deer, some ten-point buck stepping out into the open following his does to water.

Whatever it was, it made Eddy cross the field and walk through the brush to where the warm Shuswap River slides between high clay banks on its way to the Fraser and the sea. He sat there under a cottonwood for a long time by that muddy water, and then he took off his clothes and walked into the river. He looked like any boy on a hot day going for a swim. He'd fished that river three years before, him and Tom. The Shuswap is slow down there below the canyon. A branch thrown in can take a long time to float around a bend.

He waded in and then he swam, not downstream, but up, as if he had to test himself against the flow. The current moved thick as oil and he pulled against it, beating with his arms and legs, his body going steadily nowhere, stopped. He seemed to measure himself there, not moving, the water passing him by, his body the only constant, bits of sticks and bark nudging against him and then moving on. A poplar fallen from some high bank rolled slowly past and he might have taken hold of it and ridden until he was gone, but he didn't, just dove under and came up the other side of the tree trunk. He stopped swimming then, his hands raised high, his head there as if floating alone, the rest of him drowned. His arms above the water seemed to be the necks of swans, his sunburned fists their heads. Then all of him was gone.

He sank and rose, only to sink again. It was as if his body wasn't ready to die. But it was what he wanted, a boy, just fifteen, thin like such boys are with their white, white flesh, their skinny arms and legs all strings of muscle, hard bone. He went under a dozen times and surfaced at last, his red hair blazing, streaks of mud sliding down his face, and then a leaf touched his cheek and he raised his arms and began to swim toward shore until his feet found the bottom, his chest and belly and legs appearing as he walked the slick clay to the riverbank.

He sat trembling on the slurry for a long time and then he got up naked as the day he was born and headed upriver to where he'd first gone in. When he got to the cottonwood, he pulled on his clothes, the Boyco boots with their leather laces, the straw hat he'd found a few miles back on the road.

For him the story had been told and whatever was going to happen was going to be the same as what he knew when the waters refused his offering, the river flowing above him, his eyes closed as he rose up out of the murk.

18

a blue hour, the sky a skinned parchment. Tom stared out over the fields to the mountain, the day beginning, darkness wasting in the east, morning stalking him on its bright legs. When he'd got home from Hurlbert's, he wanted to be alone, so he sat in the truck for a while, fell asleep, and woke chilled. He'd washed at the water barrel and then gone into the house and got Marilyn out of bed, coffee bubbling in the percolator on the stove over the fire he'd lit, Mother up and sitting at the kitchen table, rolling yet another of her endless cigarettes. Now Marilyn was in the truck and he got in beside her and headed down Ranch Road, the land changing from fields to houses, a crow jabbing with its beak at something in a gutter, leaves blowing in the wind the truck left behind as they drove to where the road split. He took the west fork, avoiding town, then crossed the valley and turned north along Swan Lake. When she told him to, he stopped at a beaten mailbox on the lake side of the road about three miles past the town dump. He could see holes in the cheap tin where boys must have shot at it with their rifles as they drove by drunk in the night.

Marilyn got out and stood by the ditch, looking down the hill at the beat-up aluminum trailer, which sat up on blocks beside a grove of alders and cottonwoods. In front was a wooden deck with a ramp leading down. There were no signs of life, but for a heat haze rising in a wavering plume from the chimney. They got out of the truck and as he came around, Marilyn put her hand out and stopped him.

Don't you want me to go down there with you?

You just remember to come back and get me, she said. Leaning up, she kissed him on the lips, her mouth warm. She turned from him then and walked down the hill on the rough hump between the ruts to the trailer. Tom stood and watched her as she went up the ramp to the plank stoop. She glanced over her shoulder at him, then opened the door, and went inside.

He got behind the wheel again and headed back past the dump, far ahead of him the onion dome of the Ukrainian church at the edge of town, the smoke from the mill out by the lake wilting into the sky. When he got close, bits of sawdust smut from the fire already started in the burner whirled in front of him, ash blowing in through the open window.

He pulled into the yard and parked in the shade of an elm, away from the other cars and trucks down by the office, men standing around, a few of them stealing a quick drink of coffee from their thermoses. The early workers would have arrived a half-hour before, the fires burning fiercely now, diesels thumping in the power shed. Tom made a fist, his fingers stiff. He held his injured hand to his face, gazing at it as if it was some foreign object, a thing attached to him by accident. He knew the wound was infected, but that wasn't unusual, splinters, cuts, a nail, any and all had flared and healed in the past. The infection would subside. He thought of Marilyn seeing to him, the coolness of her hands when she bandaged his palm.

No one in his family went to doctors and he wasn't about to change. Only once could he remember anyone going to the hospital. It was the time Father had cut his foot open with an axe when he'd been splitting wood out by the shed, the axe glancing off a buried knot, slicing him open just below his ankle. He'd come into the house with a boot full of blood. Tom had been a kid back then, but he remembered Father undoing the bandage when he got back from town and showing him and Eddy the stitches running like a zipper across the top of his foot. His father had cursed the doctor for charging him five dollars, calling him a quack, saying he could've done as good a job stitching it with waxed thread and a darning needle from Mother's sewing basket. Eddy had broken his arm once, but father had set it himself. He'd told Eddy his bones were green sticks inside, and Mother had helped hold Eddy down when Father had straightened the arm, Eddy screaming in anger and pain. Father bound the arm with two slats of cedar, tying it there with binder twine and wrapping the whole thing in cloth he took from the kitchen. The only time you need a doctor is when he tells you you're dead, Father had told them both. That's when you don't have to pay him!

Tom saw Chooksa and the Cruikshank brothers going around the corner of the mill, Wlad following slow on their trail, and a cluster of men walking with heads bent, up onto the mill floor. Then Carl pulled into the yard and parked beside him. They both got out and stood at the tailgate of Tom's truck, leaning back as Carl rolled himself a cigarette, the paper twirling in one hand, a roll Tom knew he was proud of. A few shreds of tobacco hung from the ends and Carl tucked these in with a wooden match, then struck it on the rusty edge of the bumper and lit his smoke.

How's that hand of yours?

Coming along, said Tom.

You don't look good. You okay?

Tom was about to answer, but the warning whistle blew and they straightened up and put on their hard hats, Carl shrugging as the mill came to life, the headrig saws howling as they cut into the first log, the edger starting its chatter, the many belts beginning their whines. He walked with Carl across the yard, the last whistle choking on the dust, Carl turning left toward the forklift parked by the machine shed. Tom went down the side of the mill to the sorting yard and crossed to the chains, Chooksa and the others standing there as they watched the drop hole for the first lumber to begin pouring from the mill.

Harry had phoned the mill from Hurlbert's place an hour before quitting time and left a message at the office with Charlie Openshaw, the bookkeeper. Charlie brought the note out to the sorting yard and passed it up to Tom, Charlie's neat hand telling him to meet Eddy at Wayne's place at six o'clock. Tom didn't know why Eddy wanted him there, but it didn't sound good. He finished up the shift and drove to town. He had an hour to kill, time enough to get a sandwich and soup before going to Wayne's house.

A little before six he drove to the east hill, the side streets stuttering by the truck window, a woman in a hat and gloves out walking alone, a man with a newspaper, the paths and walks on the hill mostly quiet as he passed by the Calvary Temple with its tilted signboard telling him: The Second Coming Is Nigh. He passed the houses where the old rich used to live and pulled around back of Wayne's beside Eddy's car and got out. The Studebaker's engine was still ticking. Eddy must have just arrived. Lilacs leaned away from the fieldstone foundation, dried seed husks hanging like broken rattles from the ends of their spindly branches. Mother had told him long ago lilacs were death flowers, blooming as they did in the bite of spring, the smell of them thick with the same scent old women had, a musky smell that clogged the nose.

Tom wiped sweat from his face with his sleeve and went down the steps, the door in front of him partly open, the cellar-way at his feet littered with twigs and leaves. The day at the mill had been a long one, the fever he seemed to have not helping, his head full of too many things. He went inside. In front of him was the blanket with the Longhorn skull stitched into it hanging in the doorway to Wayne's room. Tom remembered it from when he and Eddy were kids and used to go over and trade comics with Wayne. His father had bought the blanket for him in Texas years ago. Tom and Eddy had hated him for having it. They'd believed back then that Texas was where the real cowboys lived, their movie stars, their comic book heroes, Tom Mix, Hopalong Cassidy, Lash LaRue.

He could hear Wayne's voice, plaintive, asking Eddy why he was there. He pulled the blanket to the side and stared into Wayne's cluttered nest.

Hi, Tom, Eddy said, not looking up. He was sitting on a wooden chair, staring at Wayne whose back was to Tom. Beside Eddy were shelves propped up with bricks and on them a collection of boiled animal skulls, coyote and rabbit, deer, bear, eagles, hawks, and sparrows. There's every kind of sickness in here, Eddy said, leaning over and picking up a hawk's skull. Who'd kill a bird just to boil its bones?

It's a peregrine falcon's, said Wayne. Be careful, those birds are really rare.

Eddy dropped it on the floor by his chair, the fragile bone bouncing on the cement, a fragment of skull breaking from the rim of the eye socket. And people think there are worse horrors than you.

Tom looked around and noticed a shelf above the bed with three Mason jars full of milky fluid. Wayne had bragged to him a few years ago that he'd saved every ounce of jism he'd ever come except the first, but Tom hadn't believed him. He was angry at himself that his brother had brought him to this room. Being there was trouble piled on troubles.

What're we doing, Eddy?

We're talking to Wayne, he said.

I can see that, but I think we should go.

In a little while, Eddy said.

Wayne's eyes flickered nervously in the air between Eddy and Tom. How's it going, Tom? Wayne said. He was standing now by the scratched coffee table. An overflowing aluminum ashtray in the shape of California sat on it surrounded by a cluster of empty beer bottles and glasses. Among the spill were *Classic Comics* and *Sunbathing* magazines, and by the ashtray an upside down, worn-out copy of Grace Metalious's *Peyton Place*, bulging with turned-down pages. Bits of notepaper were lined up in a cleared corner where Wayne had been doing his accounts. He'd shown Tom once how he kept track of every penny he'd ever spent. His life was contained precisely in columns of numbers with tiny notations scribbled in the margins, details of which café he'd had coffee in, the stores where he'd bought his shoes and shirts, his cigarettes, his Brylcreem. He had a record of nickels and dimes going back to school days. Wayne picked up an empty whiskey bottle and held it to the light. I'll just go up and get another, he said.

Sitting here makes me want to throw up, Eddy said. Wayne scuttled out of the room.

We're here for a reason, Eddy said to Tom.

Wayne doesn't matter.

He matters to me now, Eddy said. The thing is, Wayne does whatever he's told, no matter what it leads to. He's interfered with me and that means he's interfered with all of us. You're part of it, too.

Then Wayne was back with a bottle of Seagram's 83 and three glasses, one of them chipped and cracked. He set them down and poured drinks, passing a full glass to Eddy and the cracked one to Tom. Wayne sat then on the edge of his unmade bed, lifted his whiskey, and took a drink, gulping. Jeez, Eddy, you're not looking too good. You neither, Tom. What'd you do to your hand? When Tom didn't answer, Wayne said: So, you seen anyone around?

Tom took a sip of his drink. I don't know, he said. How's Joe?

Wayne's face twitched into a smile. What do you mean? He put his glass down and folded his hands together, tucking them into his crotch. He started to giggle, not looking at either one of them. He was staring at a spot somewhere in the middle of the room. Eddy looked only at the pool of amber circling in his glass.

Oh yeah, I saw Joe down at the café. He said the bullet went through Lester's shoulder high up and didn't touch the bone. Joe told me Lester Coombs went back to the coast. Hey, are you going to the dog fights Saturday out at Carl Janek's? He reached for the Seagram's bottle and held it out to Eddy. When Eddy didn't reach back, Wayne went over and refilled Eddy's glass, then sat back down.

Eddy looked at him and said: So Billy's big-time friend is gone.

That's what Joe said. His glass tipped, spilling whiskey on his knee. The whole time Lester Coombs was here he stayed at the Day's End Motel, the one past the willows where the old lake steamer is docked. Remember that time we were there? Those girls? What were their names?

You were never there with me, said Eddy. I'd never have let you come.

Eddy always said Wayne's weaknesses disgusted him. To him, Wayne was a rat dancing on a piece of shiplap back of a chicken house, full of brag when he was the only rat in the world, but craven when a hawk or bobcat came along. He ran to ground fast. Wayne always hung around the edges of the crowd, but he wasn't one of the tribe.

Wayne looked from Eddy to Tom and back again. Jesus Christ, Eddy.

Eddy put his glass on the floor beside the chair, stretched out his legs, and tried to cross them at the ankles, but his foot seemed too heavy to lift and he gave up and let his legs sprawl. He kept on staring at Wayne.

That old man you told Harry about wasn't there, just like you said.

Wayne nodded, hopeful, trying to understand what was happening to him.

Eddy reached into the flap pocket of his shirt and took out a fifty-dollar bill, flattening it on his pant leg. That old man left a note though. It said he wanted you to have this.

Wayne reached over, one arm leaning on the coffee table, but Eddy didn't give the bill to him. Wayne sat back, confused. Why would the old guy want me to have that? he said. I don't even know him.

Your guess is as good as mine, said Eddy.

Wayne looked like he was going to cry.

And say someone told Sergeant Stanley about that old man's house out on Priest Valley Road. You know, the place you told Harry about.

Wayne pushed his hands through his greasy hair and peered down, his eyes strained as if he were searching for something. He picked up a used toothpick burred at one end, and started poking at his teeth.

Say someone did, said Eddy, for whatever reason.

Did what?

Eddy lifted up his glass off the floor and held it loose with a finger and thumb, turning it under the single bulb hanging from the ceiling on a twisted cord. Gave the rumour to the police, he said. A fly as big as his knuckle blundered against the light and caromed off, its buzz taking it, stunned, to the table where it sat, stroking its blunt eyes.

It wasn't me, Wayne blurted. Wayne looked at Tom, pleading with his whole face, but could find no help for him there. Tom slid down the wall and perched on his haunches. I told Harry about the house, sure, Wayne said, but that's all Joe asked me to do. The toothpick was stuck between his eye tooth and a molar, a wisp of tattered wood.

Eddy just grinned at him and tucked the fifty-dollar bill into his shirt pocket. He shifted his hip, reached behind him, and pulled from his belt the pistol he'd taken from Lester Coombs.

Is that Lester's pistol? Wayne said. He giggled again, looking to Tom for support as if he'd made some kind of joke. As if, to him, the three of them were in it together, all of them knowing about the old man's house and what had happened there.

Eddy pointed the pistol at Wayne and told him to go outside.

They went up the steps from the basement, Wayne walking backward in front of the pointed gun.

Give me the pistol, Eddy, Tom said, his voice flat.

Back off, Tom, said Eddy. I mean it.

Wayne moved slowly toward the Studebaker. He spoke to Tom, not taking his eyes off the pistol in Eddy's hand: Can you help me here, Tom?

Tom stood absolutely still, looking at his brother as he went around Wayne and opened the trunk.

Wayne held his hands out as if offering a gift to some greater power.

Get in the trunk, Eddy said quietly, as if what he wanted Wayne to do was a simple thing. Eddy looked peaceful to Tom, almost asleep on his feet, innocent, there at the edge of the sidewalk in his scuffed boots and leather jacket too big for him. He seemed preoccupied, almost as if Wayne was a second thought, someone he'd happened upon by accident.

Tom went over to Eddy and grabbed his sleeve.

The pistol swung up and touched Tom's belt.

Everything stopped then. A car went by on the street on the other side of the house, and then another. Eddy smiled as if to say they were still brothers, the pistol pointed again at Wayne.

Eddy? Wayne said his name as if it were a question. He looked terrified.

Tom was sure Eddy was bluffing, but he'd gone too far. You've made your point, Eddy, Tom said.

Wayne's jaw was slung down, his mouth open, his fore-head bunched. His eyes squatted under his brows. Tom had seen that look before, in a steer when it was being pushed into a narrow chute, the animal knowing something awful was ahead of it.

Wayne spoke into the silence.

Why?

Tom figured the question was one he had asked many times in his life, but had never got a clear answer to before.

Get in the trunk, Eddy said again and lifted the pistol to Wayne's chest.

I'm warning you, Eddy, Tom said.

Wayne shook his head as if to lose all thought, turned sideways, and put his one leg, kneeling, into the trunk. He stopped there, half in and half out, never taking his eyes off the pistol. Tom heard him start to piss, could see the stain spreading on his pants, the piss running down his leg and into the earth under his bare foot.

Tom, Wayne said, his head down, crying now. Can't you help me?

Eddy pressed the barrel hard against Wayne's temple, and then, a second later, took the pistol away from his head.

Tom looked at Wayne, a rifle in the trunk catching his eye. It was the .308, the barrel tucked behind the spare tire.

You see that rifle there? Eddy said. Take it and get rid of it for me. And then he looked at Tom as if puzzled by something and said: What the fuck is so great about *Peyton Place* anyway? Superman too, for that matter.

Wayne fell away from the trunk and lay on the ground, his body shaking.

19

What had happened at Wayne's hadn't been just about the old man at the house, he realized. It was about Boyco too. Eddy had long ago told him about Wayne laughing at him at the station the day he was taken away. Tom had forgotten about that, but he knew that Eddy hadn't. All his brother's friends had been there that day to watch him leave. They looked up to Eddy, as if his getting caught had somehow made him even bigger in their eyes. But they were afraid too, for him and for themselves, the stories of the correctional school a dream they didn't want to have. Eddy said he'd seen Wayne laughing, and there was no telling Eddy it could have been about something else. Others were there too, the same curious onlookers who came to the station every time a man was sent to Oakalla prison, or a kid shipped off to Boyco. What Tom remembered most was the fear in his brother's face looking out from the train, and his father and mother not doing anything to stop it from happening.

From the moment the train pulled out of the station, silence surrounded Eddy's absence. It was as if his brother had ceased to exist. Even when Eddy returned home a year later, nothing was said by their parents. Father pretended nothing had happened to Eddy. It upset Tom more than his father's unpredictable disappearances, Father in the bush, gone for a night into town, or days and nights on the road. Mother too, her vanishing into her room. Tom had been afraid to ask them about Eddy, afraid to speak, and he came to wonder if his mother and father had been afraid too.

Eddy had got up the morning after he returned, all of them in the kitchen, Mother with her back to the three of them as Father told Eddy there'd be no more school, he had to go to work. Eddy stared blankly at him. Mother had been frying a welter of eggs in bacon grease, the boil and splatter all around them. She never turned around. And Tom had just sat there not moving as Father told Eddy he'd found him a job in the bush and Eddy looked back as if not caring what his father threw at him. Father's words were huge in the room, followed by silence.

Tom remembered a day when he'd been out hunting. He'd taken seven grouse. Eddy had been home then for two months. Tom had been walking through the orchard and was about to come down the path by the creek when he saw through the spare willows Eddy sitting on the steps leading down to the root cellar, his face wet.

He'd never seen his brother like that before. Not even when Father beat him for burning down the barn over by Black Rock when Eddy was younger. Tom figured Father didn't care that Eddy had burned it, only that he'd been caught running from the conflagration. Father said he'd told the farmer that Eddy couldn't have done it, that Eddy had been with him all that day up in Enderby where he'd been selling bootleg liquor, but the farmer had argued and left, cursing Elmer and cursing his sons, telling him the Stark family was a blight on the face of the earth. Enraged, Father took Eddy down to the root cellar. His brother never made a sound as Tom watched from the orchard, Father beating him with that belt, punishing him for everything, it seemed, for all his wanton anger and hatred, for being indulged too much, for being his mother's son.

Tom had dropped the grouse in the grass by the well. He remembered that, their falling soft onto their feathers. He'd gone to his brother then and sat down on the step beside him. It was a new kind of fear he felt, for if his brother could allow himself to cry, what safety was there in the world for either of them. Tom knew then that whatever had been broken in Eddy couldn't be fixed, by him or by anyone. And because he didn't know what else to do, he reached out and placed his hand on Eddy's arm. He touched him in the ten-tative way he'd have touched an injured animal, a dog say, hurt in a fight, or one struck a glancing blow by a car and left barely breathing in a ditch. It was just his hand on Eddy's arm, but Eddy had lifted his head and looked at him, his mouth closed tight. They had sat there together in that silence.

Tom turned now into the big park down by the creek and stopped the truck in the shadows of the grandstand where the baseball diamond was. He was sweating, his skin wet and cold. Eddy had driven away from Wayne's heading for the back roads leading to Hurlbert's farm out in the Coldstream Valley. His brother was like some outlaw now. Tom had been driving around aimlessly, thinking, and the sun had gone down. He waited there, staring into the rear-view mirror, and after a minute or two the police car that had been following him for the last while passed slowly by the turnoff and went on up Mission Hill. Tom sat there for a long time, but the squad car didn't return.

In front of him was the baseball diamond with its bags still pinned to the bases and around it the white board fence, the stands and fence both a little dilapidated, baseball a game people listened to on the radio now, not one they played. But he remembered the crowd rising to its feet, him and Eddy following the white leather sphere as it arced up into the afternoon sky, everyone there sure it would go beyond the man leaning back against the fence, his arm out-stretched as he reached for something that was falling beyond him.

He got out and walked around. A breeze stirred, a last sunflower standing against the near fence, its dried head picked clean by birds. A few black seeds studded in the hearts of the flower pans were all that was left of summer. He went over to the stands and up the worn wooden steps to the top of the bleachers. He hadn't been up there for years. This is where he and Eddy used to watch the ball games. He sat down, a spider web catching his eye. It was huge, the funnel a foot across. He stopped and gazed into the silk mouth, the splayed legs of the spider draped out. As he stared, a night-struck Bluebottle fly landed on the spider's web. He watched it trying to walk, its feet caught in the sticky mesh. For a moment there was only the fly trying to crawl off the web and then the spider rushed from its dark tunnel and placed the end of one long leg on the fly's back. Tom reached out then, the spider quickly retreating, and taking the fly gently between his thumb and finger, lifted it up. The fly battered with frantic wings, and he let it go into the night.

Descending from the stands, Tom got back in the truck. He started the engine, hung his bad hand out the window into the cool air, pushed the truck into first gear, and followed the road around the baseball field, deeper into the park. He passed under the elm trees by the railroad right-of-way. It was where he'd see the hoboes when he was a kid. They would let him sit with them around their fires as they stared into their bottles of cheap wine, beans seething in billy cans. They were the lost ones, men without friends or family and so, to Tom, beyond both safety and danger, having only themselves to care for. Now they were gone into their graves or, rare, a solitary man might be there, kneeling over a blackened stone circle, a small fire burning in the slurry of those ancient ashes.

A car swept up the incline of the railway overpass and disappeared down the road toward the Arrow lakes. He got back in the truck and, thinking of the police car that had been following him, remembered the rifle he'd taken from Eddy's trunk. He looked behind him and made sure it was still covered by the folded tarp.

He idled past the wading pool where little children had run naked through the summer afternoons to the clucking of their mothers. He'd watched them in summers past, the women all milk and sweat, their only glory the babies squeezed out of them. The barren pool glimmered under the moon and he wondered why women thought a baby an answer to the grief of this world. What hope was theirs? He asked, but like Wayne's hapless plea, he realized there was no answer adequate to the request. He thought of turning around and going back out to the valley and getting Eddy, the two of them driving away then into the night, but to go where, to do what?

He pulled the truck over at the deep end of the park where the bush started. There were no lawns there, no ponds or baseball diamonds. The night he sat in was made deeper by the remnant slab fire from a small, transient sawmill by the tracks. The mill had been set up there for the past few weeks cutting private timber off the Bar L Ranch. Tom knew the gypo outfit would be gone over the weekend, some of the equipment already loaded onto a flatbed truck that had seen better days. Back in the trees, Coldstream Creek purled into the big lake and the Okanagan River. He imagined a small woodchip falling from a saw into the creek and riding all the way to the Columbia River, the bit of wood drifting down through the desert, falling from the lip of Grand Coulee Dam and disappearing into that huge froth.

He glanced into his rear-view mirror and saw a car coming up behind him, its headlights blinking through the cottonwoods and willows. A police cruiser stopped behind his truck, its motor turning quietly over, no one getting out of the car.

He closed his eyes. Then the car door opened behind him. He heard the slick of grease in the hinges, and then the sound of boots on stones. He opened his eyes and saw Sergeant Stanley in the side mirror standing at the rear fender in his black cowboy boots. He came to the window.

Well, if it isn't Tom Stark, Stanley said. What are you doing hiding down here in the park?

The Sergeant's brush cut shone like burned stubble.

I was thinking your brother might be with you, Stanley said, his voice quiet, almost friendly, the threat buried under his words. You don't happen to know where he is, do you? Him and me, we've got some things to talk about.

Tom could feel the hate in the man. He stayed silent, staring straight ahead.

Get out of the car, said Stanley.

Tom, shaking a little, lifted the door handle and stepped sideways out of the truck, turning his body toward the cool air coming off the creek.

I went to a house out Priest Valley Road the other night, Stanley said. You know the one. It's right near Garofalo's butcher shop. I understand your brother was out that way.

I don't know what you're talking about, Tom said.

We got a tip, you see, something about a break-in out there. I followed it up. You wouldn't happen to know anything about it, would you?

I told you, I don't know what you're talking about.

Stanley put the flat of his hand on Tom's shoulder and

guided him around to the front bumper. Put your hands on the hood, Stanley said, and Tom did, his breath coming short and fast.

How's your brother these days?

His voice was casual, as if he was asking about a friend. Then he kicked Tom's legs wide and put his hand between his shoulder blades pushing him down. Tom's cheek was pressed against the metal. He knew every dint and scratch in the truck's paint, the knuckles in the chrome bumper, the pits in the steel where sun and snow had eaten it.

Stanley's hand moved up Tom's back, then he tightened his fingers around his neck as he spit out his words. Your brother's still got a fucking mouth on him!

Tom stayed there absolutely still as Stanley went on: Your brother stopped me outside the pool hall last week when I was walking with my little girl. I was taking her to the Kandy Kitchen for a bottle of Orange Crush. She's only five, for christ's sake!

I don't understand.

Your asshole brother asked if her dog was okay. How's your dog, little girl? Him with that shit-eating grin on his face. Your brother squatted down right in front of her and said: Got quite an appetite, that dog of yours!

The Sergeant's hand squeezed the back of Tom's neck. That's when he said he'd watched her when she was playing in the backyard. My daughter!

Stanley held fast to Tom's neck as his other fist swung into Tom's kidney, and though Tom knew it was coming and had tightened up, still the fist came hard. Tom sank to his knees, the vomit coming hot from his throat out onto the bumper. He looked at it, something wet on the chrome. Stanley was behind him, breathing, and then he was gone, his boots carrying him back to the car. Tom knelt there, the car lights passing over him as the cruiser turned around and drove off into the dark.

He turned down the narrow dirt road leading to Marilyn's trailer, Swan Lake ahead of him. He could see the bulrushes, their long leaves shrivelled at the tips. At the top of the ramp were two small suitcases with what looked like some sweaters and a jacket resting on top of them. He turned the truck sideways in the yard and stopped. Close up the trailer looked more weathered, the paint scratched, the aluminum gone white from the sun, worn from the steady wind that blew down the Spallumcheen. There were lights on in the back of the trailer and he tapped the horn three times. Starlight glanced off the lake, the moon just beginning to break over the eastern ridge of the mountains.

The door opened and Marilyn stepped out, leaning down to gather up her loose clothing from the cardboard suitcases. Arms full, she came down the ramp, behind her in the doorway a wheelchair appearing, her father sitting there with his hands on the polished steel. As Marilyn came to the truck, Tom opened the door and she piled her stuff behind the seat. Your father's there, Tom said.

She didn't reply, just turned and went back up the ramp.

Her father rolled the chair partway out the door, and Tom heard Marilyn say something he couldn't quite make out. Taking a suitcase in each hand, she said something else to her father, who simply looked at her, saying nothing as she carried the bags to the truck and put them in the back. Tom watched as a woman in a flowered housecoat came behind the wheelchair in the doorway and pulled it back into the trailer, neither of them saying or doing anything to stop their daughter. Then the door closed, the light shining from the small window.

He let out the clutch and drove back up to the road. They didn't look back as the truck skirted the clay hills, heading slowly toward the lights of the town. He drove along the twisting ruts, potholes and washboard shivering the truck. The lake was low as it always was this time of year, the water seeping its autumn scum into the sunken belly of the valley.

How long's your father been in that wheelchair?

She leaned back in the seat and told him about her father and how he was wounded in the war in Holland, a piece of shrapnel lodged in his spine. They crippled him, she said. Marilyn spoke softly as she told how her father spent his days in the chair or on the couch in the trailer listening to the radio and reading magazines her mother brought home from her housekeeping jobs. Her mother had told her he was changed when he came back from Europe. He isn't mean, Marilyn said, it's just that he'll blow up every once in a while for no reason. It could be anything, a piece of toast dropped on the floor, her closing the door too hard, or even just a bird hitting the window. There's no one to help him most of the time, she said. My mom's out cleaning houses most days, and I'm at school. She told him her father hated being pushed around by her or her mother. He's got some kind of pension from the army, she said. My mother gets us by as best she can.

Tom thought about the woman he'd seen in the trailer door. Marilyn said her parents had met at some small-town dance in Ontario when her father was guarding the Welland Canal. Tom hadn't heard of the canal and asked why it was so important it needed guarding from a war so far away, but Marilyn said she didn't know. She told him her mother was Irish from the Ottawa Valley. Black Irish, she said. You can tell because her hair's so dark. She said she got her brown hair from her father's side. Tom was quiet for a moment and told her he didn't know where his people had come from, way back.

The truck bumped over a large rock and Marilyn sat forward, bracing herself on the dashboard. My mother never paid me much attention except to tell me to be quiet and not to upset my father, she said. She brightened for a moment. My mother knows all about herbs and healing. She makes what she calls concoctions from things growing right under your feet. People along the lake know about her remedies.

Tom watched the hills go by, the truck lights catching at a doe in a field with two fawns beside her grown almost as big as she was, their spots faded away. The three deer looked at them as they passed, their heads lifted from the sparse grass. Ahead was a fork in the road and Tom turned sharply up the hill toward the nuisance ground, gravel spitting behind them. At the top, he drove out onto the truck flat and parked by the shed in the middle of the dump turn-around. Hubcaps from Hudsons, Oldsmobiles, Packards, and Cadillacs hung from the shed walls, the door covered in rusty licence plates the dump man had nailed up. When he was a boy, he'd loved to read the names of places he'd only heard of, Louisiana, Quebec, Florida, the word Mississippi, the sound of a river rolling. Jan Mursky had sat in the shed every day marking down each load of garbage before it was dumped into the flames. His pencil stub kept track of the drivers: Powell, Nickel, Crozier, MacDowell, whoever was hauling that day. Tom parked by the shed and they got out. Tom leaned back inside, reached under the tarp, and lifted out the .308.

What're you going to do with that?

It's just an old gun, he said. The rifling's gone in the barrel.

It doesn't look that old, Marilyn said, but he ignored her and walked to the edge of the dump. He swung the rifle in an arc and hurled it down into a dark hole where flames were licking at the apples dumped that day. The rifle struck butt-first and sank into the soft maw of mottled fruit, the end of the barrel left sticking out, pointing at nothing.

They stood there and looked at the town, the street lights ghostly among the distant trees, a car threading its way through the dark. Tom wondered if Stanley was parked somewhere along Ranch Road now, waiting for Eddy's

Studebaker. He knew Stanley wouldn't walk up to the front door of their house looking for him. No, Stanley wanted Eddy on his own.

She turned to him. You're really sweating, she said. She put her hand to his face. You're burning up.

I know, he said. I haven't been feeling all that good today.

They heard the night freight up from Kelowna, its horn blaring, the last of the apples from the valley packing houses moving north to the CPR main line at Kamloops, the apples going east to the cities. Marilyn rested against him now, her arm around his waist, and he could feel her quick breathing. She was wearing a different sweater tonight, a stitched-on rabbit chewing on a carrot above the curve of her breast. Tom stood quiet as he lifted his hand and put it under her sweater. She reached behind, undid the clasp of her brassiere, her small breast slipping like a split peach into his palm, and they stood there without moving, looking down the spill where baby carriages, wagons, ice boxes, and ancient cars had rolled into the sagebrush and cactus just beyond the flames.

You know, she said, I've breathed this dump all my life. She turned and asked him what was wrong. You're not listening to me, she said.

And he said: Eddy almost killed someone today.

She startled, and he took his hand from her breast.

Who?

He wanted to settle an old score, Tom said. He wanted to put a fear in the guy that he'd never forget.

She gripped his hip, her thumb in his belt. Wisps of ash twisted up like bats from the glowing coals among magazines and newspaper, broken boards, and shattered tree limbs. Come morning the great fires would begin again. Mursky would fling gallon after gallon of kerosene and diesel down the slope and then the battered trucks would dump their first loads, the wreckage of the town feeding the fires.

Your brother's not right, she said. Why's he like that?

Eddy's like this, Tom said, holding his hurt hand out to her. Sergeant Stanley did something to him years ago in a cell below the Courthouse before sending him away. But there were other things done before Stanley got hold of him and he's lived with them too and longer, and there's nothing that can change any of it. And Tom knew then he was speaking of both Eddy and himself and of Marilyn too, and of his mother and father, his family, the tribe, the town, the country, the valley and the mountains.

She was quiet as they walked, her face turned down in shadow. One time I was stealing makeup from Mr. Arthwright's drugstore, she said. You know, lipstick and nail polish and stuff. I thought eye shadow and mascara would help me hide my eye. Mr. Arthwright called Sergeant Stanley when he caught me with a lipstick in my purse. The Sergeant drove me out here to Swan Lake, but he talked to me before ever we got to the trailer.

She stared at the town, the Courthouse on the hill a block of stone with spotlights burning up its granite walls. She swallowed and took a breath. He told me I'd be grown up in a few more years and when I was, he'd come looking for me. She pulled Tom to a stop. That bugger, she said. There'll come a time when he'll get what's coming to him.

He didn't touch you then.

No, but I'll never forget the way he looked at me.

Did you tell anyone?

Who was I going to tell? The police? Stanley *is* the police. There's no one higher than him except maybe the judge. I couldn't tell my mother or my father. They wouldn't have believed me. Besides, I was caught stealing. All my father would've done is yelled at me. He's good at that, no matter him being crippled.

She was quiet again as she looked out over Swan Lake, the water black with shreds of light on its narrow waves.

Tom went down on his haunches, picked up a chunk of cinder and tossed it over the edge, the bit of burned coke falling in the dark. Have you ever seen someone dead?

I've seen everything dead, Marilyn said, her voice bitter. Sheep, deer, coyotes, you name it, bear and moose. My Uncle Bill's a hunter. He taught me how to shoot when I was small. I've seen people in coffins too, my aunt and uncle who died in a car crash up on the Big Bend past Revelstoke, other people too. I saw my little brother dead when he was run over. I was nine years old. One day my mother was late for her housecleaning job. She's always been nervous. Anyway, she was in a hurry when she backed the car over him. Pete was just little. My mother never got over it. My father said it was Pete's own fault. He must have run behind the car when my mother wasn't looking.

When one of my sisters died, I asked Mother why she

didn't cry and she told me she'd shed her tears a long time ago, Tom said.

My parents changed after that, Marilyn said. My mother still cries about it. I can hear her sometimes in their bedroom, my father telling her to quiet down. He says crying never does anyone any good. Most nights they just sit there in the living room saying nothing. That's when I go nuts wanting to get out of there.

She said she'd never told anyone about her little brother and now Tom knew.

You're the only one who's ever talked to me clear, she said. All I've known in my life are boys who think a girl's to screw and nothing more. She smoothed her skirt with her hands and looked up at him. I've no love for men, she said.

20

tom stood on the gravel reach with one foot on the running board and one hand on the door of the truck as Hurlbert told him what happened out at the farm that morning. He explained that Sergeant Stanley had come just before dawn with another cop. Maureen had been making breakfast when they saw the police car pull into the yard. They drove in quietly, he said. I went out and Stanley was sitting behind the wheel. The other cop was yelling out his window at the dog leaping up at his door, barking his head off.

The wind picked up, dust blowing off the garden. Tom turned his back to it and closed his eyes until the gusts blew past and died away. He shivered, his shirt damp against his skin. His thoughts were going in circles. He wondered if somehow Stanley had followed him out there two nights before. But he had been careful. He'd made sure there was no one on the valley road but him when he turned off at the farm.

Did they say what they wanted?

They said they needed to look around Harry's shack, John said. They didn't tell me why.

And Eddy?

He's okay as far as I know, John said. Maureen came out on the porch and told Stanley he'd no business on our farm, but Stanley just ignored her. He told us to stay put. Then they headed down through the orchard to the creek and that's when Maureen went over to this truck of mine and leaned on the horn. She held it down for damn near a minute.

Tom stood there feeling dazed. John said how upset Maureen had been when Stanley and the cop had come back with Harry a while later. There'd been a young girl with them, but John told him she was one he'd never seen before. Stanley had Harry in handcuffs, John said. Maureen told the Sergeant what she thought of that. I finally had to damn near push her into the house, she was so mad. Stanley told me I'd better not be hiding your brother. He said if I saw Eddy around I was to call the station and let him know. The whole time he was talking to me, Harry never said a word. It looked like they'd treated him pretty rough. Anyway, they put him in the back seat of the car with the cop and the girl in front. She couldn't have been more than twelve or thirteen, and she was acting pretty strange. Stanley told me he was charging Harry with statutory rape.

All Tom could do was ask John what happened to his brother.

He must've hid out in the orchard when he heard the horn, John said. Her leaning on it like that must have told them something. I don't know why Harry didn't take off too. Maybe the girl was a problem for him. Whether Stanley and the other cop looked for Eddy or not, I've no idea, but if they did they couldn't find him. Anyway, a while later, Eddy came up from the creek and got the Studebaker out of the shed. He didn't say where he was going, he just took off. I'm sorry, Tom. Your brother didn't look scared, he was just running.

Did Stanley say anything else?

All I know is Sergeant Stanley told me if I saw Eddy I was to call him. I'm on my way over to Harry's folks' place. They don't have a telephone. They'll want to know. I just wanted to stop by and tell you what happened. Eddy's okay. As far as I know anyways.

Tom watched Hurlbert's truck go up the driveway and down the road. He didn't know where Eddy would have gone or where he'd stay. He hoped he wouldn't be stupid enough to show up at the dog fights tomorrow.

Tom went to the house and sagged into a chair at the kitchen table, thinking of them going down the path by the creek, the night quiet but for the horn blaring in the farmyard behind them. He imagined the Sergeant cursing when he heard it. Eddy and Harry must have heard it too. He could see the girl in the backroom stumbling up from the straw tick trying to get dressed as Harry told her to hurry, and Eddy on the step out front, wrecked on junk, looking into the dark, the horn telling him that something was wrong. Then the sound of the Sergeant and his man, a flashlight probing the path by the creek, and Eddy running, knowing it had to be the police. Then they caught Harry and the girl, likely when they were coming out the door or else somewhere in the orchard under the trees, Harry not wanting to leave the girl behind, knowing she was under-age and would tell the police everything, drunk as she was and stoned on speed, afraid and confused, crying, saying she'd been raped. He pictured Eddy circling deep in the trees or on his belly in the tall grass, trying to hear what was going on.

Tom moved the ashtray and stared at the burned-out butts sticking out of the sand like the stumps of logged-off trees in a cut block. He reached out and, one by one, pushed them over with his finger.

Marilyn ladled liver and onions and fried potatoes and eggs onto a plate and put it down in front of Tom. You're going to bed after his, she said. I've seen that hand of yours, you've got poisoning in your blood. Tom looked at the food, listening as Mother sloughed down the hall, the sound of her slippers like something being dragged. Marilyn was weeping onion tears and she flattened them there with her wrist. Mother came into the room and glanced at her. Oh, you're still here. Where's Eddy? Her voice droned it out, the only question she seemed to know.

Marilyn shook her head, opened the toaster flaps, and began to scrape margarine on the toast.

I heard someone in the driveway a few minutes ago, Mother said, and she looked at Tom. Don't you have any-thing to say?

When Tom didn't reply, she said: You could at least know where your brother is.

Mother looked exhausted, Tom thought, her skin pale, stretched tight on her face. She isn't really old, he thought, but now, right now, she looks ancient. He pushed a chair out from the table with his foot, but she disregarded it.

I thought it was Eddy for sure this time, Mother said.

Quit going on about him, Tom said. You know he always comes back eventually.

He could've been here and gone away again, she said. What would you know about it? You weren't around last night when Crystal came to the house. Mother breathed deep and coughed, clearing her throat.

Tom saw a flash of guile in her quick eyes. So Crystal was here? he said.

Never you mind, Tom, never you mind. Why wouldn't a girl want to see your brother? She walked over to the counter, stepped round Marilyn, and began picking through the food in the frying pan. She scraped a few spoonfuls onto a plate and pulled a chair out from behind the table and sat down, ignoring the one Tom had pushed out for her.

So, what did she want? Tom said. I don't remember Crystal ever coming out here visiting.

Mother didn't reply as she squeezed her lower lip between thumb and finger.

What did she *say*? Marilyn asked, annoyed at the way Mother had talked to Tom.

Mother took her fork, stabbed at a piece of egg, and looked at Tom. Why wouldn't she come out here, no matter I don't hardly know her? she said. At least she showed she cared enough for Eddy to be asking to his welfare. Those drugs'll kill him someday, and why you can't do something to help your brother, I don't know. Somebody's got to put a stop to it. It's not that I can, stuck as I am in this house without a way out.

She put her fork down as if unsure what to say next.

Tom pushed his finger through the sand in the ashtray, the butts falling from the edge onto the table.

Mother pulled her plate a little closer, took a bite of onion, and then forked a tiny bit of egg, her hand barely steady. The girl wanted to know if he was home, she said. She had something to tell him. She said it was important. I told her Eddy wasn't home, probably out somewhere doing god knows what. Well, you tell Eddy I was here asking about him, she said.

Tom breathed hard through his mouth, his head splitting. I never knew Crystal to come out here by herself before, he said.

There was a car parked up on the road, Mother said. She hesitated, her fingers dibbling at her lips. I don't know. I thought at first it looked like the police come to talk to Eddy and I didn't come to the door. But then I saw Crystal outside. Why would the police be driving Crystal around? That's what I asked myself. They wouldn't have done that.

Was it the police?

I don't know, said Mother. She seemed almost desperate now, as if she wanted her story to make sense, but knew it didn't. There're those fir trees by the road and the willow and that purple maple I always hated that Father planted to spite me. Maples aren't supposed to be purple. But he drove it here a hundred miles an hour from where he'd dug it up out of someone's yard. Drove it in the back of that old truck and when he got it here every leaf was burned off by the wind. How it ever lived I'll never know.

She began to stir her fork in the liver and eggs, pushing the cold potatoes off to the side of her plate. I don't feel very well, she said. I can't seem to hold anything down these days.

Just tell us, Marilyn said, coming to sit at the table. It's all right.

I told you I didn't know who it was. I couldn't see. Mother crossed her arms and suddenly leaned toward Marilyn. What does it matter if it *was* the police? I didn't care, what with Crystal standing at the door and me having to get up thinking Eddy might have come home or was somewhere out there shooting up his drugs or dead. I told her I'd be the last to know where Eddy was. No one tells me anything. So what if I said the only place I knew was that shack out at John Hurlbert's farm. Wasn't that right to say? He always goes out there with Harry.

It's okay, Mother, Tom said. It doesn't matter now.

Mother started rocking back and forth in her chair. I'm tired of it all, she said to him. Why isn't Eddy here any more?

———

Tom stood and balanced himself against the wall and Marilyn took his arm, leading him to the stairs and then up to the attic room, the floor there littered with dead wasps. She sat him on the bed, his face beaded with sweat. You're not gonna die, Marilyn said, you're not. Tom said nothing, his eyes closed. Marilyn removed the dirty gauze from his hand and laid him back on the bed, covering him with the quilt, his breathing shallow, his lips dry. You rest now, she said. You're sick.

When he fell into sleep, she went back down. At the foot of the stairs, she listened for a moment and heard Mother's door closing. Then she walked out the door to the edge of the old vegetable garden. She knelt at a cluster of plantain and thumbed off a few leaves, pinching the stems to seal in the white sap. She found other medicinal herbs along the fence line, a few leaves of goldenseal, cranesbill, and bracken. Then she went down past the well and walked along the creek bottom. A hen pheasant with five grown chicks rose from some tangled grass, tipped her head at Marilyn, and clucked a warning cry. You too, little mother, Marilyn said, the pheasant's mostly grown chicks behind her in the grass, peering curiously at her.

She took a bubble of orange pitch from a stunted pine growing in a stand of poplars by the fence. Will not, will not, will not, she said, repeating the words over and over as if by speaking them aloud she could make them true. Pulling a handful of arrowheads up by the roots from the soft ground by the creek, she saw a worm writhing around her fingers. She placed it back, watching the dark red whip nudge into the disturbed dirt.

She'd seen her mother treat women and their children from along the lake when they'd come to the trailer for help, and knew now that she too could perform the same kind of healing. She remembered what her mother had taught her to look for among the weeds and wild plants and was thankful she'd listened and learned how to preserve a life, to cure a sickness, to relieve a woman's pains. Marilyn knew the burden of her own monthly bleeding, and knew that her womb could make a new world from the old, a kind of sacrifice her body had always known in its giving up of blood each moon. She looked down, the red worm almost gone now in the dirt where once roots were, and knew then a hand could hold a cup as easily as hold a pistol, a spoon, a knife.

Back in the house, she put the different plants on the counter, chopping them up and then crushing them with a hammer. She cooked them slowly into a thick paste, adding at the end a dust of charcoal she'd bruised from the nuggets of burned boards she found in the barrel by the shed.

While the paste cooled, she boiled willow bark with black pepper, letting them seethe into a tea. As it boiled, she tore pieces of clean cotton from the nightie she'd brought from home. Then she poured the tea into a glass and carried it upstairs with the pot of paste and the cotton strips. Tom was asleep, but she woke him and took his injured hand, creaming the poison out in a steady, rolling press, then spreading the grey paste of herbs onto a film of gauze and laying it across his palm. She bound the poultice, tying it down and cinching it with the strips of cotton. She tried to make him drink from the glass, lifting his head and dribbling the tea into his mouth, but it ran out the corners and down his chin as he tried to swallow. He turned his face away, his body shivering, smiling a little, and closing his eyes. She put the glass down beside the bed. If he woke again, he'd drink from it or not. She leaned toward him and whispered: I implore you.

She remembered one time when her baby brother, Pete, had been sick and her mother had brought him through a fever. *I implore you*, her mother had said as she sat by her brother's bassinet.

I implore you, Marilyn said.

21

In the vault of the barn, swallows wheeled below their empty nests. The roof, its main beam seized and strung by the years, curved down on itself in the sun. The beam was bent with age, wrung with its resistance to the wind and snow, rain and sun, the deep pull of the earth upon whatever had raised itself above it. The rafters attached to the beam sprayed out like a bird's feathers stretched. Light prickled through the cracks and crannies of the slant roof, shooting scattered needles across the timbered floor. The huge room shone golden against the grain of the grey pillars and studs that held the edifice still, insistent, up.

Billy and Art Gillespie, the extra man Billy always used, had gotten to the farm early, Carl nowhere to be seen, so they'd taken their dogs down to the kennels at the back of Carl's house, Billy leading Badger, and Art with Chance. When the dogs were safely caged, Billy and Art went back for the schooler dogs, bringing them to the temporary pens

Carl had banged together a few days ago with pig-wire and cedar posts. They went back to the truck then, the heater on against the morning's chill, drinking coffee from Art's thermos, the two of them waiting for the sun to break over the mountain and for Carl to come up from the house. They'd sat there and talked about the possibility of a storm coming late in the day, about past fights and pits, the different dogs coming in from out of town. Billy had said he supposed Carl's wife was off visiting her brother again down in Omak. Art had laughed and told Billy she'd taken off yesterday. She doesn't mind him raising dogs, Art said, she just doesn't like seeing them fight.

Billy's truck backed up to the barn doors, Carl driving, craning his head out the window as he nudged the tires against the planks in front of the barn. Billy stood in the early light, watching Art as he cut the yellowed twine on the last two bales at the back of the barn. Art and Carl had been working with forks and rakes, covering the worn floor six inches deep in straw. The bales had filled the barn back in the days when Carl's father eked out a living there, felling trees and blowing stumps with black powder to clear the quarter section Carl now sowed with oats and alfalfa. His father had dropped from a stroke thirty years before when he was scything a crop, his tractor broken down and no money to fix it. Carl said he had followed the crows to his downed father. He'd been Catholic, but Carl had said he'd always wanted to be buried with the dogs in the meadow behind the house. When he did die, the church had its way and Carl, just a kid then and intimidated by the priest, put his father in the cemetery. His mother, Baptist to the core, had wanted her husband anywhere else so long as it was in a place where dogans didn't pray over him, but she'd been unable to say or do much one way or the other, bed-ridden as she'd been with pleurisy and glad to be left alone. She was dead now too, and Carl had told Billy more than once he regretted listening to the priest and putting his father where he did, separate from his dogs and far from where his mother was eventually laid to rest.

Billy leaned against the barn, staring out into the first of the sun, and thought about what Art had told him earlier that morning, when they'd been sitting in his truck, gazing at the lakes in the distance and talking dogs, Art going on about Chance and how he thought his dog would win its fight against Mike Stuttle's pit bull. Art told Billy his nephew was a dog man too. He'd been helping Art with the training, working with Chance when his shift at the station was over, building the dog up on the treadmill. Billy had forgotten about Art's nephew being a corporal in town and asked Art what was new down at the detachment. Art said his nephew had been over the night before and had talked about the usual stuff, a fight at the Venice Café, some kids picked up for drag racing on Main Street, a young woman with a baby coming in to complain that she couldn't find her husband, and an anonymous tip alerting them to a possible break-in at some old man's house up on Priest Valley Road.

Billy knew more about the so-called break-in than he'd let on. The day after the party on Ranch Road, he'd seen Joe down at the pool hall. They'd shot some stick, Joe ranting about people who thought they were better than anyone else. Joe went on about the Starks, how it was always the same with Eddy, him thinking he could do what he pleased, the whole family acting like they were a whole lot better than everyone else. Billy had listened, saying little or nothing. He was still mad about what Eddy had done, Lester Coombs getting shot and having to go back to Vancouver and him having a pistol held to his head. Joe said it was about time Eddy Stark got taught a lesson, and he'd figured out a way to do it. Billy asked him how, and Joe said he knew about a secluded house up on Priest Valley Road, so he'd passed on a rumour to Wayne that there was money to be had there, the old man who owned it out of town visiting a sister at the hospital up in Kamloops. Joe said he'd told Wayne to be sure to mention it to Harry, because he knew Harry would be sure to tell Eddy all about it too. Joe told Wayne to keep quiet about where he'd got the information from. What Joe didn't bother saying to Wayne was that the old man's grandson had once told him that ever since his grandmother died, his grandfather never left the house. Joe said that evidently no one had seen much of the old man in years, but for the kids who delivered food and sundries from Olafson's every week. Christ, he'd said, if Harry and Eddy broke into the guy's house they'd get one Jesus scare and maybe a nice little run-in with the police too. Billy had gone along with the scheme, but he wasn't sure about it now. Eddy Stark was a fuck-up, yes, but Joe getting the police involved didn't seem like such a good idea any more.

Billy had asked Art if there had been a break-in, and Art said the police hadn't received a call from out there, but the Sergeant had gone to the house later to check on things and found that the old guy who lived there was nowhere around. His nephew had said the funny thing about it was there was no sign of a break-in, but the Sergeant reported he'd seen a little blood on the floor in one of the rooms. Billy had heard Jim Garofalo that afternoon at the Venice Café talking about how the police had asked him if he'd seen anything going on at the old man's house the night before. Jim said he'd told the Sergeant he'd seen two cars leaving late and one had looked like Eddy Stark's green Studebaker.

It had been Joe who'd tipped off the police. Now the old man was missing and they'd found blood there. Billy knew Eddy Stark never carried a gun, but he also knew he had Lester Coombs' pistol. Something must have happened out there, but what exactly was anybody's guess.

Billy rubbed his back against the wall, scratching his shoulders on the rough boards. He looked to the west where a few wisps of high cloud were threading across the sky. The field sloping down in front of the barn was empty, but soon enough there'd be cars and trucks there, men and their dogs, and the day would start. He glanced over as Art and Carl came out of the barn. They looked like they were done with spreading the straw. They stood in front of him by the doors, the two men leaning forward, hands hanging from their wrists as if their bodies were about to break into some kind of stumbling run if Billy would only give the command to do so. Carl and Art could hardly wait for things to begin.

They'd been fighting their dogs at smaller pits around the valley, working them hard on lesser animals. To them, Billy's pit was the high end of the summer circuit. Carl, especially, had said how proud he was Billy had chosen his place again to hold the fights. Billy knew both men wanted time to hurry faster, wanted the sun to move higher above the pines so everything could begin. They'd worked with their dogs for a long time, the fight in the pit today one more measure of their animals' worth. Billy listened to them talk about their dogs' fighting prowess, but Billy knew dogs would fight whether they were in the pit or not. They always had, they always would. It was in their nature.

Supposed to get some weather later today, said Carl as he brushed straw off his shirt. His head was covered in a beaked cap, streaked with rust and grease, the cap bill long ago broken in the centre so he could stuff it into his hip pocket. His overalls were tucked into his round-heeled boots. Art, beside him, had on his cowboy hat with the narrow brim, the sweatband made of braided leather with two bronze hawk feathers arched by the knot.

Billy told Carl and Art to get the pit set up. It was just gone eight and people would start arriving in a couple of hours. He swung the door beside him out against the wall, the hinges crying. Art stepped inside and placed his shoulder against the other door, forcing it against the uneven floor until it broke free of its bite against the sill. It swung out into the bright glare, the sun flooding in to form a square of light on the barn floor as swallows fled past them into the day.

Art dropped the tailgate of Billy's pickup as Carl came up and the two of them pulled the first of the curved pit shells from the pile. The wood was a pale gold, the slats cut from oak somewhere back east. He had inherited the pit from his grandfather who had loved fighting dogs. He'd brought dogs and pit with him on his third trip from Portland, Oregon, to the valley back in the last century. Billy's grandfather had followed the Okanogan Trail in 1865 that had led from Wallula on the Columbia River up through the Cariboo to the gold fields of Barkerville. He'd stopped at Father Pandosy's Mission in the Okanagan Valley, and after hanging around for a couple of weeks, figured it was easier to live halfway between Oregon and Barkerville and reap the money coming and going from the Cariboo. Following him were cowboys and gold seekers, farmers and settlers, all of them believing the valley was God's own country. He brought the dogs and the arena with him, he'd once said, for three reasons: he needed money, he liked gambling, and he loved dogs. It was his son, Billy's father, who'd first brought pit bulls up from San Francisco to fight, back in the early Thirties. Billy often said he was half dog himself, raised as he was with them.

When the pit wasn't being used, Billy kept it in a shed out behind his house. His dog-fighting implements were kept there too, the things he used to repair whatever injury an animal might have, and drugs he'd got from a married doctor he sold his little sister to for a weekend out at a line cabin back of Cousin's Bay on Kalamalka Lake. He'd made the doctor pay for the indiscretion for years, having taken pictures of him at his pleasures. In his kit were all the things he needed to make a dog fight go more smoothly, to prolong a life, or make a death go easily. Billy knew by the time a dog needed to be put down, it took to dying with welcome ease.

They cleared the area where the pit would be, pushing the straw back with their boots. It took a little over an hour for the shells to be unloaded and bolted together, the assembled ring held down by lag bolts screwed through angle-iron into the wood floor. Then Carl and Art were on their knees stapling down carpet in the fifteen-foot ring. Its tight pile would give the dogs purchase when they fought. While they were working, Art started whistling an Elvis tune as he turned the socket wrench, and Carl smiled to hear it. That Elvis is a helluva singer, he said.

You got that right, Art replied. The wife loves him all to hell. He ratcheted down hard on the wrench until the nut closed tight to the washer. She says he's great but, let's face it, nothing beats Frankie Laine in the end.

Billy walked away and headed down to the kennels, the dogs in Carl's runs beginning their hopeful growls and roars. Billy had an instinct for breeding animals who would fight to the death. Some dogs showed early, but that didn't mean they'd mature into one that could stay the pit. He'd learned from his father and grandfather how to groom a good pit bull. He knew what to look for in a pup. He'd said more than once that it wasn't just a willingness to fight that counted. A good fighting dog had to want to go past hurting to another place entirely. When Billy found one, he'd separate the dog from the litter, hand-feeding it until the dog imprinted on him. He trained all his best dogs by having them hang in the air from leather thongs, building them up to twenty hours without relaxing their jaws, running them on treadmills until their paws broke blood. He would set them early against schoolers, pushing his dogs past mauling and biting to killing.

His best was Badger, the dog never having lost a fight in four and a half years even though one ear had been torn off and the other wasn't much more than a few rags of skin. Everyone knew he was fighting him today against Carl's dog, King. Billy squatted by the kennel and put his hand through the wire to scratch the black dog's neck. Badger could smell the pit shells on his hands and he whined and stretched, standing high with his nose questing the air for the smell of another dog arriving, the sound of a truck on the farm road, one he would recognize when he heard it, a pickup or modified horse trailer that only showed up for the fights. Billy leaned close to the cage, Badger's nose poking through the wire. He saw no greater destiny than for a dog of his to die as it had lived. Meanwhile he'd stood the six-year-old at stud for four years, and the early pups, trained on treadmills and schooler dogs, had won fights all over the northwest. Billy had made better than three thousand dollars on Badger's fights and another thousand in stud fees.

Moving down the kennel line, he appraised the dogs, the way they stood, the way they held their heads. After them were the schoolers he'd brought. Billy kept a supply of animals he'd bought out of the back door of the animal shelter for fifty cents a dog and no questions asked. He also bought feral strays from boys hired to catch them, as well as flawed animals from breeders who had no desire to raise worthless dogs. The schooling dogs never lasted long, and Billy kept up a regular supply for his own use and for others to bring their animals to so they could learn aggression and endurance. The schoolers were there so an owner could find out if his dog had the desire to finish. If it couldn't, then it was sold off as a pet, used as a schooler itself, or was put down, the owner cursing the weak bitch it came out of.

The schoolers were in their pig-wire cages, legs shivering, some of them limping from injuries sustained in earlier matches. In a small run next to them was a rust-coloured dog that looked to be a mix of hound and pit bull. As he got near, the dog rose up and growled and Billy stepped back, looking at it more closely, surprised by its aggression. Carl usually brought his pups and yearlings over to Billy's when he wanted to work them, but this animal looked like one Carl was using here. Carl had mentioned to him the other day that he'd bought a rough-looking, cross-bred dog for a couple of dollars from some hitchhiker he'd picked up a few weeks back on the road north of Armstrong. He said he was planning on using the dog when he started training his young pit bulls later in the fall, and this animal looked like it was the one. Billy stared for a moment at the animal as it chopped its jaws and growled low in its throat. Fuck you too, Billy said with a laugh.

He was paying Carl fifty dollars for the use of the barn. It was cheap at the price, but then he didn't charge Carl for anything he might have to do for a dog if one of them got injured. Men who came to see the fight paid Billy five dollars to enter the barn to watch and gamble and thirty dollars for each dog they placed in the pit. It was up to Billy to call for the fight, to have the dogs set, to stop a match if a dog rolled, or to say, if there was doubt or argument, which dog won or lost, on the outside chance they refused to continue. Any betting done today would be handled by Joe. Small side bets were okay, but the odds were laid down by Billy. The gambling was his to run. If the day went well, he stood to take home better than five hundred dollars. There would be more if he used his amphetamines, depressants, and oxygen right.

He'd arranged with Lucky Johnson for blocks of ice, cases of beer, boxes of pop for women and children, and rye whiskey and rum for those who liked to drink their liquor hard. He'd keep the beer chilled in washtubs under the betting table. The hard stuff was sold by the bottle or glass. He didn't bother to bring in food. Women usually brought potato salads, sausages, and hamburger with them in their hampers, chops and steaks if their men were flush. There'd be fires with marshmallows and hot dogs for the kids. People shared, it was their way. Carl had a home-built concrete block barbecue big enough to fry a quarter of beef on. No one had to go hungry and those who did would just have to drive to get what they wanted. The Queen Victoria in Armstrong with its take-out or sit-down chow mein and chop suey was only a few miles away down in the valley.

Billy started walking back toward the barn. When he

passed King's pen, Carl's dog leapt from the corner toward him, hackles up and teeth bared. King leapt at Billy, the wire cutting the scarred skin above the dog's eye. Billy looked at the tongue hanging straight out and down between the front teeth, the huge incisors like braised pearl, the back molars perfect scissor blades. He picked up a blunt spear of wood by the door and when King snarled and leapt at him again, he poked the wood through the wire, catching the dog in the chest, slaver whipping from the jowls as the pit bull continued to snap at the splintered wood. Billy smiled as he rattled the stick against the wire, the dog lunging again and again, silent but for its heavy breathing, intent in its fury the way all crazed things are.

The noon sun raked the open field below the barn, a breeze stirring the dust where children ran and played among the cars and trucks. What mothers who weren't in the barn yelled at this one or that, but the children paid them no mind. A few men lingered by a trailer, drinking beer and talking, but everyone else was inside watching the last moments of the fight between Caesar and Chance.

The crowd grew still as Billy opened the gate in the wall of the pit, and sidling carefully, he placed the muzzle of the .22 at the front of Chance's skull where the hide was torn. The skin lifted up like a wet curtain on a line when he squeezed the trigger. Caesar, the black pit bull, his jaws on Chance's neck, jerked but didn't release. At the sharp *snap* of the sawed-off rifle, Chance slumped forward. The left paw, cut bad and leaking blood, blunted at the wine-dark carpet, seeking purchase and finding none even as he died, held up by the jaws of Caesar.

Mike Stuttle stepped onto the killing floor and gripped his dog by the nape as Billy pried the pit bull's jaws apart with a wooden cable pin. A woman at the end of the second row of seats cried out as the animal let go with a sudden jolt and snapped at Billy's hand, teeth grazing his knuckles as he kneed the dog in the shoulder. Stuttle looped a choke chain around Caesar's neck and hauled the dog to the gate, Caesar surging toward Art as he dragged Chance away. The men who had bet on Caesar to win began to come down from their seats and go to collect their bets from Joe, who was sitting in a chair behind the gambling and drinks table.

Art was quiet as Mike Stuttle went by with his muzzled dog, Caesar's paws jamming at the carpet as he tried to get back to Chance. When Mike got Caesar through the gate, the dog went wild in the trodden straw, Mike tightening the chain, choking him down, Caesar twisting inside the throttle. The crowd of men and women back at the ring leaned in as Art knelt down and gathered his dog up into his arms.

Chance gave a good fight, he said to Billy, who was standing just inside the gate, the .22 out of sight along his thigh. Yup, he said, nodding his head in respect.

People here and there began to move slowly toward the barn doors and the field where the women had started cooking. Men were buying drinks from the betting table, others began to form a half circle around Caesar, some peering close to look at his wounds. Mike gripped the chain collar in his fist. Billy, he said, his voice unsteady. We got to get Caesar fixed.

Billy followed Mike to the tables at the back, Caesar quieter now, subdued by the muzzle Mike had put on him, the adrenalin in him from the fight starting to burn off. Mike lifted the dog onto the table, and Billy checked out the cuts on his shoulders and neck, telling Mike that most of them didn't need stitches. He dribbled hydrogen peroxide in some of the deeper ones, put in a few stitches here and there, then looked to the dog's leg, washing bits of straw and dirt from the exposed muscle. He told Mike to lay Caesar down and hold him there. Once the dog was helpless, Billy swabbed iodine where the hide had been ripped away. The dog struggled and Mike put his weight across him, holding him down. Caesar whined as Billy tugged the rippled skin back up to the dog's shoulder and stapled the wound together. Mike leaned down and spoke quietly into his dog's cropped ear. There, there, he said. It's okay.

Silk threaded in a curved needle, Billy began a rolling back-stitch, snugging the edges together with each pull of the thread. He lifted the hide where he hadn't sewn it yet. Look at those tendons and muscles, he said to a couple of men at the end of the table. Now that's a pit bull.

You got that right, one of them said.

Is my dog going to be okay? Mike asked. His forearm was across Caesar's neck, knots of rug wool and slobber congealing on his shirt.

All things being equal, Billy said.

He's a good dog.

Pit bulls, said Billy. They're the best.

He knotted a stitch below the dog's shoulder, snipped off the end, and picked up more silk to thread into the needle. He glanced up at the barn and saw Tom Stark come through the doors with the girl he'd seen him with at the party, the one with the funny eye. Then he saw Carl go over and speak to Tom, Tom then leaning down to the girl, saying something before going with Carl back out the doors.

He saw the girl hesitate, look around, and, noticing him and the wounded dog, cross the barn to where he was working. She came up to the table and stood quietly as he began to put the last stitches into Caesar's shoulder. Billy ignored her as best he could, the needle slipping in and out of the dog's tough hide, the pulled thread looking like one of those skinny worms Billy had seen in bloated carcasses in the hills, the worms sticking out into the sun, twisting there like wild morning-glory.

The wind had come up, bits of straw lifting from the floor and flittering across the table. Finished with the stitching, Billy wrapped the dog's leg in gauze and tape, covering the bandages with a sock of tanned and supple deer hide he bound lightly with leather thongs. He liked working on animals. Sewing a dog up was to him like fixing an intricate motor, some needle valve, some slim and delicate bolt that had to be threaded perfectly so what was broken could run again.

You're going to have to keep the muzzle on him a while, Billy said to Mike. He'll worry this off in a minute if you leave him alone. Mike nodded.

I've never seen a real dog fight before, the girl said to Billy. He squinted at her and she said, My name's Marilyn.

He looked at her, the tight pedal-pushers and white blouse. She placed the tips of her fingers on the oilcloth as Billy finished cleaning a few shallow cuts on the dog's shoulder, Mike stroking his dog's head.

I like dogs, she said.

Yeah, well, maybe some day you'll get one, Billy said, not looking up as he took a small blue bottle from a pan that had been full of ice chips a few hours ago and was now only soiled water. He opened the bottle, filled a syringe, and gave the dog a shot in the hip, rubbing it into the heavy muscle. He set the syringe down, stretched, as Mike stood up, his fist tight around Caesar's choke chain. Billy scanned the barn, marking each cluster of people, the men and women in the stands drinking beer and others looking over Lucky's young pit bull as he paraded it around.

I hope your dog is going to be all right, Marilyn said.

Mike nodded as he lifted Caesar down, snapping a short leash to its collar, holding the dog to heel. Caesar shivered against his leg. Mike reached in his hip pocket, slid out a thin billfold, and spread it with two of his fingers. Take the two tens and the five there, he said.

Billy took out the bills and put them in his shirt pocket. Helluva fight, he said.

Caesar whimpered as Mike Stuttle gathered him up and carried him across the barn. Marilyn picked up the needle Billy had used and held it close to her eye. I never saw a curved needle before, she said.

Billy took it from her and placed it in a saucer of alcohol. Don't touch my things, he said.

When's the next fight?

Pretty soon, Billy said. A young pit bull's trying out against a schooler.

What's a schooler?

It's a dog other dogs learn from. It's why they're called that.

Marilyn reached out, looking directly at him as she pushed her finger through the landscape of blood, skin, and hair.

Billy suddenly felt awkward, her stare unsettling him. Unable to break her gaze, he knelt beside his kit under the table and began to put some of his tools away. He clicked the lock on the metal box and stood up, Marilyn heading for the pit where a crowd was beginning to gather.

Billy started walking toward the door when Weiner Reeves, looking dazed, bumped into him. Billy put out his hand and pushed him away. The guy had been wrecked on booze and amphetamines at the party, but he looked even worse now, his whole body vibrating. He looked to Billy like someone risen from a grave. As Weiner wandered off, Billy wiped his hand on his shirt, the smell of the formaldehyde an oily vapour in his nose. What kind of kid would live in a basement with a bunch of corpses? Billy wondered.

The fight between Caesar and Chance had followed hard on the heels of Badger and King's. His dog had won easily, King rolling hard after Badger scissored him deep in the throat. Billy had saved King, Carl grateful for his skill with caustic powder and sutures. He'd had to put a dog down in the match before Badger's, and he'd sewed up one other besides King and Caesar, a pit bull from Walla Walla that'd gone almost forty minutes in the second fight.

Mike Stuttle carried Caesar to the doors. He put the dog down, Caesar jerking at the steel links of his chain. Weiner Reeves leaned out from a group of men and Caesar turned and lunged at him, the dog's teeth biting the air a foot from his leg.

Get the fuck out of the way, Mike said. Billy watched as Weiner tried to laugh, but his eyes betrayed his flinch.

Billy followed the same route Mike had taken, not stopping as people tried to talk to him about the fight. He stepped through the barn doors and a sudden gust of wind caught at him, swirling the dust at his feet. Sid Morton was standing there spread-legged, a beer in his hand.

That dog of Art's fought hard, he said to Billy. You gotta be proud of an animal like that.

Yeah. He's not bad, he said, his fingernail picking at a crevice in his tooth where a bit of meat was lodged. Rain coming, he said. Take a look at the hills over there.

Art was standing behind his truck. Chance was lying in the back, a man by the fender reaching in and touching the mottled flank, saying to Art that his dog had put up a good fight. When Art didn't reply, the man asked if there was anything he could do, and Art shook his head.

Then Billy noticed Norman Christensen and Vera Spikula coming up the slope. He moved a few feet away, looking at the house where Carl and Tom were putting some dog into an empty kennel. He'd taken one look at Norman and that had been enough, the bandage on the guy's face taped from his jaw to his temple.

As he stood there he heard Norman say something to Sid about a seeing a kid playing with a whip down by the barbecue pit.

Billy bent down and began to fiddle with his bootlace as he tried to avoid Norman. He didn't want to get provoked. He'd heard his bullshit too many times.

The thing is, Norman was saying to Sid, that kid I saw liked it. He was trying hard to get good with that whip. It's like he was practising for his life.

What the hell are you going on about? Sid Morton said.

I don't want to be here, Norman, said Vera.

Norman scratched at the edge of his dressing where a few stitches poked out near his nose, Vera pulling at his elbow. He shrugged her away.

Hi there, Billy, Norman said as he went on into the barn, Vera beside him, talking a mile a minute into the ear on his good side.

Art covered Chance with a soiled Hudson's Bay blanket, closed the tailgate, and then just stood there in the dust, arms at his sides, his head down. Some men close by moved a little away, not wanting to intrude. A woman with two barefoot kids went around Art, her lips pursed, looking like she'd seen it all before, this thing men had about dogs, their certain grief.

Dark clouds were building along the crest of the Bluebush hills on the other side of the valley, their shadows dark on the lake, the wind twisting around Billy's feet, broken grass and bits of bark and woodchips rattling against the barn wall, the trees at the edge of the field a green clatter of needles, limbs thrashing in the blustering air. He stared out over the cars and trucks parked below the barn. Out in the field a few men were kicking dirt on their fires as the women with them gathered remnant food and utensils into boxes and hampers. Here and there one or another of them would look up at the hills and the storm building, hurrying their kids along as they packed their stuff away. A few trucks had already pulled out, but a good number of people were paying the coming storm no mind as they passed through the barn doors.

Billy stood in the sunlight and gazing out at the road leading up from the valley saw Eddy Stark's Studebaker turn into the farm, Eddy parking it away from the cars and trucks. He got out and stood by the door, looking up to the barn. Even from where Billy was standing, he could see Eddy was worn down. For a moment he wondered if Eddy would leave town, but he knew Eddy was like most people in the valley, no one ever straying far from home, no matter the trouble they might be in. He remembered one winter a few years back when a guy down the road from him killed his wife. Some men from Lumby found him in the bush the third night, less than a half mile from his house. The guy was half-frozen in a bivouac he'd built out of pine branches and a hunk of tarp, his small fire leading the pursuers to him. Billy stood there waiting as Eddy wove his way across the field, women and men watching him curiously as he passed them by.

When Eddy came close, Billy nodded his head, knowing what Eddy wanted.

Sixty bucks, Eddy said, holding out his hand.

Not here, said Billy. There's too many people around. Let's take this down to the car.

Eddy crumpled the bills in his fist, turned, and started back down the slope, his scruffy red hair whipping around his ears. Billy followed along behind, saying nothing, Eddy in front of him, thumbs hooked in his pockets, women parting as he threaded through the last fires to the car. He opened the door and got in, slamming it behind him. Billy could see Eddy looking at him in the side mirror as he came up, his hand out the open window, fingers gripping around the money against the wind.

Billy took the money and reached into his pocket, filching a packet out of a small bag. Eddy took it, tucking the drugs down between his legs.

Billy put his hands on the door and looked in. I heard about your troubles with the cops and all, he said. Something about a house getting broken into?

Eddy rubbed a hand against the light beard on his cheek and rolled the window partway up, Billy pulling his hands away. What house? What are you talking about? Eddy said.

Forget it, said Billy, taking a step back. Anyways, he said, be careful with that stuff. I didn't have time to cut it yet.

Yeah, sure, Eddy said, starting the car. He put it in gear and let the clutch out, the wheels spinning on the hard clay, the car swerving out onto the main road. A moment later a police car came out of the trees farther up the road, heading down the hill behind the Studebaker. Billy couldn't see who was driving, but he was sure the cop had to have been waiting up there to appear like he did. He stood and looked for a moment at the empty road. The clouds on the other side of the valley were boiling now, thick knots of black rising into the sky. High above the road a solitary turkey vulture balanced on its column of emptiness. Billy shook his head and started back toward the barn.

He saw some kids gathered at the door of his truck, one of them with a long willow whip dragging from his hand was standing on the running board staring through the window at Badger. Billy could see Badger's head through the windshield, the window beside him open a few inches. Billy yelled at the kid to get the hell away from the door. That dog in there will bite your arm off, given the chance, he said.

The kids ran off, but not far, the one with the whip in his hand standing by the back fender. Get the hell away, Billy said. He turned and looked in the window at Badger, who was breathing steady and slow, a blood pearl in the corner of his eye where he had stitched it shut.

The boy with the whip never moved.

Billy motioned to Sid, who was still leaning against the wall of the barn, and Sid nodded, coming over to Billy's truck, the boy retreating a few steps.

Fuck off, you little prick, Sid said. The boy slashed his willow whip into the dust between them, Sid making a grab for him, the boy laughing crazily as he ran away.

A few men were standing inside the doors out of the wind, arguing about different breeds, one of them saying there was nothing that could match a pit bull's bravery in the end. It's not bravery and it's not stupidity, Billy said as he passed them. All you need is the desire to finish hard.

He walked into the barn, and over to the pit, opening the gate, and telling the men around him to make sure no one got in the way when the dogs came up. He turned and shouted to the people gathered at the ring and up in the stands that the fight between Lucky's pit bull and the schooler would start shortly. He saw Marilyn standing up on something on the other side of the pit wall, Tom beside her, rubbing at a bandage on his left hand. She reached out and placed her hand on Tom's forehead, holding it there. He shook it away, and walked into the gathering crowd.

Billy was going to send someone down for one of his schoolers, when it occurred to him that that rust-coloured dog of Carl's would be a good one to go up against Lucky's Rebel. It had looked like it had some spunk in it. Carl had come back from the kennels and was in the pit now, stapling down the carpet where it had come loose in the last fight. Billy walked over and asked him if he was interested in putting that particular dog in against Lucky's pit bull. Carl seemed to think about the idea for a second or two, then said he'd been planning to save it for training a few young ones of his own. Billy waited, knowing Carl was still hurting about King losing the fight to Badger. Carl hesitated a little longer, and finally said it was okay with him if Billy really wanted to use the dog. Billy said he did, and told him that when he was finished, why not go down and bring the dog up from the kennels. I'm done here, Carl said, tucking the stapler into his hip pocket and getting up off the carpet. A gust of wind broke through the far wall. That storm's coming fast, Carl said. We'll be lucky to get this fight done by the time it's here. He hitched up his pants and headed toward the doors.

Billy watched him go, then went over to the betting table where Joe was selling drinks and taking some last bets. He looked at the Winchester .30-30 leaning against Joe's hip. Joe, as usual, showing off to people that he was guarding the money, that he was bigger than he really was. He sold a few last drinks, nothing revealed behind his half-closed lids. The men and women in the beer line had mostly thinned out, everyone looking around for a good spot to watch the match from, the crowd around the pit already three or four deep.

Joe said: You made good money from Badger's fight earlier. That dog of Carl's rolled a lot faster than I thought it would. King's lucky he got out of there alive.

Billy popped the cap from a bottle of Old Style, took a long drink, and stared at the cracks in the roof, shafts of sun breaking through here and there.

Chance should've won this last fight, Joe said as he leaned down and brushed some straw from his pant leg.

You don't know near enough about dogs to have an opinion, Billy said. How much did I turn on the fight?

A hundred and fifty easy, said Joe. A lot bet on Chance.

People try their luck any which way, Billy said. Take Eddy, for instance. He was just here and when he left he had a cop on his tail.

Joe leaned his rifle against the table and smoothed back the thin hair over his ears. There was a smug grin on his face and for a moment Billy felt like hitting him.

He turned away and started counting the money in the cash box. He was tired of Joe and tired of the Starks too. He folded a wad of bills into his pocket, leaving a few dollars and coins for Joe to use making change. Right then, all he wanted to do was run his fights and make a living.

He handed the box to Joe and elbowed his way to the gate, a few frantic swallows veering in the air above him. Lucky was sitting on his haunches on the far side of the pit, Rebel's neck chain in a tight grip. The stands were full again now and there were still people coming in from the field. Billy looked at Tom's girl on the far side. She all eager, standing there on her apple box, head and shoulders above the men around her. People in the stands were talking and drinking beer as they waited for the match to begin, some younger men on the top tier laughing too loud, an older guy in front of them turning around and hollering at them to take it easy. Let's have some respect, he said. There was something about watching a schooler getting maimed that seemed to get certain people too excited. Beyond the crowd, he saw Carl heading toward the ring, his schooler held close to his side on a short rope lead.

The crowd quieted as Carl crossed through the beaten straw, the wind shifting around the barn as it found its way through boards and shakes. Dust swirled in the random beams of broken light. Carl led his dog up to the gate.

Billy saw Tom walking around the outside of the crowd,

looking for a way to get closer to his girl, but there were too many people. He watched him circle back to where the betting table was.

———

Tom knew Billy didn't like people standing near the betting table during a match, even though that's where the liquor and beer were sold, but a few men had crowded around to see this last fight and, Joe, who might have said something, was in front of the table, not seeming to care one way or another. Tom could see Billy glancing over in their direction, looking surly, but he had his hands full and wasn't about to do anything. Tom blinked, his eyes sore, the headache he'd had mostly gone, the last of his fever a faint shadow between him and the world. His hand throbbed.

The crowd's muttering turned to shouts. Marilyn was standing up on her apple box on the other side of the pit, crowded round by men, her hand on the shoulder of some thin guy, balancing herself there, everyone caught up in the excitement.

He'd never liked the dog fights, yet he was somehow drawn to them each year, the violence a thing he'd always known lived in both dogs and men. Dogs fought dogs, sometimes to the death. That was bad enough. But when Billy killed a dog after it had been savaged in the ring, he had a look in his eyes. Tom had seen it in others, the doing of an ordinary task. It wasn't triumph and it wasn't sorrow, no matter what they might say afterward.

You could think you knew a man, and know nothing about him, because men lied about blood, especially when it came to killing men. And it wasn't killing like a hunter does, the moving downwind from prey. He'd hunted all his life, almost always alone, though when he was young he'd hunted sometimes with Father, but shooting a deer at dawn up by Cheater Creek wasn't the same as shooting a wounded animal in the pit. It wasn't killing for food or for a prize, a ten-point buck, or the bear they'd hunted one autumn, the one who broke a heifer's neck on a neighbouring farm with a single blow and was brought down at last by Father in the fall of '49. There was some justice in the taking of the bear, just as there was a kind of pleasure in taking a prize buck. The pit was different. Billy was like the hangman Eddy had told him about when he came back from Boyco. He accepted killing a dog as a job to do, a *thing* to be done, what he was good at, as a carpenter with his level, or a mason with his chisel.

Lucky Johnson was in the ring across from the gate, holding his dog close, the animal straining against the choke chain, cropped ears pricked forward. The young pit bull was thick through the shoulders and chest, lean-muscled, and was gazing through the open gate at Carl and the schooler as they came up. Billy nodded at Carl, and stepped through the gate with the dog Carl had shown Tom when they were down at the kennels earlier. Billy held the gate partly open so Carl could get back out once the fight began. As soon as the dog saw the pit bull, it surged up on its hind legs, Carl holding tight to its leash. Tom pushed sideways between a couple of men so he could see into the pit better, the two dogs stretching at each other, teeth bared, slavering as Carl and Lucky yarded on their tethers, holding the dogs apart, the men around the ring telling Billy to give the word and let the dogs go.

Seize him! Lucky cried as he yanked at his pit bull. You seize him! He urged Rebel to the limits of his chain, the pit bull raging.

You take him! Carl yelled at his dog. The schooler turned and bit at the rope lead, Carl slapping it across the side of its head, loosing the rope and then pulling it short again, the dog maddened even further by the noise of the crowd and the snarling pit bull a few feet away.

The wind had come up stronger and the eaves and rafters, timbers and struts, whistled above Tom. He looked out through the barn doors and saw a dark curtain of rain on the far side of the valley. The swallows, knowing the wind, and the rain on its heels, swept into the barn and criss-crossed the air above the pit as the dogs, frenzied now, jerked to the limits of their tethers. Billy raised his hand, Lucky and Carl freeing the dogs from their collars at the moment he cried out, *Let Go!* The dogs leapt toward each other, and Lucky clambered out over the pit wall, people staggering back to give him room as Carl slipped out through the gate, Billy closing it quickly behind him.

The dogs looked like something sprung whole from the earth, the two animals reaching through space for each other, as if eager for blessed release. A gust of wind whirled in the pit, straw glinting in broken spears, tufts of dog hair, ripped bits of rug flicking up from the dogs' claws, the hands of men and women moving around the wooden wall as if in benediction, cigarettes burning, bottles clinking, and among all this Marilyn crying out, her voice lost in the din.

Behind Tom's eyes, the dogs hung in the air in their first wild leap, then the maul and bite, the growl and thrust, as they heaved at each other to gain some kind of hold. He saw the tip of Rebel's left incisor, a stained green line running down to the gum, the dog's head high as if seeking a throat to grip. Its hackles were raised up, startled there in a crest, its paw touching Rebel's paw perfectly, the other paw pressed forward, almost but not quite on the pit bull's shoulder. Rebel's teeth were huge, pricks of light reflected from the scissoring line of peaks that were the cutting molars. The blunt head was turned slightly to the side, searching for a neck hold that was there and wasn't. The back legs of the dogs held braced to the torn rug, their bites coming and not coming, the yelling of the men in the stands, some who were on their feet now, the cries of the women, the dogs quick and savage.

And then Tom saw Rebel feint, chesting Carl's dog, who shouldered off and rounded the wall of the pit, snapping at the other dog who replied in kind, the two of them set and rearing again, neither getting a solid hold. Rebel lifted with a thrust of his back legs, tail stretched stiff, and Carl's dog went under the pit bull's maw, taking the front paw deep in his teeth. He wrenched down as a press does on metal. Rebel was locked hard to the back of the schooler's neck, his jaws closed on the loose hide, shaking his head viciously until

Carl's dog let go, twisted, and bit up into Rebel's throat, finding purchase there in the tendons and veins. Rebel gave a strangled gulp, trying to pull in a deeper bite, one paw down for a brace, the leg crumpling under him, the ruined paw blunting at the dark carpet.

The crowd stopped shouting when the pit bull faltered. Marilyn stood with a small fist raised up and clenched, her mouth open, soundless. It seemed to him as if the men around her were there only to hold her up, the skinny guy on one side bent forward, Marilyn's hand gripping his shirt at the shoulder, and on the other side a man standing tall, his chest heaving. Tom looked down the wall and saw Art Gillespie push his way back through the crowd and start walking away, Mike Stuttle going with him, his arm across Art's shoulders.

Lucky urged his dog on as if somehow Rebel might yet attack in spite of his crushed paw. Carl's dog let go of Rebel's neck and the pit bull sat back on his haunches, the muscles along his flanks quivering, a thin spray of bright blood rising from a cut in his throat.

Lucky cried at his dog one last time: You seize him!

Rebel cringed, looking up at his owner as a pup might who had been struck. He gave a choked bark, and the schooler, coppery hackles up, heaved at his throat again, biting hard, shaking the other dog, the pit bull trying to roll and show his belly, his head held up by the schooler's jaws even as he tried to twist his haunches down. Lucky, his dog finished, climbed back over the wall, dropping beside his dog and trying to wrap a choke chain around Rebel's neck.

He yelled at Billy to get in there and pull the schooler off. As he shouted, he kicked the schooler in the ribs, the dog not releasing his grip on Rebel's throat. Billy opened the gate, the .22 loose in his hand, Carl trying to get past him, but Billy put his arm out and stopped him.

Shoot that fucking dog! yelled Lucky as he yarded on the choke chain, Rebel freed from the other's grip. The schooler, confused, settled to the carpet, unsure of what it was to do, then looked up at the crowd and whined. Marilyn stepped up on the wall then and jumped into the pit. Tom, amazed, tried to push through the men who'd moved in front of him, but they shouldered him back. Billy moved into the ring, Carl's dog backing up to the wall. Billy turned to Lucky, who was squatting beside his injured dog. Get Rebel the hell out of here, Billy said. I don't want that dog over there any madder than it already is. Lucky put his arms under Rebel, lifted him up, and carried him hurriedly from the pit.

The barn was suddenly quiet.

For chrissake, get that girl out of there! someone shouted.

Tom jammed himself between the men and started to climb up onto the table, but a man pulled him back down, telling him to get the hell out of the way, the two of them struggling there for a moment and Tom breaking free.

Billy lifted his gun.

Don't you dare hurt that dog! Marilyn screamed.

Billy hesitated and then Tom saw Joe in front of him raise his own rifle, pointing it into the ring. Tom pulled himself across the table, then fumbled in his pocket for his clasp knife, taking the edge of the blade in his teeth and opening it. He moved close behind Joe, laying the blade across Joe's throat, saying: Put the fucking rifle down, Joe. That's Marilyn in there.

That girl's going to get hurt! Carl cried, pushing against Billy who was still blocking the gate.

Carl! Tom shouted. Don't go in there. That dog could attack her.

People turned to look at him.

You cocksucker, Stark, Joe said, turning under the knife, the razor edge of the blade scoring a thin, red line from his throat to the back of his neck. He stood there then, facing Tom, and, letting his breath out slowly, he placed the rifle on the table, and took a step to the side.

Move away, said Tom.

Joe backed to the pit wall, watching as Tom put the knife down and picked up the rifle, aiming it at Joe's chest, the rifle balanced there in one hand, his elbow pressing the stock against his ribs. Tom kept the rifle trained on Joe, wanting him to make some kind of move so he could have it over and done with. Years of Joe's misery, now some old man dead, and his brother's life on the line.

You bugger! Marilyn screamed at the back of Joe's head. You tried to shoot this dog. Marilyn turned toward the schooler, its growl lowered to a rumble now. She held her arm out, her hand dangling loosely from her wrist.

Tom kept the rifle on Joe, watching Marilyn, knowing the dog would bite her if someone made the wrong move.

It's just a dog, said a man behind Tom. That's all it is.

The dog settled to the floor, and Marilyn got down on her knees. The men around the wall leaned forward, not moving, the people in the tiers standing, waiting to see what would happen next. Everyone was silent.

The dog chopped its teeth twice and Billy began to move slowly toward Marilyn. When she held her fingers directly under its nose, he stopped dead. The dog sniffed at them, a single canine tooth clinging to its lip, the nostrils flared. A long moment went by as she grazed her fingers over the muzzle, then across the wounds on the side of the dog's head, passing lightly back to a torn ear, stroking the fox ruffs of hair. Tom watched, transfixed, as she shuffled gradually forward on her knees, bringing herself right beside the dog.

Then Carl came through the gate, going around Billy, and crossing the pit. He crouched beside Marilyn and said something to her that Tom couldn't hear. Marilyn stood and Carl reached down and put a collar around the dog's neck, taking the rope lead in his hand. He pulled at the lead gently, and the schooler stood up, its legs shaking.

Marilyn looked over at Tom as if seeing him for the first time, and he lowered the rifle.

Carl kept the lead short as he left the pit, the dog holding close as it padded beside him out the gate toward the doors of the barn. Billy stepped out of the ring and came around the pit over to them. Tom handed him the rifle.

Cold gusts of wind blasted through the walls, the roof beginning to rattle from the first heavy drops of rain. Billy hefted the Winchester lightly in his hand, then reversed it, holding it out stock-first, Joe taking it from him with a half-smile, tiny blood beads ringing his throat.

Some fucking families leave nothing behind them but trash, Joe said.

Billy gave Joe a long, slow look. This's over, Joe. You and your games. Get your truck and go.

Joe didn't say a word. He cradled the rifle across his arm and walked away, the wind buffeting him so that he staggered a moment as he neared the barn doors, his head down as he went out into the storm.

Fucking DP immigrant, Billy said under his breath, then glanced at Tom.

Tom looked away and walked to the pit. He swung himself up and over, and went to Marilyn.

The rain struck the walls, water pouring in crystal streams through the holes in the roof, the doors obscured, gone in the deluge. Men and women stumbled from the stands and out of the barn, seeming to swim away, disappearing into their own shouts and cries, fleeing through the water as if they'd been turned into fish with legs, scrambling back into an original element they'd long forgotten, drowning in the air as they ran toward their trucks. The rain had ruptured the hanging dust, turning it to mud in the air, a browned and beaten stew that smeared the bodies of children, pants and boots, shirts and jackets, men and women yelling at each other, dogs seeming to float on the earth, following their chains to whatever cage they were being led to in their cringes, barks, and howls.

Tom led Marilyn from the pit, her hanging on to his arm as they walked from the barn. All Tom could see were the backs of people bent over as they ran past them, each man and woman gone into what was neither above nor below, somewhere out in the downpour cars and trucks starting, windshield wipers beating time to curses, the rain beginning to slow suddenly, turning into a steady, drumming fall.

Tom and Marilyn headed toward Carl's, where his truck was parked. Carl came out from behind the house, the dog beside him, and called Marilyn over, handing her the lead. Carl looked at Tom who was standing by the side of the truck, nodding his head at what Tom couldn't find the words to say.

Billy turned at the doors and looked back into the barn, which was empty now, but for a few swallows weaving in and out of the now frail threads of water wavering down from the roof.

Who cares about Joe anyway? he thought. Who cares about any of them? Even Eddy Stark, running around the back roads with a cop on his tail. There wasn't anything he could do about that. He walked over to his truck and looked in the window at Badger. The dog raised his head and when Billy made no move to open the door, Badger lowered it again to his paws.

He'd have to go find Carl and Art so they could take the pit apart and load it up. He went around the back of the truck and dropped the tailgate, taking out the tarp he used to cover the pit shells. He shook the canvas out, bits of wet straw falling to the ground. When he looked up, he saw Tom Stark's truck crossing the field, moving away, vanishing in the rain, as it headed toward the clay-slick road.

22

read between the lines, Mother would say when he was little, cunning in her deceptions. Tom had sat beside her on the couch and stared into the book she was reading from. He could see the cramped white space between the lines of letters and he imagined a secret code embedded there like lemon writing only a flame could reveal. Learning from her was like trying to read the story of a blizzard. It was like going out into the February snow and finding the tracks of animals and birds, small stories left behind in the drifts.

Everything you saw was the past of a winter hunt. It was the story of snow. You followed the trail of a rabbit and saw how it stopped at a red willow sapling and stood up on its two back paws to nibble the buds from the bare branches. You got close, hunkered down, and marked the cut of its sharp teeth in the bark, the delicate bites it took from next year's leaves. The branch was bare. The rabbit stayed close to the willow and sagebrush and the tall grasses pushed up through the snow. The animal was white, the fur turned to the same cold of the land it wandered for food. Only the nose, the ear tips, could tell you where it hopped. You saw the rabbit sometimes on the snow, black specks moving like summer flies across a pure white tablecloth.

And you followed the tracks because you were a boy and the story of the rabbit was who the rabbit used to be, as it went this way and that, and always to the spare seeds hidden inside grass heads, the alder and willow buds. You saw how the rabbit moved at last, hesitant, careful, out into the open. The rabbit had come out from the safety of the creek brush and was crossing the orchard to the other side where the old fence hung its rusted wire. There was food over there, frozen, windfall apples under the snow kicked to the margin of the field by Father one night in autumn when he was out visiting his graves.

You stepped out into the open and followed the tracks into the field. You imagined yourself white as snow, crossing a great emptiness, imagined yourself with slender ears ending in tips of black fur, tiny reminders of the past summer, and you had a small black nose, and eyes looking to either side, seeing two landscapes, and how your mind brought them together like playing cards shuffled on a table before Eddy laid down a hand of Patience. The old fence with its fallen, tangled wire, the slender icicles hanging from the barbs, and the tall grasses were only a few hops away.

The rabbit didn't hear the Great Horned owl as it rode the white sky. The owl was the story of silence. And you stood there in the small disturbance and saw the outline of the grey hunter, its mark on snow. It was as if the rabbit grew sudden wings and beat them down once before lifting into the sky.

The tracks of the rabbit stopped there and you waited. It took time to step past the broken snow and into the perfect whiteness beyond and as you did you looked behind, looked at the horizon and the sun low in the south where it crawled among the clenched branches of the poplars and the cottonwoods by the creek. You saw the sun. You looked at that pale orb riding the hills and then you moved through the unbroken snow toward the safety of the far fence and the willow and the sage, the apples, and the spare grasses.

Rabbit stories.

Mother had told them to him and Eddy.

You had to watch a long time to see through her words. You'd listen to her read aloud and then you'd read between the lines to find the story beneath the story, the one she'd hidden. There were always clues, a word, a phrase or two, a small fragment that told you there was something hidden, but you had to imagine it, you had to piece it together bit by bit and supply the parts left out, the silences, the moments when she turned away and told you to go to sleep, the times you hid behind the door and listened to her and Father, the arguments, the shouts. But mostly it was the silences you found in the other rooms of the house when you had to invent what you read in their eyes, the sideways glance, the blink, the hesitation, the quick anger that told you there was something left unsaid, something you needed to know, but no matter your begging they never told you.

Didn't you?

You had to find it for yourself.

You had to find the story.

You imagined your father still a boy and walking away from his home down a Saskatchewan road that cut in a straight line from the dwindled forest to the open plains. Father was only thirteen then, bare feet in huge boots, his father's hunting knife strapped in the knotted baling twine that held up his threadbare pants. Tom could see him coming out of the sparse trees at the edge of the north, the Black spruce country where the deer were small and timid and there were coyotes and bears, wolverines and wolves.

He knew almost nothing of Father's early childhood except how he hated his father and loved his mother and his sister, Alice. And how his grandfather strung her from a beam in the barn, hung her there in the shadows, her body swinging slow, and he took the bullwhip out of the rain barrel where it was kept to keep it supple and whipped her methodically, carefully, spacing the blows so no cut touched another and how he cursed when he made a mistake as the long blade of the leather bull-cock whip crissed the air. Tom remembered the story, how his grandmother knelt in the dust and chaff at the door and begged him to stop. But Tom never learned why he whipped his daughter. That part wasn't told, and he didn't invent a reason because he couldn't think of one. Tom couldn't think of a reason why a father would do that to his daughter.

Did Father tell that story?

Or was it Mother? She hated Father going on about how her own father killed himself. He said her father was a coward, a worthless man who couldn't look after his own. When he said that, Mother would retort: And what about you? When did you ever look after *your* family?

The story of Alice being bullwhipped was a tale told *on* him, not about him. But what part of the story was his and what part Mother's? Was it the part about the precision of the blows or the part about the dust and chaff? When she told the story, Tom could see the swirls of dust and the bits of straw and hay on the worn boards, and the barn, its dank darkness smelling of cows and horses, chickens, rats, and mice, the earless barn cats, yowling, the tips of their tails gone, frozen off by the terrible cold from the north. He could see his Aunt Alice hanging from her tied hands as her father wrote his name on her skin. He could see the grandmother he never met, still young, on her knees in the doorway of the barn, the barn door pushed partly open and the great shadow splitting her in two, half her body darkness, the other light, while she prayed to whatever god she knew for him to stop, the whip moving from her daughter's buttocks to her thighs.

Where were you hiding, Father? In what stall, what grain bin, straw pile, behind what harness rack? Was it you, Father, told Mother how Alice was laid down in the poplar-log lean-to behind the house, how she almost died, how her wounds took months to heal? Did you go to her? Or did you leave the barn to follow the stone-boat as the horses pulled it through the fields, your father on the other side bending to lift scattered boulders, dropping them into the sledge, and you afraid to speak her name for fear of what he'd do?

And when you finally ran, what then? That first night, did you hide yourself away? Did you find some gulch or gully and build a fire, or were you afraid to light one for fear your father might see that small light in the darkness and track you down? Did you lie awake, thinking a rock falling was your father's boots come walking? Were you afraid, Father? Or did your anger and your hate turn you into who you'd always be? Who were you when you were told to walk away from the bush farm, leaving behind your mother and your sister, their lives in the hands of that man. You knew what he'd do to your mother, your sister, when he found you gone. Did you know then you'd carry the memory of the boots and fists, the whip?

What about the one time Aunt Alice came out from Saskatchewan to visit? She was always covered from ankle to throat by a long cotton dress, the top button made of pearl. Tom saw the button the rare times she lifted her head and let the sun touch it and it seemed to be a jewel then, a rare and mysterious jewel, something hard and bright she fastened there with her long white fingers each morning behind her door. That was her, Father's sister, girl and woman, eggless in the Eden she made of herself, a single name writ large on her living skin. She sat in the kitchen late one night and told her brother that the day she finally left the family farm she swore to herself she'd never marry, never carry a child. She said: I bear his name and that is curse enough. What? And bear another Stark into the world? That name ends with me.

There is another story, there always is . . .

She said.

He said.

Read between the lines.

A rabbit takes a single hop from the shelter of the brush. It stops and sits up on its long back paws and touches the air with its black nose, nervous, testing the wind, almost ready to move into the open.

Through a break in the clouds, Tom saw the glint of stars, little fires in the firmament, bright suns turning to ash. When he was a boy, he'd watched a meteor crash through the sky, leaving behind its bull head a breath of smoke that reached from mountain to mountain. He sat swaying on the wellhead, staring up into the night as if from the bottom of a mine shaft. How he had got from the house to the well he didn't know, the journey beyond him.

He could hear metal breaking, the wrench of steel coming apart, and see a car flying over a ditch, cedar fence posts ripping out of the ground, the strands of barbed wire snapping, thin whips singing as they hurt the air, a windshield bursting into a million shards, the car going over a cliff above an arroyo, rocks raining down, two hands gripping a steering wheel in fists.

The stars were soft balls of exploded light, glistening mysteries that moved in an immense circle, always returning to their place as if tied to the North Star, the darkness everywhere being created by light as Tom tried to think of what it would mean to leave forever.

The telephone kept ringing, and he was trying again to get up from the chair in the kitchen, but his legs this time were full of dense water, his bones melted, and as he tried to rise, he fell, and he was on his hands and knees in the house, crawling like a small child across the kitchen floor and into the living room where the telephone was on the wooden side table, the telephone screaming at him as he reached up, the ringing stopped, and a voice spoke to him: *Is this the Stark residence?* And he said: *Yes, this is where we are,* and a man asked who he was speaking to. *Tom Stark,* he said into the telephone, *This's Tom Stark here,* and the man said he was the corporal down at the police station and he asked if Mrs. Stark was home, and Tom said, *No, she's in the bathtub,* and then: *What is it you want?*

The corporal didn't say anything for a moment and Tom said, *Hello?* And the corporal said there'd been an accident, and Tom said, *What?* he said, *Where?* The corporal cleared his throat and said there had been a police pursuit of a speeding car out on the Coldstream Road, a green Studebaker registered to Eddy Stark, and the car had gone off the road, and the man asked him if this was where Eddy Stark lived, and Tom said, *Yes, Eddy Stark lives here. He lives with us,* and the corporal said that the driver of the car had died in the crash. *You mean my brother?* And the corporal said: *Eddy Stark. The driver was Eddy Stark,* and when Tom didn't say anything because he couldn't, suddenly not knowing how to speak, his knees hurting because he was kneeling on the floor, his hands shaking, the corporal asked him again if this was the Stark residence and was he talking to Tom Stark, as if he needed to be reassured he had the right place, the right person, and Tom held the telephone out, some creature caught in his hand, a weasel or a black-snake, and lifting it to his head again, said, *Yes, this's Tom Stark. This's him here*, and then, when the corporal didn't say anything more, he said, *I'm listening*, and the corporal said, *Good*, but Tom didn't know what that meant, *good. What do you mean?* he asked, and the corporal said, *There's been an accident*, and Tom said, *Where?* wanting to know the precise spot on the Coldstream Road, because it mattered if it was a bad corner or the bridge over the Shuswap River or a deer stunned in the road, and, *Where?* he said again, the corporal somehow misunderstanding, and saying to him, *Eddy Stark's body is down at Reeves Funeral Home.*

They were quiet then, listening to each other breathe, and then the corporal coughed, clearing his throat again, asking him if he was all right. *No*, Tom said, *No, I'm not*, and he hung up.

Because his father was shouting at him, and Mother was hiding under the stairs with Eddy. Father was carrying sacks and boxes down to the basement, potatoes and carrots, onions, cabbages, and squash rumbling into the vegetable bins. Jars of fruit glowed on the shelves beside the saws and hammers, the cans of nails and screws. His father placed the rifle in his hands and sent him out into the world, and he shot the Percheron, the horse so large he could bend his head and shoulders and pass under its belly. The huge body collapsed in on itself, the sound of it striking the earth, and he came home, Mother telling him with a smile that he was *the keeper of the vineyards*.

You made me, he said, but she didn't hear him offer the words. The sawdust furnace burned its fierce fire in the basement as his father dug his sisters' graves in the orchard, boards breaking across his knee, his huge hands tearing straw from a rotten bale of hay, and Tom stopped. Father was shooting his dog, and why did he shoot Docker? He didn't know why, and he wanted to know, but there was no one to ask, his father dead, and the red rag of his dog lying on the floor of the root cellar, as he picked up the shotgun where it leaned against the wall, the barrel smell a grey grease inside his mouth and nose. He went out into the night, his father wheeling around, the bottle in his hand a flail, and Tom, hating this man, hating what he had done, and then shooting him, shooting his father.

It was Eddy who told him that everything would be okay, and not to think, and never to remember. But he *had* remembered. And he'd tried to understand, because now, right now, none of it seemed to matter.

The sparse tales became legion in his mind, pieces of the past falling around him. He'd listened closely to the few stories he'd been given. It was strange how things came down to almost nothing, a single image that stayed alive. The moment when his father touched a stallion's neck in Fort Qu'Appelle, and heard the horse's flesh, both of them alive there in the chute. A young boy, his sister left behind, following the Saskatchewan River into the west with a stolen knife and boots that were too big for him.

The stories that belonged to him were sometimes couched in curses, things always going wrong, a boy breaking his knuckles on a frozen bolt, his father telling him to put his whole body into it and Tom lifting his forty-five pounds and throwing himself onto the handle of the monkey wrench, thinking praise could be gained by the blood on his childish hands. What did his father think when he took the wrench from him and broke the bolt loose from the rusted metal, laughing at his son's uselessness, his weakness? He knew a child could never break it free. Was it the shame, the failure he saw on his son's face? Is that what he wanted?

Tom tried to comprehend what his father's life had meant, but he couldn't, he could only know that his father had guarded his secrets and carried them into the years, and that he had visited them upon Eddy and upon him and upon his Mother too. Tom closed his eyes, the vast plains spread out before him, the miles of rolling grassland, coulees ripped into it as if a hand had torn the earth open. A boy was crouched in a cave in the badlands along the border, wolf hides stretched and drying on the rocks, a pony tethered to a sagebrush, patient, hobbled, waiting for him to go on with the life he was making, the life he had made.

Tom sat there, his sisters flying around him, spirits from another time, their cries the night he looked to as if the lights he saw glinting above him were his sisters' eyes, small windows leading him finally to another life.

He got up slowly and walked back to the house. When he went through the door, he saw Marilyn at the kitchen table, looking worried, a plate of half-eaten pork chop bones and partly thawed hamburger on the floor at her feet, the red dog hunched over, choking down the meat she'd placed there, growling as he came in.

Who was it you were talking to on the phone?

When he didn't reply, she asked him what the matter was, what had happened, putting out her hand as if to stop him. What's wrong? she said. What's wrong?

He didn't stop, but walked past her to the bathroom where his mother was. He opened the door.

Mother was sleeping in the warm water, her mouth slightly open, strands of hair floating out from her face. She seemed, as she'd always been, a stranger to him, her hair, long threads twining toward the tub walls, her wrists thin and white. He leaned forward, crazy, thinking he could just push her head under and hold her there. Tom knelt down, gripping the edge of the tub against what he knew he had to do. He could see her eyes moving under her lids. He stared at the bubbles rising from under her body, the spheres trickling up from her breasts and shoulders, her belly, hips, and thighs. The bubbles rose in tiny, imperceptible columns and Tom put his ear close and listened to them burst. The spheres held sounds, a language inside them he could almost understand: rants and canticles, outcries, teases, and wheedles. A Bible opened in his head, the fragile pages turning. He could hear his mother reading to him when he was a boy, page following page: *And of thy sons that shall issue from thee, which thou shalt beget, shall they take away.* Words upon words: *Every wise woman buildeth her house,* and on and on, Tom's heart beating, a sledge in his skull, slow and huge, resonant, resigned.

She opened her eyes and, startled, looked up at him.

Mother, he whispered.

She rose up, water streaming from her hair, and pulled the shower curtain across, a single red fish seeming to thrash in her hand, the rest swimming around her. Her bare arm reached out as she bent to snatch her housecoat from the floor. She slipped it on behind the veil, pushed the curtain aside, and stepped from the tub, water dripping from the bottom of her housecoat, her hand holding the top of it closed at her throat, shaking slightly, a tremor so small as to be almost invisible. She stood in a pool of water, her hair plastered to her skull. The hand kept trembling, and he saw her fingers gripping the collar of her housecoat tighter, his mother not wanting her body to betray her.

When is Eddy coming home?

And he told her.

Things seemed to constrict around her, the air, the light above her shrinking to the size of a burned marble, the tub with its curtain, the tin medicine chest, its mirror, and he tried to reach to where she was, but he couldn't find the way in.

She followed him into the kitchen. You go and bring your brother home, she said, staring at him, her words clear and cold.

Marilyn, at the kitchen table, asked: Is it your brother?

He looked at her. Yes, he said, Marilyn huddling back in her chair, the dog at her feet, the sound of it eating, and Tom stepped wide and went out the door.

He got in the truck and drove, the trees rolling their

black limbs out of the tail of the storm, the road a clutter of needles and broken branches. He stared into the shadows beyond his lights, a thin rain beginning again, speckling the windshield and him drowning.

Weiner Reeves stood at the bottom of the ramp, opened the basement doors, and Tom went in. There were polished steel sinks along the counter by the wall, faucets hanging over them, a black hose coiled like a lasso, looped over the handle of what had to be a pump beside a drain in the middle of the floor, and beside it a table on wheels. On it was what looked like a makeup kit, the kind women used, and other things that Tom didn't want to think about. Weiner stood there, jumpy, wringing his hands as he told him how his mother and father were away in Grand Forks, but they'd be back tomorrow. Tom asked him who'd brought Eddy there, and Weiner told him the body had come with the ambulance, Don Sparrow driving it, and a corporal in a police car who'd followed the body in.

Not Sergeant Stanley.

It was Dave Gillespie, Weiner said, Tom just staring at him. You know Dave.

Tom waited, Weiner going on, saying how he'd been meaning to phone out to the house, but Dave, the corporal, had said the police were looking after that part, that they were the ones who'd be doing the calling to the Starks. Anyways, Weiner said, they told me not to tell anyone about Eddy being dead and all.

Weiner raised up on his toes and told Tom how he was real sorry about Eddy getting himself dead, and how the police had said it was a bad accident and all. At least, that's what the corporal told me, said Weiner. He said the Studebaker was a complete write-off.

Where's my brother?

Weiner walked over to what looked like a cooler in the back wall. It was the same as one he'd seen at Jim Garofalo's. Weiner lifted the steel handle, opening the door, a light coming on inside.

Tom went to the gurney sitting there in the cold on its black wheels. His brother was under a kind of rubber sheet, and he lifted the corner of it up. Eddy's head lay crooked on a plastic pillow, his face caked with dry blood, flakes of glass glittering in his red hair.

Weiner stood back as Tom pushed the gurney out of the cooler. Where are you going with him? Weiner asked, coming behind, their feet sounding wet on the grey linoleum, Tom trundling it to the truck, one of the wheels rattling on the cement. Weiner told Tom he wasn't supposed to be taking the body away, that his father always made people sign papers before they ever got one, and the police too. That they, for sure, weren't going to like him taking the body away like he was. Weiner pleaded with Tom, saying how he was going to get into trouble if this went on.

Tom grabbed him. You don't know who took Eddy away, he said. This never happened.

I won't say a word, Weiner said, even as Tom knew he would, that he'd tell the police whatever they asked, Stanley or Gillespie or whoever else wanted to know, but Tom didn't care what Weiner said or did now. He saw him slip some white pills into his mouth, his throat moving as he swallowed them, then he said, he, for sure, wasn't going to tell anyone. Tom paid no attention then, as Weiner, stupid, tried to help him get Eddy off the gurney and into the front seat. Tom made him hold Eddy upright until he got around to the other side and sat behind the wheel. Weiner closed the truck door and scurried away. As Tom backed the truck up the ramp and turned toward home, Eddy slumped to the side, his head against the window, as if he was sleeping there.

He wanted to wake his brother up and ask him exactly how he'd driven the Coldstream Road. He could see each hill, each valley bottom, the hairpin turns, the poplar trees past Lavington that obscured the one bad corner, and the different bridges across the creek, the cliffs above the deep gully near Lumby, every place a car could go wrong, the police following close behind, red lights flashing, going too fast, the brakes, or not the brakes, the gas pedal then, the car leaving the road, flying through the air.

Blood is blood and sometimes never gone.

He could see the turn onto Ranch Road in the distance, and he was suddenly twelve years old again, walking home from school, Eddy pulling alongside him in a car he'd stolen. They drove together down the back roads at the foot of the mountain, the car careening around corners, Tom holding on as they slewed from side to side, yelling at his brother, telling him to slow down, asking again and again where they were going. *Where are we going, Eddy?* Then they rode wild over the bridge at Cheater Creek, and, with a howl, Eddy cut the wheel hard, taking a sharp turn into the blind side-road, grass and branches ripping at the car's belly, a deer startling and running frantically ahead of them. Eddy gunned the car a moment and the deer, crazy with fright, leaped off into a tangle of brush.

Finally, they stopped in front of the old shack where Father had taught them to shoot a few years before when Tom would have been kneeling at the edge of the trees, the old Lee-Enfield rifle heavy in his young arms as he aimed it at the crude target his father had drawn with chalk on the wall.

He and Eddy got out, and he stood by the back fender as Eddy opened the trunk and dragged out a five-gallon can. Eddy told him to open the passenger door, and when he did, Eddy tilted the can sideways, the purple farm gas chugging onto the seat and floor. The gas lay pooled in the leg space under the glove compartment, his brother trailing the spout over to the driver's side, the gas spilling out. Then he hefted the can, carrying what was left to the trunk. He emptied the rest of the gas there, fumes around him in a shimmer of blue and gold, and Tom, as if in a spell, moved away slowly to the edge of the clearing.

His brother closed the car door, and, taking a folder of matches from his pocket, struck one and held it to the red tips of the others. The folder flared and he quickly tossed it through the open window, turning to run, taking only a few short steps before the gasoline exploded, the force of it driving him face-first into the dirt, smoke and flame billowing from the car.

Tom stumbled across the clearing toward his brother when the trunk exploded, the gas bursting out, the trunk lid flying up and the fenders above the tires shearing out like crooked blades. Eddy had crawled a foot or two, no more, the back of his shirt starting to smoulder. Then the back end of the car lifted up, the gas tank exploding, the car falling back on its burning tires like an animal held by a chain. Smoke boiled out of the windows and trunk, the shack behind the car on fire now, the old wood engulfed in flame, the images being eaten, the bullet holes Tom and Eddy had put in, erased in the fire. Alders and poplars reared back, their yellow leaves shrivelling, the fretted bells of their branches blossoming into torches. A single tongue of flame touched Eddy's ankle and Tom grabbed his brother by the arms, dragging him to safety where the road entered the clearing, Tom urging him to go a little faster, leading him back to Cheater Creek. There he made Eddy lie down in the rivulets, cold water soaking up into his shirt and pants. The creek slid along the skin on the backs of his legs, cooling the burns, while Eddy lay there, defiant, a grin on his face.

The house rode toward him now, faint lights in the gloom, his brother beside him, someone he'd looked to and watched for. What he had left was who he was, himself, alone now, driving down Ranch Road to where the three of them had lived.

The headlights glanced off the side of the house, Marilyn standing at the kitchen window, arms crossed, looking out. He turned off the motor, and Mother came down the porch steps then, pulling on the door of the truck.

Eddy, she said, and Tom leaned across his brother and lifted the lock, the door swinging open, Mother staggering back, her hand hooked in the handle, and then she clambered into the truck.

Tom got out, his brother fallen over by the steering wheel, and Mother, her arms around his neck, tried to lift him up.

Marilyn came out of the house then, the dog beside her, and he called to her to come and help as he untangled his mother's hands and pulled her out, turning her away from the truck. Mother twisted in his arms, her body unyielding as she struggled. He tightened his arms around her.

Don't, he said, Mother sagging then against him.

He let her go, and she turned around, her face utterly naked, her eyes telling him to do something so that all this could be undone. She peered at him from her thin eyes as if she'd only now recognized who he was.

Are you all right? Tom said, and she raised her arm and slapped him in the face. When he didn't move, she raised her hand again, Marilyn yelling at them to stop, that it was enough.

The last clouds butted against the mountain, the blade of the moon bright in the sky. His mother stood there, her hands at her sides, as if unsure what to do next. She seemed pathetic to him now, and he wondered how he could ever have been afraid of her.

Go inside the house, he said.

Marilyn made a move toward him, but he shook his head. Mother turned and Marilyn went with her, walking to the light coming from the kitchen, passing from him through the door.

After a moment, Marilyn came back out onto the porch. She called to the dog, then asked Tom if he'd seen it. Tom said he hadn't, and she turned and walked back in.

He lifted his brother from the truck, stumbling as he took the weight, and carried him to the house. As he came up the steps, Marilyn was at the screen door, saying he should take Eddy to his mother's room. She rubbed her wrist against her eye, seeming to him to be somehow lost. She let him go ahead, Tom turning sideways in the doorway, taking the body through, and down the hall to the room at the end.

Mother's bed was swimming with red fishes, and for a moment he thought he'd gone mad, and then he saw she'd torn down the shower curtain in the bathroom, spreading it on top of the quilt. When he hesitated, she told him to lie Eddy on the bed and he did, his brother's knees bent awkwardly. She placed her hand on Eddy's shoulder as if to her he was a child hurt in a game he'd played too hard.

Tom looked at her, a small woman standing beside her dead son. He leaned over to straighten his brother's body.

Haven't you done enough, she said.

What have I done?

You tell that Marilyn girl to throw some wood into the stove and get the water in the kettle hot. There's nothing here for you to take care of, she said.

He turned to Marilyn, who was standing just outside the door, and when he said her name, she nodded and went down the hall.

Tom stayed where he was, his mother putting on an apron, suddenly busy, pushing back her sleeves, no hesitation in her now, as if this was something she was destined to do. Her hands undid his brother's buttons, moving down to Eddy's waist, pulling his shirt out of his pants, and spreading it open. He watched her take a pair of scissors from the drawer in the bedside table and cut the sleeves open from wrist to neck, then she peeled the shirt from him and stripped it away. His brother's skin glistened like old wax through the dry blood on his face, his caved-in chest, bruises and cuts among the freckles on his shoulders and face, and the other, older bruises lying like shadows on his arms and in the cups of his elbows.

His face is all bloody, she said, as if distracted. I don't even know what time it is.

He looked away, leaving the room. He went to the front door, opened it, and walked out to the road, the huge limbs of the old fir tree stretching above him, which he had once climbed to wait for his brother to come home. From where he was standing, he could see his mother through the bars on the bedroom window. She was leaning over, Marilyn beside her, holding out a dish pan, Mother dipping a cloth in and then wringing it out, her hands disappearing, her arms moving, and then her hands lifting, dipping the cloth in the water again in a simple ceremony of grief.

A dog barked somewhere out in the orchard. The sound echoed in him, the night suddenly quiet, and then the dog barked again. He turned and walked around the back of the house and down the path. He called to the dog, but there was no answering bark.

The creek before him was a silver wand. In a tiny pool left behind by the rain, a water-strider dimpled on its diminished sea, everything that had supported it slowly vanishing as it strode within the limits of the puddle. He looked over at the path and saw the marks of his boots filling in, bits of clay crumbling, stems of grass bending back over the scars, seed heads dribbling next year's roots onto the disturbed earth. A Spadefoot toad, refusing to believe the coming cold, had found a hole where a stone had been thrown out by an iron wheel. The toad squatted low, blinkered in dampness, its mottled throat silent, its golden eyes staring over the water-strider's pool to the creek flowing past the orchard.

He remembered how once his father had told him that he'd kept a magpie in a willow cage when he was a boy back on the farm, his pet, his wild bird tamed, its tongue slit with a razor so it could talk. He told him that the morning he left home forever he'd set the magpie free, but the bird had followed him for miles with his name on its split tongue until later that day it disappeared for good. Tom had always wondered how long a bird like that could live in the wilderness. He knew the other magpies would kill it when it came to them for comfort, its call a human cry, the smell of Father on its feathers.

He thought of the men down by the railroad tracks at night, sitting in front of their small fires, sufficient to themselves in the flickering light, him beside them, listening as they talked about where they'd been, drawn to their lives, his own somewhere else, forgotten in the hours. A few nights later he'd return, but those men would be gone, the fire pit still warm, empty bean cans and bottles lying in the ashes. He'd sit there, thinking of them in the gondola cars of a freight train, leaning on the iron walls, staring out at the passing cities and towns, as they rode into the night.

There were the times years ago when he'd crouch in the mouth of the cave up Cheater Creek, a snared grouse he'd cooked beside him, cooled on a flat rock, his pup sleeping, full of breast meat, stolen milk, and eggs. He built careful fires, hoping the smell of smoke and the glow of the flames wouldn't give him away. It was always Eddy who found him, Eddy who brought him back.

He heard a slight sound now, an animal coming through the brush by the creek, and he saw the red dog come out of the willows. It stopped by the water-strider's pool, looking at him for a second or two, as if curious who he was, why he was there. Hey dog, he said. But it just lapped at the water briefly, and went on by. He began walking, the dog moving on its steady paws past the house, and on up to the road. It stopped, turning for a moment to see if he was following, then lifted its head and coursed the light wind coming out of the north. Tom felt a nameless thing inside him, and he took a breath and then another.

The dog crossed over the road and passed under the barbed wire on the other side of the ditch, moving out into the ploughed field, padding between two deep furrows, heading toward Black Rock, the far lakes, and the valley beyond.

ACKNOWLEDGEMENTS

I especially wish to express gratitude to my editor, Ellen Seligman, who was so inspiring during the last stages of my six-year-long journey with this book. Her support, her insights, and her tireless care helped this novel to find its final shape. Also at McClelland & Stewart, thanks to Jenny Bradshaw, for her sharp eye, and to Morgan Grady-Smith, for her astute comments. My thanks as well to my agent Dean Cooke, and Suzanne Brandreth, and to the Canada Council and the B.C. Arts Council for their support during the writing of this novel.

I wish to give a nod to the presence of Friedrich Nietzsche and Grace Metalious, and to the authors of the Book of Psalms, Proverbs, Isaiah, Jeremiah, and Job from the King James Bible.

Lastly, I owe a deep debt of gratitude to my wife, Lorna Crozier, who suffered the years of my writing this novel with tolerance, patience, and grace. My heart goes out to her.

A NOTE ABOUT THE TYPE

The text of *Red Dog, Red Dog* has been set in Goudy (often referred to as Goudy Oldstyle), a face designed in 1915 for the American Type Founders by the prolific typographer Frederic W. Goudy. Used with equal success in both text and display sizes, Goudy remains one of the most popular typefaces ever produced. It is best recognized by the diamond-shaped dots on punctuation; the upturned "ear" of the g; and the elegant base curve of the caps E and L.

Hillary Jordan

Mudbound

Winner of the Bellwether Prize for Fiction

'A page-turning read that conveys a serious message without preaching'
OBSERVER

When Henry McAllan moves his city-bred wife, Laura, to a cotton farm in the Mississippi Delta in 1946, she finds herself in a place both foreign and frightening. Henry's love of rural life is not shared by Laura, who struggles to raise their two young children in an isolated shotgun shack under the eye of her hateful, racist father-in-law. When it rains, the waters rise up and swallow the bridge to town, stranding the family in a sea of mud.

As the Second World War shudders to an end, two young men return from Europe to help work the farm. Jamie McAllan is everything his older brother Henry is not and is sensitive to Laura's plight, but also haunted by his memories of combat. Ronsel Jackson, eldest son of the black sharecroppers who live on the farm, comes home from war with the shine of a hero, only to face far more dangerous battles against the ingrained bigotry of his own countrymen. These two unlikely friends become players in a tragedy on the grandest scale.

'This is storytelling at the height of its powers'
BARBARA KINGSOLVER

'Jordan builds the tension slowly and meticulously, so that when the shocking denouement arrives, it is both inevitable and devastating ...
A compelling tale'
GLASGOW HERALD

Lauren Groff

The Monsters of Templeton

Shortlisted for the Orange Broadband Award
for New Writers 2008

Willie Cooper arrives on the doorstep of her ancestral home
in Templeton, New York in the wake of a disastrous affair
with her much older, married archaeology professor. That
same day, the discovery of a prehistoric monster in the lake
brings a media frenzy to the quiet, picture-perfect town her
ancestors founded. Smarting from a broken heart, Willie then
learns that the story her mother had always told her about her
father has all been a lie. He wasn't the one-night stand Vi had
led her to imagine, but someone else entirely.

As Willie puts her archaeological skills to work digging for
the truth about her lineage, a chorus of voices from the town's
past rise up around her to tell their sides of the story. Dark
secrets come to light, past and present blur, old mysteries are
finally put to rest, and the surprising truth about more than
one monster is revealed.

RACHEL HEATH

The Finest Type of English Womanhood

It is 1946, and seventeen-year-old Laura Trelling is stagnating in her dilapidated Sussex family home, while her eccentric parents slip further into isolation. A chance encounter with Paul Lovell offers her the opportunity to alter the course of her destiny – and to embark on a new life in South Africa.

Many miles north, sixteen-year-old Gay Gibson is desperate to escape Birkenhead. When the girls' paths cross in Johannesburg, Laura is exposed to Gay's wild life of parties and inappropriate liaisons. Each in her own world, but thrown together, the girls find their lives inextricably entangled, with fatal consequences ...

ANDROMEDA ROMANO-LAX

The Spanish Bow

When Feliu Delargo is born, late-nineteenth-century Spain is a nation slipping from international power and struggling with its own fractured identity, caught between the chaos of post-empire and impending Civil War.

Feliu's troubled childhood and rise to fame lead him into a thorny partnership with an even more famous and eccentric figure, the piano prodigy Justo Al-Cerraz. The two musicians' divergent artistic goals and political inclinations threaten to divide them as Spain plunges into Civil War. But as Civil War turns to World War, shared love for their trio partner – an Italian violinist named Aviva — forces them into their final and most dangerous collaboration.

ANDRE DUBUS III

The Garden of Last Days

*'This book is so good, so damn compulsively readable, that I can hardly
believe it . . . read it now'*
STEPHEN KING

A SEPTEMBER NIGHT IN FLORIDA.
A YOUNG MOTHER FACES A TOUGH CHOICE . . .

April's usual babysitter has had a panic attack that has landed
her in hospital. April doesn't really know anyone else, so she
decides to keep her three-year-old daughter, Franny, close by,
watching videos in the office where she works. But April is a
stripper. And tonight she has an unusual client, a foreigner
both remote and too personal, and free with his money. Lots
of it, all cash. Meanwhile another man has been thrown out
of the club. He's drunk, angry and lonely, but he's not quite
ready to leave. And Franny is growing restless, bored of
waiting for her mother to return . . .

The Garden of Last Days is the explosive new novel from the
author of the international bestseller *House of Sand and Fog*. Set
in the seamy underside of American life at the moment
before the world changed, it is a big-hearted, passionate and
unforgettable novel about sex and parenthood, honour
and betrayal from a truly great storyteller.

*'More than cements Dubus's status as one of America's finest writers . . .
Tension and confusion are wrought from every spare yet evocative sentence'*
GUARDIAN

'You cannot help but be mesmerised'
SUNDAY TIMES

THE POWER OF READING

Visit the Random House website and get connected with information on all our books and authors

EXTRACTS from our recently published books and selected backlist titles

COMPETITIONS AND PRIZE DRAWS Win signed books, audiobooks and more

AUTHOR EVENTS Find out which of our authors are on tour and where you can meet them

LATEST NEWS on bestsellers, awards and new publications

MINISITES with exclusive special features dedicated to our authors and their titles

READING GROUPS Reading guides, special features and all the information you need for your reading group

LISTEN to extracts from the latest audiobook publications

WATCH video clips of interviews and readings with our authors

RANDOM HOUSE INFORMATION including advice for writers, job vacancies and all your general queries answered

Come home to Random House

www.rbooks.co.uk